'Is everything a matter of profit?' Kathryn said angrily. 'Tell me, how much did Lord Mountfitchet pay you to rescue me?'

Raising her head proudly, she looked into his eyes. 'Perhaps you should know that I am an heiress, and my true worth is what my father will give to have me back.'

'I shall bear that in mind,' Lorenzo said, his eyes glinting. 'Perhaps I shall not take your uncle's ransom after all, Madonna. It might be that you would fetch a higher price elsewhere.' He moved towards her, towering above her so that she felt shivers run down her spine. For a moment she thought he meant to take her into his arms, but then he shook his head and stepped back. 'You are a troublesome girl and I have better things to do! Be careful, or I may find it easier to be rid of you.'

Kathryn stared as he turned and walked from the cabin. He could not mean that! No, of course he didn't. And yet what did she really know of this man? He guarded his feelings so well that anything might be going on inside his head.

Kathryn sat on the edge of the bed, hugging herself as she tried to come to terms with her feelings. For a moment, as she'd gazed into his eyes, she had wanted him to kiss her. How foolish she was!

Anne Herries, winner of the Romantic Novelists' Association ROMANCE PRIZE 2004, lives in Cambridgeshire. After many happy years with a holiday home in Spain, she and her husband now have their second home in Norfolk. They are only just across the road from the sea, and have a view of it from their windows. At home and at the sea they enjoy watching the wildlife, and have many visitors to their gardens, particularly squirrels. Anne loves watching their antics, and spoils both them and her birds shamelessly. She also loves to see the flocks of geese and other birds flying in over the sea during the autumn, to winter in the milder climes of this country. Anne loves to write about the beauty of nature, and sometimes puts a little into her books, though they are mostly about love and romance. She writes for her own enjoyment, and to give pleasure to her readers.

Recent titles by the same author:

THE ABDUCTED BRIDE
CAPTIVE OF THE HAREM
THE SHEIKH
A DAMNABLE ROGUE *

Winner of the Romantic Novelists' Association
ROMANCE PRIZE

and in the Regency series *The Steepwood Scandal:*

LORD RAVENSDEN'S MARRIAGE
COUNTERFEIT EARL

and in *The Elizabethan Season:*

LADY IN WAITING
THE ADVENTURER'S WIFE

and in *The Banewulf Dynasty:*

A PERFECT KNIGHT
A KNIGHT OF HONOUR
HER KNIGHT PROTECTOR

RANSOM BRIDE

Anne Herries

MILLS & BOON®

All the characters in this book have no existence outside the imagination of the author, and have no relation whatsoever to anyone bearing the same name or names. They are not even distantly inspired by any individual known or unknown to the author, and all the incidents are pure invention.

First published in Great Britain 2005
Paperback edition 2006
Harlequin Mills & Boon Limited,
Eton House, 18-24 Paradise Road, Richmond, Surrey TW9 1SR

© Anne Herries 2005

ISBN 0 263 84635 0

Set in Times Roman 10½ on 13¼ pt.
04-0206-82520

Printed and bound in Spain
by Litografia Rosés S.A., Barcelona

RANSOM BRIDE

Chapter One

Kathryn stood at the top of the cliff, looking down at the sea as it swirled about the rocks far below her. The wind tore at her hair, catching at her cloak, buffeting her from all sides as she stared out to the far horizon, her thoughts returning as always when she came here to that day in her childhood—the day when the bravery of her companion had saved her life. Never would she forget how they had gone down to the cove in direct disobedience to their fathers' commands; how their curiosity about the strange ship in the bay had brought disaster.

Kathryn's cheeks were wet as she wiped the tears with the back of her hand. There was no point in weeping. Dickon had gone from her, from his family, taken by the Corsairs who had come ashore to find water and food. It seemed that some of the villagers had been trading with these evil men who plagued the seas of the Mediterranean and occasionally ventured as far as the coasts of England and Cornwall. How often she had regretted that she had not been more mindful of her duty, for it was she who had prompted her companion to go down and investigate the strange ship.

Shivering, Kathryn recalled the way the fierce pirates had suddenly swooped on them as they walked innocently towards where the pirates were plying their trade with the rogue villager. That man had long disappeared from the village, for when Kathryn escaped from the clutches of the men who had tried to seize her, he must have known she would tell her story. But her beloved Dickon had not escaped. He had pushed her behind him, telling her to run for help while he had bravely fought against the men who attacked them. At the top of the cliff, she had stopped, turning to see that they were carrying Dickon on board the boat that had brought them ashore, and that he appeared to be unconscious.

Kathryn had run as fast as she could to her father's house, spilling out her tale of abduction and treachery, but when the party of men had arrived at the beach it was to find it empty, with no sign of the brave lad who had fought against impossible odds. He was but fifteen when they took him, but Kathryn knew he would have been sold as a slave, perhaps to work in the kitchens of some eastern potentate. Or perhaps, because he was tall and strong for his age, he had been chained to an oar in one of the raiders' galleys.

She had wept bitter tears, for she had loved Dickon. He was her friend and her soulmate and, though their families lived some leagues distant from one another, they had known each other well. Kathryn believed that it was the intention of both fathers that they should marry one day, when she was nineteen. She was almost nineteen now and soon her father would make arrangements for her to marry someone else. But in her heart she belonged to Richard Mountfitchet—her own Dickon.

'Dickon…' Kathryn whispered, her words whipped away by the wind, drowned by the cries of seabirds and the crashing of the waves against the rocky Cornish coastline. 'Forgive me. I never thought it would happen. I did not know that such evil men existed until that day. I miss you. I still love you. I shall always love you.'

It was ten years to the day, Kathryn thought, and every year she came here at the same time hoping to see Dickon, praying that he might return to her and his family. Yet she knew it was impossible. How could he return? Their fathers had sent men to search the slave markets in Algiers. They had contacted friends in Cyprus, Venice and Constantinople, the city that the Turks now called Istanbul, but which was still known in the Christian world by its old name. Always, there was unrest between the Turks and the Christians; wars, quarrels, and differences of religion and culture made it difficult to conduct a search within the Ottoman Empire. For Sultan Selim II was constantly seeking to push out the boundaries of his empire and had boasted that one day he would stand victorious in Rome itself. However, there were a few men who could help and one of them was Suleiman Bakhar.

Suleiman had an English wife. He was a clever, educated man and travelled tirelessly, trading, trying to reach out to the world beyond the Ottoman Empire, and hoping to bring about peace, though there was such hatred, such a history of conflict between their peoples that it seemed the breach could not be bridged.

Kathryn knew that Suleiman Bakhar was in England at this time. He had promised to make inquiries on behalf of Lord Mountfitchet, but as far as she knew he had discovered nothing that could help them. Sir John Rowlands and Lord Mountfitchet had gone to London to speak with him, for they had other business of which Kathryn knew nothing, and it would suit them to meet with Suleiman at the same time. But they were expected to return today, and Kathryn felt a flicker of hope as she turned her steps towards the beautiful old manor house that was her home. It had once been fortified against attack from the sea, but, in these more peaceful times of Queen Elizabeth's reign, it had become simply a family home rather than a fortress, with many improvements to make it more comfortable.

As she reached her home, she saw that a cumbersome travelling coach had pulled up in the courtyard and she began to run, her heart racing. Perhaps this time there would be news of Dickon...

Lorenzo Santorini stood on the steps of his palace. It was built at the edges of the Grand Canal, the huge lagoon that wound through the city and beneath the many bridges of Venice. The city had established trading arrangements with the Muslim world that had helped it to become one of the most powerful seagoing nations on earth a hundred years earlier. It was from here that the great Marco Polo had set out on his voyage of expedition that had taken him as far as the court of Kublai Khan, opening up the known world far beyond what it had been previously. However, the Turkish invasions and the unrest of recent years had led to gradual erosion of the Republic's supremacy.

The Venetian galleys were, however, still thought to be some of the best craft available and remained a force to be reckoned with; the merchants of Venice were rich and influential—and Lorenzo Santorini was one of the most powerful amongst them. His galleys were famed for their speed, fighting abilities and the discipline of his men, none of whom were slaves.

He frowned as he saw the galley making its way towards the small jetty where he stood waiting. It was one of the fleet that he owned which guarded his merchant ships, and it was late returning from what should have been a routine trip to Cyprus to buy wine. As it drew closer, he could see that it had taken part in some fighting—which could only mean that it had been attacked by a Turkish or Corsair galley.

'Welcome back, Michael,' Lorenzo said as the captain mounted the steps towards him. He extended his hand, helping him jump up to the steps of the palace. 'I thought there must have been some trouble—was it Rachid again?'

'Is it not always Rachid?' Michael dei Ignacio replied with a grimace. 'He hates us and will harry our vessels whenever he gets the chance. Fortunately, I had left Cyprus in company with three other galleys and the ship that carried your wine. We lost one of our fighting galleys, but the merchant ship is safe. It is but an hour behind me, accompanied by two galleys. We came ahead because we have several injured men on board.'

'They must be tended by the physicians,' Lorenzo said with a frown, 'and all shall be compensated for the hurt they have suffered.' In Lorenzo's galleys the men were paid for their work, not chained to their oars the way the wretched prisoners were in the galleys of those men most feared in these waters. The Corsairs, or Barbary pirates, as some were wont to call them, roamed the seas from the Mediterranean and Adriatic to the Barbary Coast and the Atlantic. They were fearsome men who were a law unto themselves, owing no allegiance to anyone, though some paid tribute to the Ottoman Empire.

'It shall be attended to,' Michael promised. Lorenzo was a good master to work for, and a mystery to most, for few knew anything of his history. Michael himself knew that Lorenzo was the adopted son of the man whose name he bore; of much of what had gone before he was as ignorant as the next man.

'I know I can leave their welfare in your hands,' Lorenzo said. His eyes were the colour of violets, a dark blue and as unreadable as his thoughts. His hair, the colour of sun-ripened corn bleached white at the tips, was worn longer than the fashion of the time; thick and strong, it curled in his neck. 'I leave for Rome in the morning. I have been summoned to a meeting concerning these pirates.' His lip curled in scorn, for he included the Turks, who had caused the merchants of Venice so much trouble these past fifty years or so and now had the audacity to demand Cyprus of the Doge, something that would be fiercely resisted by the Venetians. 'As you know, there is talk of gathering a force to curb Selim's power, otherwise he will sweep further into Europe. The Emperor is concerned and he hopes to bring in Spain as well as other allies to break the power of the Turks.'

Michael nodded, for he knew that his friend was considered an important man by certain men of influence in the Holy Roman Empire. Lorenzo owned twenty fighting galleys besides his fleet of four merchant ships, and he would certainly be asked to join any force that attempted to sweep the menace of the Turkish invaders from the seas. There was a widely held belief that, could they but break the power of the Ottoman Empire, many of the Corsairs would lose much of their own power.

'They need to be curbed,' Michael agreed. 'In the meantime, we have captured one of Rachid's oarsmen. We sank one of his galleys and this man was brought out of the water, still chained to the wooden spar that prevented him from drowning. We shall see what information we can persuade him to give us about his master's stronghold—'

'I will not have him tortured,' Lorenzo said. 'No matter that he is a Turk and an enemy, he shall be treated as a man. If he is willing to help us, we shall offer him employment in our ranks. If he refuses to co-operate, we will see if he can be ransomed to his family.'

Lorenzo rubbed at one of the wide leather bands he habitually wore on his wrists, his eyes as dark as the deepest waters of the Mediterranean and as impenetrable.

'I do not believe he is of Turkish origin,' Michael said. 'He will not answer when spoken to, though he understands the language of his masters, also some French and, I think, English.'

Lorenzo looked at him in silence for a moment. 'This man is not to be ill treated,' he said. 'You will leave his questioning to me when I return, if you please, my friend. And now you must rest, enjoy the benefits of home and family for a few days. You have earned them. When I return from Rome we shall meet again.'

'As you command,' Michael said, watching as his friend signalled to a small gondola that was waiting to ferry him out to his personal galley, which was further out in the lagoon. He was curious as to why his commander had suddenly decided that he wanted to interrogate the prisoner himself, but he would obey his orders. The reason Michael, born of good family, had chosen to sail with Lorenzo Santorini was because he respected him; he was a fair man, not cruel—though he would not suffer disobedience lightly.

Lorenzo was thoughtful as he boarded the galley, which was the flagship of his fleet, the fastest and newest of the vessels he owned, with the benefit of three sails, to be used when the wind was fair, thus giving the oarsmen a chance to rest. Such galleys were still much faster and easier to manoeuvre than the top-heavy galleons the Spanish favoured. Even the smaller, lighter craft of the English merchant adventurers, who had begun to be a considerable force in these seas, would find it difficult to keep pace with this galley. Turkish galleys seldom attacked his ships—they knew that he was a man to be reckoned with.

His real quarrel, however, was with Rachid the Feared One, a man of such cruelty that his name was well earned. The pitiful creatures that served at the oar in his fleet were wretched indeed, few surviving more than three years of beatings and torture.

Lorenzo's eyes darkened as he remembered one such object of pity, a man who had survived by chance. He would never rest until Rachid was brought to justice, either at the end of a rope or by the sword. He had vowed it at the deathbed of the man who had adopted him, and one day he would keep his promise.

He regretted that he had lost one of his galleys in this struggle, for men must have died, though their comrades would have saved all they could. Rachid had also lost men and galleys, but for him life was cheap. He would replenish his oarsmen from the slave markets of Algiers or simply send a raiding party to one of the islands of the Aegean to capture men, women and children. The men would serve in his galleys, the women and children would be sold as house slaves—a trade that revolted all good Christian men and women.

It would be interesting to hear what plans were afoot in Rome, for he would welcome any fight that lead to the demise of such men. Rachid paid tribute to the Sultan of the Ottoman Empire and was free to pillage and murder as he would in these waters. If the power of the Turks could be curbed, it would make his enemy that much more vulnerable.

But even if he had to enter his very stronghold to do it, one day he would find and kill the man he hated.

'It is so good to see you, sir.' Kathryn kissed the cheek of their visitor. Lord Mountfitchet was almost as dear to her as her own father, and she looked forward to his visits. They had been rare enough since Dickon was stolen all those years ago. 'Did you see the man of whom Father told me—Suleiman Bakhar?'

'Yes, we spoke with him at length,' Lord Mountfitchet told her with a sigh. 'But there is no news. He has made inquiries for us, for, as you must know, his influence is far reaching in that part of the world. However, he has not given up hope—though he says that it would be rare for a man to survive that long in the galleys. It depends what happened to Richard when he was taken. If he was sold as a house slave...he could be anywhere.'

'We must pray that he was,' Kathryn's father said, shaking his head over the sad business. 'Otherwise...' He looked sorrowful. For his own part he believed that Richard Mountfitchet must be long dead, but his friend had refused to give up his search and he did not blame him. If it had been his own son or—God forbid—Kathryn, he might have felt the same.

'I do not believe that Dickon is dead,' Kathryn said. 'I am sure that I would have felt it in here.' She pressed her clenched hands to her breast as if in prayer. 'You *must* go on searching for him, sir.'

'Yes, Kathryn.' Lord Mountfitchet smiled at her. She was lovely with her dark red hair and green eyes, a sweetness about her mouth that was testament to her tender nature, but more than that she had helped him to retain the hope of his son being restored to him one day. 'That is why I have come to stay with you for a while. It is in my mind to visit Venice and Cyprus. As you know, I have recently begun to import wine from Cyprus and Italy to this country. I began to take an interest in the region when I started my search for Richard, and I am thinking that I might decide to live out there in the future.'

'You would leave England?' Kathryn stared at him in surprise; she had heard nothing of this before now. 'But what of your estate?'

'The house and land could be left to my agents to administer. It might be that I shall want to return one day, but there is little for me here now. In Elizabeth's England,

Catholics like myself and your father are not given an equal chance. I mean no disrespect to the Queen, for I know she must take the advice of her ministers—and they live in fear of a Catholic plot against her. I have taken no part in such plots nor would I, for she is our rightful Queen, but there is nothing to keep me here. If our poor Dickon lives, he must be somewhere in that region of the world— perhaps Algiers, or Constantinople.'

'We shall miss you,' Kathryn said and her throat caught with tears at the thought that she might never see him again. 'How shall we know if there is news of Dickon?'

'I should write to you, of course,' he said and smiled at her. 'But if I live there I shall need a good friend in this country to keep an eye on my affairs. I have asked Sir John if he would join me in this venture of importing wines, and he has been good enough to agree.'

Kathryn looked at her father, who confirmed his satis- faction with the arrangement. 'Then at least we shall hear from you sometimes.'

Lord Mountfitchet nodded, looking at her thoughtfully. 'Your father is too busy to accompany me on this voyage of exploration, Kathryn, but I would like him to have first- hand knowledge of what I intend to do there. He has sug- gested to me that you might accompany my party. My sister, Lady Mary Rivers, was widowed a few months past and has agreed to make the journey with me, for she has nothing to keep her here either and we shall be company for each other in our dotage.'

'You are not yet in your dotage, sir!'

'No, you are right—but it comes to us all in time, Kathryn. Mary and I get on well enough, and I have no wish to marry again. She thinks me a fool to search for Dickon, but keeps a still tongue on the subject. She will be your chaperon on the journey, and I believe we shall find a suitable guardian to accompany you on the return journey—unless you meet someone that you would wish to marry.'

'Oh…' Kathryn looked at her father, a faint colour in her cheeks.

'I had it in mind to look about for a suitable husband for you, daughter,' her father said, and paused. 'But Lord Mountfitchet is right. There is little opportunity for Catholics in this country these days. If you should chance to meet someone suitable who you liked while on your travels, I should be pleased. I know that Mary and Charles would take care of you and make sure that any suitor was worthy of you before advising me. Indeed, I shall probably make the journey to fetch you home myself. If I were not so busy at the moment, I would come with you. Your brother Philip will be home from Oxford next year and, if I cannot come myself, he will be happy to take my place, for he longs to travel.'

'Yes, I know.' Kathryn gave him a look of affection, for she was fond of her brother. 'Would you truly not mind if I went with Lord Mountfitchet and Lady Mary?'

'I should miss you, Kathryn,' her father said, his eyes warm with affection. 'Had your mother lived I might have been able to introduce you to a gentleman you could like before this. I have been too busy to see to it, and, besides, I think you need a woman to help you make such a decision. When Lady Mary told me she was to accompany Charles I thought it an opportunity for you to see a little of the world. I fear you must have been too often lonely since your dear mother left us.'

Kathryn smiled, but it was true enough. She had her good friends, neighbours and the elderly nurse who had been almost as a mother to her, but she had missed the time she had spent with her mother, talking and working at her sewing. It was nine years since the fever had taken her, just a year or so after Dickon was abducted.

'Where do you intend to go first, sir?' she asked, turning her clear green eyes on Lord Mountfitchet.

'We should return to London and my sister,' he replied. 'Then we should travel to Dover, and from thence to Venice. I have made contact with a merchant there, a rich, powerful man from whom I have been buying fine wines these past three years. It is he who has encouraged me to expand my business. I shall consult with him before I make my final choice, though I believe Cyprus will suit me rather than Italy itself. I have it in my mind to establish a vineyard there.'

'May I think about this for a little and give you my answer in the morning?'

'Yes, of course. I know it is a grave decision—it would mean that you would be away from your home for many months.'

'I believe I know my answer, but I would think about it,' Kathryn said and smiled at him. 'If you will excuse me now, sir, I shall leave you both, for I have things to attend to.'

'Until the morning, my dear.' Lord Mountfitchet bowed to her as she walked away.

'She is a good girl,' Sir John Rowlands said as the door

closed behind her and sighed regretfully. 'Her feelings for Dickon went deep and she has never forgotten him. I think they made some childish pact between them, but she has not told me the details. Until she accepts that all hope of Dickon is gone, I believe she will resist the idea of marriage with another.'

'It would be a shame if she were to waste her life,' Lord Mountfitchet said. 'Much as I hope that we shall find some news of him in Venice, I would not have Kathryn grieve for my son for ever. She is young and beautiful of face as well as nature, and she deserves some happiness.'

'Do you think this merchant of whom you spoke may have news?'

'I pray it may be so. Suleiman Bakhar knows him well. He told me that Lorenzo Santorini has helped several slaves who have managed to escape from their masters. He sometimes buys them in the slave markets of Algiers or takes prisoners from the pirate galleys he sinks, and he will ransom a Corsair captain for galley slaves. I think he exchanged ten slaves for one such man just a few months back. He gives them the chance to work for him, and sometimes he will return them to their families. He might ask for a ransom for his trouble, but for myself I would gladly pay it.'

'He sounds a man to be reckoned with?'

'Indeed, he is. Suleiman admires him—they have a mutual respect, I believe, though Santorini hath no love for Corsairs or the Turks. Indeed, I have heard that he hates them.'

'Yet Suleiman Bakhar calls him friend.'

'Suleiman is a man of enlightenment, as you know. He

has only one wife, Eleanor, though his religion allows him to have several, and he adores her. They travel together and though she adopts Muslim dress when in his country, she wears English garb in ours. Suleiman says that if anyone can find Dickon, it is Santorini.'

Sir John nodded. 'And that is the true reason you want Kathryn to accompany you, isn't it? You believe that Dickon will need both you and her if he is found.'

'What will he be like if he has survived?' Lord Mountfitchet said, his face grey with grief. The abduction of his son had haunted him these many years, giving him no peace. 'He is bound to have suffered terribly. He will need nursing and care if we are to teach him how to live again.'

'Yes, I fear you are right,' Sir John agreed. 'Perhaps Kathryn is the only one who might help him. They were so close as children.'

'I have not told her my thoughts on this matter,' Charles Mountfitchet said. 'It would make her feel that she ought to accompany us—but I would have her come only if she wishes it.'

'Yes, it must be as she wishes,' Sir John said. 'I would not have it otherwise. Yet if she should want to marry…'

'I shall write to you at once,' his friend promised. 'But Mary will have a care to her. We shall not allow some ruthless fortune hunter to snare her.'

'Her fortune is adequate, but not huge,' Sir John said. 'I have my son to think of and, as you said, Catholics are not given the chance to rise these days. Philip will not be given a post at court as I was when Mary was Queen.'

'That is why you do well to join me in my venture,' Lord

Mountfitchet said. 'We may trade where we will, for the world is bigger than this country of ours.'

'Yes, I believe you are right,' Sir John said, 'though for myself I would be loath to leave it as you intend.'

'Perhaps I might have thought as you if…' Lord Mount-fitchet sighed and shook his head. 'It does no good to repine. If Santorini can give me no hope, then I may accept that I shall never see my son again.'

Kathryn looked at herself in her small hand mirror. It had come all the way from Venice and had once belonged to her mother. She touched the smooth silver handle with her fingertips. The merchants of Venice were known for the quality of their wares, and it was from that city that the beautiful glass posset set, which her mother had treasured, had come.

It would be a great adventure to go with Lady Mary and Lord Mountfitchet. She had never expected to leave the shores of her homeland, for her father was not a great traveller. Yet she had read the histories in his library, those rare and valuable books and bound manuscripts that she was privileged to share, and her mind was open to new things. And of course Venice was renowned as a centre of publishing, particularly of the poets and of great histories. She thought that she would like to see new countries, new places—and there was always the possibility that they might discover something concerning Dickon's whereabouts.

Her hair was hanging loose about her shoulders, a dark, shining red mass of waves that gleamed with fire when it caught the candlelight. She got up and went over to the window, gazing out into the darkness. She could see very little for there were no stars to light the sky that night. Her father had spoken of her finding someone she might wish to marry—but how could she ever do that when her heart belonged to Dickon? She had given him her promise as a girl and he had taken his knife and cut her initial into the back of his wrist. She had cried out in alarm, for it had bled a lot, and had given him a lace kerchief to bind it.

'Does it hurt very much?' she had asked and he had laughed, his eyes bold and daring.

'It is nothing, for I know that this blood binds you to me for ever.'

She had kissed the wound then, tasting his blood, and had known that she would always love him. She would resist any attempts to marry her to a man she did not love. She would behave modestly when travelling and listen to Lady Mary's advice, but she would not let them marry her to a man she did not respect or feel some affection for. Perhaps one day she would feel inside her that Dickon was dead. If that happened, she might consider marriage. If not...

Her thoughts seemed to come up against a blank wall, for she did not know what she would do if Dickon never returned to her. There was no alternative to marriage for a woman of her class, unless she wished to retire to a convent. Women married or became nuns, unless their male relatives had a use for them. Perhaps Philip would accept her as a dependent in his household if she grew old and past the age of being a wife.

It was a sad prospect, but what else was there for her? Laying down her mirror, Kathryn went to her bed, which was a heavy box base with four posts and a carved tester overhead. A handsome thing, it was piled high with soft mattresses filled with goose feathers, for the slats were wooden and hard. Slipping beneath the luxury of silken quilts, she wondered what life was like on board ship.

Yet she would put up with any discomfort if, at the end of the journey, she could find the man she loved.

The momentum was gathering, Lorenzo thought as he left the meeting to which he had been summoned. There had been talk of forming an alliance to fight a campaign against the Turks for a long time, but now, at last, it looked as though it might actually happen later that year. Pope Pius V had formed the Holy League with Spain and Venice, and it was hoped that others would bring their ships to help fight the menace that had haunted the Mediterranean seas and the Messina Strait for so long. Many had thought the talking would simply go on and on, and negotiations would probably continue for a while. However, after these latest threats against Cyprus and Rome itself, it seemed that His Holiness was determined to strike against the enemy that had for so long threatened the nations of Christendom.

Leaving the palace, Lorenzo was thoughtful as he walked, his mind dwelling not on the conference that he had attended, but on a letter that had reached him shortly before he left Venice. It was from an Englishman with whom he had done business in the past, telling him that he was coming to Venice and asking if he could help to trace a youth who had been abducted from the shores of his homeland over ten years previously.

Lorenzo frowned, for it was a thankless task. He knew

as well as any man how unlikely it was that the youth had survived.

He would, of course, do what he could to help Lord Mountfitchet, for although they had never met he had heard good things of the gentleman. His father, Antonio Santorini, had visited England some years previously and had spoken of meeting Lord Mountfitchet, saying that he was both honest and decent. Therefore, Lorenzo would help him, but to trace a man who had been taken by Corsairs so long ago…

Lorenzo's instincts remained alert even while his mind wrestled with his problems, and he was aware that he was being followed. So when the attack was made, he was ready for it, drawing his sword as he turned to meet the three ruffians who rushed upon him out of the darkness.

'Come, my friends,' he invited with a cold smile that only served to intensify the ice of his eyes. 'Would you have my purse? Come, take it if you can…'

One of the three, bolder than the others, took him at his word. They clashed swords, contesting the fight fiercely, but the rogue was no match for a master swordsman and called for help from his comrades. The other two came at Lorenzo warily, for they had seen that he was no easy mark. Outnumbered three to one, he held his own for some minutes, slashing to left and right as each one attacked in turn, whirling out of reach, retreating, then advancing as he fought with the skill and ferocity his years as master of a war galley had brought him. Even so, the odds were against him and it might have gone ill with him in the end had not a newcomer joined in the fray, bringing his own skill and courage to Lorenzo's assistance.

Lorenzo's sword found its mark, disabling one of the

three. Finding that the odds were now even and that they were being driven back, the other two rogues broke and ran, whilst the wounded fellow leaned against a wall, clutching his arm, blood oozing through his fingers.

Lorenzo had sheathed his sword when the others ran, but the stranger who had come to his aid still held his, regarding the would-be assassin speculatively.

'Shall we kill him?' he asked of Lorenzo. ''Tis what the dog deserves—or do you wish to question him?'

'His purpose was to rob me,' Lorenzo answered with a careless shrug. 'Let him go to join his companions—unless he would prefer a quick death?' His hand moved to his sword hilt suggestively.

The man gave a squeak of fear, suddenly finding the strength to run in the wake of his comrades. A harsh laugh escaped the stranger, who turned to Lorenzo.

'You are merciful, sir. I think he would have killed you if he could.'

'I do not doubt it.' Lorenzo smiled. 'I thank you for your help, sir. I am—'

'I know you, Signor Santorini,' the stranger said before he could continue. 'I am Pablo Dominicus and you were pointed out to me at the conference we both attended. I followed you because I wish to speak with you.'

'Then good fortune followed me this night,' Lorenzo said. 'Shall we find an inn where we can sit and talk, if you have some business you would discuss?'

'My business is twofold,' Pablo Dominicus said. 'I am on the one hand an emissary from His Holiness the Pope—and on the other I am a man seeking revenge. I believe we have a common enemy.'

'Indeed?' Lorenzo's eyes narrowed. It seemed the stranger was a Spaniard. He had no great love of the Spanish, for the Inquisition was a fearful thing, practised by many in the name of Catholicism, but stronger and more powerful in Spain than most countries. And it was known that Spain resented Venice for its independence, and considered that some of its inhabitants would benefit from the attention of the Inquisition. There were men who served in Lorenzo's galleys who had known what it was to suffer torture and beatings at the hands of the fanatics who ruled the religious order. Yet there was only polite inquiry in Lorenzo's voice as he said, 'Pray tell me more, *señor*. I would know how I may serve you?'

'Let us find somewhere we can be private, Signor Santorini. I have a request from His Holiness, for your name is well known to him—and another of my own.'

'There is an inn I know in the next street,' Lorenzo said. 'If your business is secret we can take a private chamber and be sure that we are not overheard.'

Lorenzo drank sparingly of the rich red wine Dominicus had ordered, listening to the request being made of him. In the darkness of the streets he had been unable to see the face of Don Pablo clearly, but now he saw that he was a man in his middle years. Heavily built, he wore a small, dark pointed beard, his hair short and thinning at the temples. And there was a faint unease in his manner that Lorenzo found interesting.

'His Holiness requests that you pledge your support to our cause,' Don Pablo said. 'Your galleys are some of the finest and your men are strong and brave, and, I am told, loyal to you. If you join us in the League, others will surely follow.'

'It was my intention to make my offer once I had consulted with my captains,' Lorenzo said, his eyes thoughtful as he studied the other man. Why was it that he did not quite believe him as honest as he appeared? 'I shall join your cause for it is also mine, but the men who serve me are free to choose. I believe most will follow me, for they have cause to hate the Turks and their allies.' Some hated the Spanish just as much, but he would not say that. 'Now, perhaps you would care to tell me the true reason you chose to follow me this evening?'

Don Pablo smiled. 'They told me you were clever. I shall not insult your intelligence by holding to the claim that I am here on the Pope's behalf, for that might have been left to others, though I know His Holiness intends to approach you. I followed you because I believe you have good cause to hate Rachid—he they call the Feared One. I have heard it said that you hate him and would see him dead if it were possible.'

Lorenzo was silent for a moment, then, 'What has Rachid done to you?'

'Three months ago his galleys attacked and captured one of my merchant ships,' Don Pablo said and his fist clenched on the table. It was clear that he was suffering some deep emotion. 'That cost me a great deal of money— and one of the men he killed was my son-in-law.'

'I am sorry for your loss, sir.'

'My daughter and grandchildren are living in Cyprus,' Don Pablo went on and his hand shook as if he were in the grip of some strong emotion. 'Immacula wants to return to Spain with her children. I would send ships to fetch her myself—but I have suffered other losses of late. Those accursed English privateers, as they call themselves, have been harrying my ships as they return from the New World…'

'You are asking me to bring your daughter to you?' Lorenzo's brows arched as he studied the other's face.

'I am willing to pay for your time, of course.' Don Pablo's eyes dropped before Lorenzo's intense gaze.

'My galleys are meant for war. They are not suitable for a woman and children. I think you must look elsewhere for your escort, Señor Dominicus.'

'You mistake me, *signor.* Immacula will naturally travel in our own ship. I but ask for an escort to see her safely to Spain.'

'You want my galleys to escort your ship?' Lorenzo nodded, his gaze narrowing as he studied the Spaniard. Something was not right about this. His instincts were telling him to be wary, and they were seldom wrong. 'My men work for me. They are not for hire to others.'

'Surely they would do as you bid them?' Don Pablo's eyes were dark with suppressed anger and something more—was it fear? Lorenzo could not decide, but sensed that there was more to this than he had been told. 'I believed you commanded. Do not tell me that those who serve you dictate what you do, for I should not believe it!'

Lorenzo's mouth curved in a strange, cold smile that sent a shiver down the spine of his companion. 'Forgive me if I speak plainly, Don Pablo. Some of my men have suffered at the hands of the Spanish Inquisition. They would spit in your face rather than fight for you.'

Don Pablo's face suffused with anger, his neck a dark red colour. He started to his feet as if he would strike out in anger. 'You refuse me? I had heard that you were a man of business. Surely my gold is as good as the next man's?'

'For myself I would take your money,' Lorenzo said, his face a stone mask that revealed nothing of his thoughts, 'but I cannot expect my men to fight for a Spaniard.' He stood up and inclined his head. 'I am sorry, but I believe you may find others willing to assist you.'

'You may name your own price.' Don Pablo flung the words after him, seeming desperate. 'I beg you to help me, *signor.*'

'My answer remains the same, Don Pablo.' Lorenzo turned to look at him, his eyes cold and resolute. He was certain now that his instincts had been right; this was not a simple matter of business. 'When you decide to tell me the truth, I may reconsider, sir—but until then, farewell.'

A look of fear mixed with horror came to the Spaniard's eyes and for a moment he seemed as if he would speak, but he shook his head and in another moment Lorenzo closed the door behind him.

His instincts had served him well as always. He believed that the attack on him had been planned, not random, a ploy to make him grateful to Dominicus—to make him accept the commission that was offered in a sense of friendship and trust. Lorenzo had learned in a hard school that few men were to be trusted.

There was more behind this than met the eye, and it smelled wrong. If his enemies had set a trap, it would need to be baited more cleverly than this.

Chapter Two

So this was Venice! Kathryn looked about her eagerly as their ship weighed anchor in the great lagoon. They were too far out to see the shoreline clearly, but the grand palaces of the rich merchant princes lay shimmering in the sunshine, the waters of the lagoon lapping over the steps at which brightly coloured gondolas were moored.

'What do you think of Venice, my dear?' Lady Mary asked as she came to stand beside the girl. 'Is it what you expected?'

'It is beautiful. I did not know what to expect. I have seen a pastel of the Grand Canal and its palaces, ma'am, but reality far exceeds the artist's imagination. Those palaces seem almost to be floating.'

Lady Mary laughed. She was a stout, good-tempered lady, who had been pretty in her youth, and her smile was warm with affection, for she had grown fond of Kathryn on their journey. They had been together some months and it was now the spring of 1570. In England it would still be very cool, but here it was much warmer as the sun turned the water to a sparkling blue.

'Yes, it has a magical appeal, does it not? My late husband was an enthusiastic traveller in his youth. He told me of his visit to Venice. We must visit St Mark's Square and gaze upon the Doge's palace while your uncle is at his business, Kathryn.'

It had been decided that she should look upon her kind friends as Aunt Mary and Uncle Charles.

'We may not be blood related,' Charles Mountfitchet had told her at the beginning of their journey, as they set out to London to meet his sister. 'But we shall be together *en famille* for some months and must be comfortable with one another.'

Kathryn had been very willing to accept him as an honorary uncle, for she had long felt close to him. They had comforted each other throughout the years since Dickon's abduction and she was fonder of him than anyone other than her father.

'Oh, I want to see everything,' she said now. Her eyes had a glow of excitement that had been missing for a long time. The journey had suited her for she had not been seasick, as Lady Mary had for the first few days of their voyage. 'And you will feel so much better to be on land again, Aunt.'

'Indeed, I shall. I might wish to go no further,' Lady Mary said with some feeling. 'I fear that this is but a temporary respite, for my brother wishes to settle in Cyprus and so we must put to sea once more.'

'He plans to grow his own wine,' Kathryn said. 'But who knows? His plans may change.'

'You are thinking of Richard, of course.' Lady Mary frowned. 'I know that both you and my brother hope for a miracle, my dear, but I fear you will be sadly disappointed.'

'But it does happen,' Kathryn said. 'Suleiman Bakhar told my uncle that sometimes slaves may be either rescued or bought from their masters. If Dickon was sold as a house slave, it is possible that we might be able to find him and purchase his bond.'

'My brother has tried to find his son,' Lady Mary said, sighing deeply. She did not believe their search would come to anything and feared that they merely brought more pain on themselves. 'For years he petitioned men of influence to help him in his search, to no avail. I believe that Richard is dead. I am sorry, but I think that some trace of him would have come to light before this if he were alive.'

'I know what you say is sensible,' Kathryn said, her eyes bright with the fervour of her belief. 'But I feel that he lives. Here inside me.' She pressed her hands to her breast. 'I cannot explain it, for it must sound foolish, but if Dickon had died—a part of me would have died too.'

Lady Mary shook her head, but said no more on the subject. In her own opinion Kathryn was living on false hope. Even if her nephew had somehow survived, he would not be the same. Any man who had endured years of slavery must have changed; he might be hard and bitter or broken in spirit. Either way, Kathryn was doomed to grief. It might be better if no trace of Richard was ever found, for surely in time she would learn to love someone else.

The girl had blossomed under her care. While in London they had visited the silk merchants, buying materials to make into gowns suitable for a warmer climate. Lady Mary had been pleased to take the girl about, introducing her to her friends, giving her a taste of what life could be, and the change in Kathryn had pleased her. She smiled more and her laughter was warm, infectious, though there was a stubborn streak beneath her pretty manners. Yet she had thrown off the air of sadness that had haunted her lovely face and was revealed as a charming, intelligent girl.

Lady Mary had great hopes of finding a suitable husband for her charge before the time came for Kathryn to return home.

'I believe this is the gondola come to take us ashore,' Kathryn said as she turned to her companion. 'We are to be taken to the house Uncle Charles has hired for our use, but he is to meet that friend of his immediately. Signor Santorini, I believe he called him.'

'He hopes for news, I dare say.' Lady Mary smothered a sigh. 'Well, at least it will give us time to settle in. Men are always in the way at such times.'

Kathryn smiled, but made no answer. Given a free choice she would have wished to go with her uncle to the meeting, but she had not been asked. She would be of much more help to Lady Mary—but she would be impatient for news.

'I trust your journey was a good one, sir?' Lorenzo rose to meet his visitor. He had chosen to receive him in one of the smaller salons to the right of the grand entrance hall, for it was more welcoming and more conducive to privacy. 'I am pleased to meet you at last, Lord Mountfitchet.'

His words were spoken frankly, his eyes going over the older man and finding that he was drawn to him in a way that was not often the case with strangers. He saw suffering in the other's face, the greying at his temples and in his beard; it was a face grown old before its time. It was the face of a man who had known terrible grief. For some reason Lorenzo was saddened by his grief, though the man was a stranger to him.

'Come, sir, will you not take a glass of wine with me? Pray be seated.' He indicated the principal chair, which was of a kind not common in England, the seat well padded, and the low back comfortable and shaped to accommodate a man's bulk. 'I dare say you are weary from your journey?'

'Indeed, a glass of wine would be welcome, Signor Santorini,' Charles Mountfitchet said as he took his seat. 'My sister and niece wanted me to accompany them to our lodgings and rest for a day or so, but I was impatient to meet you.'

'Unfortunately, I have no definite news of your son,' Lorenzo said. 'However, there is a man I would have you meet, sir. He was rescued from a Corsair galley two months ago, but has been too ill to question. We believe that he may be English, though as yet he has hardly spoken a word.'

'What does he look like?' Charles asked barely able to contain his excitement. 'What colour are his hair and eyes?'

'What colour hair did your son have? Were there any distinguishing features?'

Charles thought for a moment. 'It distresses me to say it, but I can no longer see Richard's face. His hair was fair—darker than yours, but of a similar texture. His eyes were blue…' He frowned. 'I might be describing a thousand men. I fear I have given you but poor help, sir. But loath as I am to admit it, I spent little time with my son when he was young. He was there and I took my good fortune for granted. It was only when I lost him that I understood what he had meant to me.' His voice broke with emotion.

'Yes, it is often so, I believe,' Lorenzo said. He was not certain why he felt affected by Lord Mountfitchet's story, for he was not a sentimental man. 'We all take what we have for granted. My father died some months ago and I miss him sorely. I was away much of the time and afterwards regretted that I did not show more gratitude towards him.'

'I was sorry to learn of Antonio's death. We met only twice when he visited England, but we were drawn to each other.' Charles hesitated, then said, 'I did not realise at the time that he had a son.'

'I was adopted some years ago,' Lorenzo said, revealing more than was his wont. 'My father was a good and generous man. I owe him much. He was not a wealthy man, so it was given to me to improve our fortunes and I was happy that I was able to see him end his days in comfort.'

'He was fortunate to have you. I have tried to preserve my estate for Richard, but it would have been a relief to me to have him with me. I fear I grow old and the days seem lonely.' His eyes were clouded with grief, the years of futile searching carved deep into his face.

'The man I would have you meet has blue eyes,' Lorenzo said with a frown. 'As for his hair—it has turned grey from the suffering he endured at the hands of his captors. I must warn you that this man has terrible scars on his arms, back and legs.'

'The poor devil,' Charles said and his hands shook as he sipped his wine. He took a deep breath, trying to control the images in his mind—images that had haunted his dreams for years of his son being beaten and tortured. 'This wine is excellent.' He made an effort to banish his nightmares. 'A new one, I think? You have not sent me this before?'

'It came from a vineyard in Cyprus,' Lorenzo told him. 'I have been trying it before adding it to the shipment.' He refilled his guest's cup. 'I shall speak to the man I mentioned myself, ask him if he will see you.' He saw the surprise in the other's eyes. 'He is not my prisoner. He was saved from the wreck of a galley and we have nursed him through his illness. Now that he is well, he will be given a choice. He may work for me as a free man or return to his homeland. If he asks me for help to find his family, I shall give it.'

'Do you ask a ransom for him?'

'If his family can afford to pay. I am a man of business, sir.'

'And if he has no family?'

'Then he is free to go where he will—or stay with me.' Lorenzo's eyes held a glint of ice. He lifted his head defiantly. 'He has his life returned to him. What more would you have of me?'

'Nothing you have not given,' Charles replied. 'For myself, I would be glad to pay for the return of my son.'

'I wish that I might give you more hope,' Lorenzo said. 'But let us speak of other things. You have an idea of settling on Cyprus, I believe?'

'I have thoughts of my own vineyard.'

'Then I may be of more help to you there,' Lorenzo said. 'Come to dinner tomorrow evening. Bring your sister and niece to dine. I may have more news for you by then.'

'Thank you. I shall look forward to it.'

Charles was thoughtful as he took his leave. He believed Lorenzo Santorini an honest man. His manner was somewhat reserved and at times his eyes were cold. He was clearly unsentimental about his business, a man of purpose. Some might think him harsh to take ransom money for men he rescued from slavery, but Charles found no fault in his seeking some profit from what he did. There were others who would simply have left the galley slave to die or even have sent him back to the markets to be sold again.

No doubt it was Santorini's keen intelligence and lack of sentiment that had made him wealthy. Yes, perhaps he was a little harsh in matters of business, but who knew what had caused him to be that way? He sensed some mystery in the man's past, but it was not his affair. Santorini would deal fairly with him and he could ask for no more.

His thoughts turned to the man he had been told of—a man who might be English with blue eyes. Could he possibly be Richard? Charles felt a flicker of hope. Yet it was ridiculous to allow himself to hope. There must be many blue-eyed Englishmen who had been lost at sea and taken as galley slaves, and not only by the Corsairs. Some served in Spanish galleys and there was little to choose between their masters, for they were beaten and tortured, made to work until they collapsed at the oar and were tossed into the sea to die. The Spanish hated the heretic English and it was often said that they were crueller than the Corsairs to those they took in battle.

Charles closed his eyes, trying to shut out the pictures that crowded into his mind. God forgive him, he could almost wish his son dead rather than know that he had suffered such a terrible fate.

'But that is wicked!' Kathryn exclaimed as Charles spoke of the ransom he would pay if the man he had been told of should by some extreme chance be his son. 'Why, this Lorenzo Santorini is little better than those evil men whose business is to trade in slaves.'

'No, Kathryn,' he said. 'You do not understand, my dear. I would be willing to pay any sum for Richard's return and should be grateful to the man who found him for me.'

'But a decent man would not ask for money, Uncle Charles.' She was outraged, her eyes scornful of this man she had yet to meet.

'Hush, Kathryn,' he chided. 'We must not judge him. He does much good, I think, and if he makes a profit by it…' Charles shrugged his shoulders. 'I found him honest. He is a man I can do business with. You may feel it wrong to take money for restoring a man to his family, but others would have let the poor fellow die.'

'Please, Charles,' Lady Mary said with a little shudder, 'I wish you would not say such things. You will give Kathryn nightmares.'

'No, dear Aunt Mary,' Kathryn said and smiled at her. 'My nightmares have become a thing of the past since we began our journey. I do not know why, but my heart has become much lighter.' It was as if she felt that she was going to meet Dickon, that she would find him at her journey's end. In her dreams he seemed very close and he was no longer in pain or distress. She seemed to see him smiling at her, opening his arms to enfold her and kiss her.

'Well, I am happy for it,' Charles said with a smile. 'But it would be too much to expect to find Richard so swiftly. It may be months or years—or perhaps never—but Signor Santorini has promised to do what he can. I pray you, Kathryn, do nothing to antagonise him this evening.'

'Of course I shall not, Uncle Charles,' Kathryn said. 'If you believe he can help us, then I shall do nothing to make him change his mind. I may think him unprincipled and wrong, but I shall not say it.'

He smiled at her, nodding his satisfaction with her promise. It was time for them to leave, and the gondola was waiting at the steps outside their house to take them to Lorenzo Santorini's palace.

Kathryn's eyes widened as she saw it, for it was surely one of the most important and attractive of the many beautiful buildings built by the Grand Lagoon. This Signor Santorini must be very wealthy; if that were so, he did not need to ask for money from the families of the poor wretches he rescued from cruel masters.

Her antagonism was growing towards the man she had never met, her feelings of outrage at the obvious trappings of his great wealth building a picture in her mind so that, when the tall, golden-haired man came towards them, she did not at first imagine that he was Lorenzo Santorini. She had seldom seen a more attractive man, Kathryn thought, and as she looked into his deep blue eyes her breath caught and she felt very strange. She had only ever known one person with eyes that colour and so strong was the emotion that gripped her then that she almost fainted. Indeed, she swayed and put out her hand to steady herself, finding her arm gripped by a firm hand.

'Are you ill, Madonna?'

His voice was so deep and husky; yet she heard only the echoes of the sea against a rocky shore on a windswept night, her mind whirling in confusion. For a moment she was there again, looking down as the Corsairs carried her beloved Dickon away with them, her feeling of terror so strong that she almost fainted.

'Kathryn? Is something wrong, my dear?'

Lady Mary's voice brought her back from the edge of the precipice and her head cleared. She looked at the man, who still held her arm in a vicelike grip, her eyes suddenly dark with revulsion as she dismissed the foolish notion that had come to her. How could she have thought even for one moment that this man was her beloved Dickon? His face was deeply tanned, with sculptured cheekbones and lines about his eyes. Richard Mountfitchet would be no more than five and twenty; this man must be some years older, of course, the set of his mouth harsh and unforgiving, so different from the easy smile that she had been wont to see on Dickon's lips.

Why, from what she had heard of him, he was little better than the evil men who had abducted her dearest friend!

She moved her arm and his grip relaxed, releasing her as her head went up proudly, daring him to touch her again. 'I am all right, Aunt Mary,' she said, smiling at the woman who was clearly concerned for her. 'It was just a moment of faintness. Perhaps the change from the bright sunlight to darkness?'

It was a weak excuse, of course, for it was not truly dark in the palace, which was a place of colour and sunshine from the many windows high above that gave the grand hall a churchlike feel.

'It has been very warm today,' Lorenzo said, his eyes narrowing as he sensed her hostility. What ailed her—and why had she looked at him so oddly for a moment? 'And I believe it may be cool in here. Please come through to my private chambers, ladies. I believe you may be more comfortable there.'

Lorenzo led the way to another, smaller chamber, which was lavishly appointed with beautiful tiled walls and floors, the colours rich and vibrant. It was furnished with the most exquisite things that Kathryn had ever seen, some of them with a distinctly Byzantine look to them. For surely those silken couches belonged more properly in the harem of an eastern potentate?

'I have never seen such a lovely room,' Lady Mary declared, echoing the thoughts Kathryn would not for pride's sake utter. 'Where did you find all these lovely things, Signor Santorini?'

'Some of them were given me in gratitude for saving the life of a precious son,' Lorenzo told her. His eyes were on Kathryn as he spoke, a mocking gleam deep in their mysterious depths. 'It was in Granada and the boy was a Moor, the son of a merchant prince—a man whose wealth would make me seem a pauper by comparison.'

'How interesting,' Lady Mary said. 'Pray do tell us more, sir.'

'It was nothing,' Lorenzo told her with a fleeting smile, his eyes becoming colder than deep water ice as he saw that

Kathryn's mouth had curled in scorn. 'I happened to be in the right place at the right time—and the grateful father showered me with gifts of all kinds, some of which you see here.'

'You must also be a very wealthy man,' Kathryn said and her tone made it sound like the worst of insults. 'Might it not have been nobler to refuse the gifts and be satisfied with the pleasure of saving a life?' Her eyes flashed with green fire, challenging him so clearly that the air seemed to crackle between them.

'No, no, Kathryn,' Charles reminded her uneasily. He was afraid she would antagonise the Venetian, and Santorini was his best hope of ever finding his son. Indeed, since they had met, he had been filled with new hope. 'You must not say such things, my dear. It is not for you to judge these matters.'

'Kathryn's fault lies in her ignorance,' Lorenzo said easily and she saw that there was an amused curl to his mouth. His eyes glinted with ice and she felt her heart catch, for something about him drew her despite herself. 'To have refused the gifts from such a man after rendering him a significant service would have been to offer him a deadly insult. Had I been unwise enough to do so, he would have thought that I believed he owed me more and would simply have increased the size of his gift—even to beggaring himself, if I demanded it. But of course, your niece could not know anything of the customs, or indeed the pride, that prevails amongst such people.'

He was looking at her as if she were a foolish child!

Kathryn felt as if she were in the hands of her old nurse, being scolded for some childish misdemeanour. He was humiliating her, stripping her to the status of an ignorant girl, making her feel foolish—and she hated him for it. If she had not remembered her promise to Lord Mountfitchet at that moment, she might have given him an honest opinion of his morals, telling him what she thought of his habit of asking a ransom from his victims.

'I bow to your superior judgement, sir,' she said, her nails turned inwards to the palms of her hands as she fought her instinct to rage at him. Dickon's father was relying on his help. It was through him that they might learn something that would lead them to find Dickon. She must remember that, no matter how great her disgust of this man and his trade. 'Forgive me, I did not know…'

The apology was the hardest she had ever had to make and she tasted its bitterness; she was determined to say nothing more that evening, for it would kill her to be civil to him! She could not know that the look in her eyes and the tilt of her head betrayed her, nor that he found her defiance amusing.

'No, do not apologise, sweet Madonna,' he murmured and the mockery in his voice stung her like the lash of a whip. 'We should be churlish indeed not to forgive such beauty a small mistake of judgement.'

Kathryn inclined her head. Oh, he was so sure of himself, so secure in his position of power and wealth! She would like to wipe that mocking expression from his face and were she alone with him she would do it! But no, she must not let him drive her to further indiscretion. She would behave as befitted an English gentlewoman.

'I bow to your generosity, sir.' The look she gave him was so haughty that it would have slain any other man, but he

merely smiled and turned his attention to Lord Mountfitchet.

Wine was served and there was a choice of a sweeter
wine for the ladies, but Kathryn stubbornly chose the same
as he and her uncle drank and nearly gagged on the dry-
ness of it. She took one sip and set the glass down, her irritation mounting as she saw that he had noted her distaste.
When they were directed outside to a small courtyard garden, where a table had been set for them, she noticed that
he made a small signal to his servant, and when she looked
for her wineglass her wine had been changed.

Oh, was there no ending to this torture? Kathryn asked
the servant who served her from the many delicious vari-
eties of fish, meat and rice dishes to bring her some water,
refusing to be tempted by the wine, which Lady Mary had
declared was delicious.

The food was wonderful too. Used to the more heavily
spiced dishes her father's cooks served at home and sick-
ened by the awful food on board ship, she could not resist
trying the delicious prawns and unusual fruits and vegetables that were served to her. After each main course a cold
ice sherbet was served, which cleared the palate, and the
sweet courses included a delicious sticky jelly that she
simply could not resist.

'I see you approve of one of the gifts my friend from
Granada sends me from time to time,' Lorenzo said, smiling at her. 'You see, as his son grows to a man, his gratitude increases and he will not allow me to forget that he
considers me as another son.'

Kathryn had been reaching for another piece of the
sticky sweet and her hand froze in mid-air, then withdrew,

her eyes darting a glare at him that would have made most men retreat in confusion. His answer was to smile so wolfishly that it sent a chill through her, the flash of white teeth sudden and menacing, as if he would devour her.

'Please continue to enjoy them, Madonna,' he told her. 'It will please my friend mightily to know that his generosity is not wasted. He fears that I do not appreciate it, but now I can tell him quite truthfully that it brought me favour in your eyes.'

'I am glad that your friend will be pleased,' Kathryn said and defiantly took the piece of lemon-flavoured sweetmeat that she desired, biting into it with such venom that she saw his eyes flicker with laughter. He enjoyed taunting her! She could see it in his face, but there was nothing she could do, for she was at his mercy. Please God, let this meal be over soon and then, perhaps, she need not ever see him again.

'I was thinking,' Charles said, seemingly unaware of the duel going on between Kathryn and their host. 'I have cudgelled my brains to think of a distinguishing mark that might help you find Richard, sir—but I cannot recall a thing.'

'Oh, but—' Kathryn began and then stopped as all eyes turned on her. She shook her head. 'I cannot be sure that it would still be there.'

'If you know of something, you should tell us, Kathryn,' Charles said. 'I believe you knew Richard better than anyone.'

'Pray do give me any information you can,' Lorenzo said and reached for his wineglass. As he did so she caught sight of a leather wristband chased with silver symbols.

The wristbands were so at odds with the richness of his dress that she was mesmerised for a moment and he saw her interest. 'You are admiring my bracelets, Kathryn?' He pulled back his sleeves so that she could see that he wore the curious bands on each wrist. 'The symbols may not be familiar to you, for they are in Arabic. One stands for life, the other for death.' There was something in his eyes that made her shiver inwardly, an expression so different to any other that she had seen in him that her stomach clenched with fear. 'It is to remind me, lest I should forget, that one is the close companion of the other.'

'Surely…' The words died on her lips, for now she felt a sense of desolation in him and it touched her, reaching down inside her so that she shared his grief, his pain, and it almost sent her reeling into darkness. 'They are remarkable, sir,' she said, fighting to pull herself back from that deep pit. 'But you asked about a distinguishing mark. There was one that Uncle Charles would not know about.' She paused, for the memory was so strong in her mind then that it made her ache with the grief of her loss. 'Dickon was my closest companion, my dearest friend. One day he told me that he would always love only me, even though I was but nine years to his fifteen. I said that when he grew up he would forget me, and he drew his knife. He cut my initial into his arm, just above his wrist.' She saw Lorenzo's eyes darken, his gaze intensifying on her face. 'It bled a great deal and I was frightened. I gave him my kerchief to bind his wrist, but it was deep and the bleeding would not stop. My nurse bound it for him when we went home and scolded me for allowing him to hurt himself. When it began to heal, there was a livid mark in the shape of a K.'

'You have never told me this, Kathryn,' Charles said and frowned. 'It might help in the search—if it still remains.'

'It might have been obliterated by other marks,' Lorenzo said and he looked thoughtful, serious now, all mockery gone. 'I do not wish to distress the ladies, Lord Mountfitchet, but you must realise that the manacles galley slaves wear leave deep scars. Even if the scar that Richard inflicted on himself remained, it might not be easy to see after so many years of being chained to an oar.'

'If he was a galley slave,' Kathryn said. 'He was but fifteen, sir. Might he not have been sold as a house slave?' She had prayed so often that it might be so, otherwise there was little hope that Dickon would have survived.

'It is possible—but if he was strong for his age he would more likely have been put to the oars. The rate of death amongst such unfortunates is high and anyone with the strength to pull an oar might be used if the Corsairs had lost some of their oarsmen.'

'Yet that makes it all the more likely that the mark may still be there,' Kathryn said. 'For if he lives, it is unlikely that he was in the galleys.'

'You speak truly, for I doubt that any man could survive ten years in the galleys,' Lorenzo told her and the expression in his eyes sent a shiver down her spine. 'We must hope that for at least some part of the time your cousin was more fortunate.'

Kathryn looked at him, seeing an odd expression in his eyes. What was he thinking now?

'Would your friend in Granada help us to find Dickon?' she asked.

'Yes, that is possible,' Lorenzo said. 'I will write to him

and ask if he will make inquiries, though after so long…'
His words drifted away and he lifted his shoulders in a gesture that made her want to defy him all the more.

'You think it is impossible, don't you?' Kathryn saw the answer in his face. 'But I don't believe that Dickon is dead. I am certain he lives. I feel it in here.' She put her hands to her breast, her face wearing an expression of such expectation, such hope, that he was moved. 'As we journeyed here my feeling grew stronger. I believe that he is alive and may be closer than we think.'

'All things are possible,' Lorenzo said, for he found that he did not wish to dim the light in those beautiful eyes by telling her she was wrong. 'My friend would tell you that it is the will of Allah, but I believe it is the will of man. If Dickon was strong enough, if he wanted to live badly enough, he would find a way to survive. And perhaps he might have been fortunate. Not all slaves are ill treated, Kathryn. Some masters are better than others.'

'You speak as if you have some experience of these things, sir?'

Lorenzo smiled oddly. 'Perhaps…'

Kathryn would have pressed for an answer, but he turned to Lord Mountfitchet and began to talk of Cyprus and the land most suitable for wine growing. Kathryn sat and listened, her first disgust of him waning a little as she realised that he was a man of knowledge and influence.

She could not condone what he did in the matter of the ransoms he demanded from the families of those he rescued, and yet she began to understand that it could be but a small part of his business and not the source of his vast wealth.

She could not like him, she decided, for he was too arrogant, too certain of his position, and he could not understand how she felt—how Lord Mountfitchet felt—about the loss of Dickon. But perhaps Uncle Charles was right and he would deal honestly with them.

Besides, what right had she to judge him when she did not know him?

Lorenzo turned his gaze on her again for a moment, and she felt that strange sensation that had almost made her faint when they first met. Why was it that she felt as if they had met before?

'This is so beautiful,' Kathryn exclaimed as they wandered about the square that was the centre of Venice. 'Is it true that the Church of Saint Mark was built to house his body when it was brought from Alexandria?'

'That is what I have been told,' Lorenzo answered her though she had addressed her question to her aunt. 'The building you see near by is the Palazzo Ducale—and over there is the Cathedral, which was first begun in the ninth century and rebuilt after a fire in the eleventh. Notice the architecture, which bears a distinctly Byzantine influence.'

'It is very fine,' Kathryn replied. 'I had thought the people of Byzantium were barbarians, but it seems that they knew how to build.'

'They knew many things,' Lorenzo replied with a smile. 'It was a great empire that demands our respect.'

'You seem to know so much,' she said, a little overcome by all the things he had told them as they explored the beautiful city of Venice and its waterways. 'What, pray tell me, are those buildings over there?'

'That is the Procuratie Vecchie, and used by the proc-urators or magistrates, from amongst whom the Doge is chosen, and is built, as you see, in the Italian style, as are many of the palaces themselves. And those columns were erected in the twelfth century. That one bears the winged lion of St Mark and the other portrays St Theodore on a crocodile.' He looked at Kathryn, a faint smile on his lips. 'Would you wish to visit the Bridge of Sighs—or would you prefer return to my home and take some refreshment?'

'Tell me, why is it called the Bridge of Sighs?'

'I imagine Signor Santorini has had enough of your questions for one day,' Lady Mary said. 'It was kind of him to accompany us, but perhaps like me he is ready to return home for some refreshment.'

'Oh, forgive me,' Kathryn said, for she was not in the least tired and might have carried on exploring for another hour or more. 'Yes, we shall go home—at least, we shall return to your home, *signor.*'

'It is also yours for the duration of your stay,' Lorenzo said. On discovering the previous evening that the lodg-ings they had taken were less than they had hoped for, he had sent his servants to remove their baggage, insisting that they stay with him until they left for Cyprus. It was also his suggestion that he accompany Lady Mary and Kathryn on their tour of the city, for Lord Mountfitchet had other business and, despite Kathryn's protests, he did not think it suitable that they should go alone. 'And as to the matter of why the bridge has that name, it is because the palace connects to the prison and the bridge is the route by which prisoners are taken to the judgement hall.'

'Ah, I see,' Kathryn said and smiled. 'I had thought it might have had a more romantic story attached to it.'

'Perhaps a lover who had cast himself into the water after having his heart broken?' Lorenzo laughed huskily. 'I can see that you are a follower of the poets, Madonna. You have come to the right country, for this is a land of beauty and romance. You have only to look at our fine sculptures and paintings.'

She blushed, looking away from the mockery in his eyes, for her heart was behaving very oddly. 'I have noticed some very fine paintings in your home, sir.'

'Tell me, which ones do you admire?'

'I noticed one that had wonderful colours…' Kathryn wrinkled her brow. 'It was in the great hall and I saw that the colours seemed to glow like jewels when the sunlight touched them. Most of the paintings I have been used to admiring were tempera, but I believe that one was done in oils, was it not?'

'Indeed, you are right,' he said. 'The artist was a man called Giovanni Bellini and my father bought the painting some years ago. I have others that I have bought that you might like to see one day.'

'Yes, I believe I should, if you have the time to spare, sir. I know you must be a very busy man and— Have a care, sir!' Kathryn gave a little cry as she saw someone suddenly lunge at his back with what looked like a curved and deadly knife.

Lorenzo whirled round even as she spoke, catching the would-be assassin's wrist as he raised his arm to strike. There was a sharp tussle and she heard something that sounded like a bone cracking, and then, before she knew what was happening, three men rushed up and overpowered the assassin, dragging him away with them.

'Forgive us, Madonna,' Lorenzo said and his face had become the customary hard mask that she found so disturbing, all trace of softness and laughter gone. 'I believe your safety was not in doubt, but it should not have happened. My men were instructed to keep a look out for anything that might cause an unpleasant incident.'

'What a terrible thing,' Lady Mary said, looking distressed. 'I trust you are not hurt, sir?'

'I thank you for your concern,' he said, but his eyes were on Kathryn, an odd expression in their depths. 'Perhaps now you will understand why it would not be safe for you to wander at will in this city.'

'But why did he attack you?' Kathryn had been startled by the incident, but he had dealt with it so swiftly that she was not frightened, though Lady Mary looked shaken. 'Do you have enemies, sir?'

Lorenzo frowned. 'I believe that any man in my position must have his share of enemies, but I did not know until today that I had one prepared to attack me here in Venice.'

'Do you know who the man was?'

'A hired assassin,' Lorenzo dismissed the man with a twist of his lips. 'I dare say I know who paid him.'

'Someone who hates you?'

'He has cause enough,' Lorenzo said. 'He belongs to that fraternity you despise so much, Kathryn—a Corsair by trade and inclination. He is called the Feared One, for his cruelty exceeds that practised by most of his brethren. Even they fear and hate him, but they do not dare to betray him.'

'Why does he hate you enough to pay someone to kill you?'

'Because I have made it my life's work to destroy as many of his galleys as I can.' Lorenzo's eyes were colder than she had ever seen them. Gazing into them, she was caught up in an emotion so strong that it robbed her of breath. 'I have nineteen galleys at the moment—we recently lost one in a battle with Rachid—but I have ordered six more. Soon my fleet will be large enough to meet him wherever and whenever he takes to the seas—and then I shall destroy him, little by little.'

Kathryn gazed into his eyes, feeling herself drawn into a vortex that had her spinning down and down, drowning in the bottomless depths of his eyes. 'Then I must tell you that I owe you an apology,' she said when she could breathe again. 'I believed that you were as guilty as those men who enslave others because you asked for a ransom for those you rescued, but if you have dedicated your life and your fortune to destroying such an evil man, then—'

'Pray do not continue,' Lorenzo said and she saw that his eyes had lost their haunted look and were filled with laughter. 'You run the risk of flattering me, Madonna. Say only that you approve of what I do and I'll not ask for more.'

'You are mocking me,' she said and could not quite hide her pique.

'Indeed, it is very unkind in me,' he said, 'but do not grudge me the pleasure that teasing you has brought into a life that has hitherto known very little, Madonna.'

Once again she was aware of powerful emotions swirling beneath the mask he showed to the world and was silent for the moment. They had been walking as they talked, a little ahead of Lady Mary and two men who now shadowed them more closely than before, and had now reached one of the canals where Lorenzo's gondola was waiting to convey them to his palace.

'You are not what you seem,' she said. 'Will you tell me the reason you hate Rachid so much? For there must be other pirates almost as feared, and yet it is he whom you wish to destroy.'

'That is something I have told to very few,' Lorenzo replied. 'One day perhaps I may tell you, Kathryn. But for the moment I think I shall keep my secret.'

Chapter Three

~~~ oooooooo ~~~

Here within the courtyard garden, where brightly coloured flowers spilled over from warm terracotta pots, their
perfume wafting on the soft night air, Kathryn could almost believe that she was in the knot garden of her home.
It was odd, but there was something English about this garden, though many of the flowers were Mediterranean. The
roses were fully bloomed and scented, very similar to
some that her mother had grown at home.

She thought of her father, wondering if he was missing
her. But Philip might be home from college now and so he
would have company, though she was sure enough of his
love to know that he would think of her. She missed her
family and yet she was moving in a new world that she
found interesting and colourful.

Her thoughts turned to the incident in St Mark's Square
earlier that day. Had Lorenzo not acted so swiftly it might
have ended very differently. It was true that she had called
a warning to him, but she did not flatter herself that she
had saved his life; he had acted instinctively, as if he had

heard or perhaps sensed the assassin's approach. What kind of a man was he that he needed to be so alert to danger?

He had begun to haunt her thoughts, for she had dreamt of him the previous night. He had been in danger and she had tried to reach him, but a strong wind had been blowing, carrying her further and further away. She had woken from her dream with tears on her face, though she did not understand why she wept.

Kathryn's feelings were mixed—she did not know how she felt about Lorenzo Santorini. He was such a strange mixture, at one moment as cold as ice, his features rock hard, his mouth an unforgiving line. Yet when his eyes were bright with laughter…it was then that she had this strange feeling of having known him for ever.

What had he meant when he said he would keep his secret for the moment? That he was a man of mystery she did not doubt, but—

Her thoughts were interrupted by the sound of voices. Charles Mountfitchet and Lorenzo were talking together. They spoke in English as always, for Lorenzo's grasp of the English language was much better than their grasp of Italian. He, of course, spoke several languages.

'It may be that it would be better for you to buy land in Italy,' Lorenzo was saying. 'With this threat of invasion from the Turks…'

'Do you really believe that they will try to invade the island?'

'I cannot say, sir. I merely sought to warn you of the possibility.'

'I doubt there is much danger for the moment,' Charles

said, for he had set his heart upon buying land in Cyprus, an island rich in sugar, fruit and fertile wine-growing soil. 'I visited the man you told me of—poor fellow.'

'Would he speak to you?' Lorenzo was saying.

'He asked if I had come to buy him,' Charles said, sounding distressed. 'When I told him that I was trying to find my son he wept, but would not answer me. I could not tell him that he would not be sold to another master, for it was not in my power, despite what you have told me, sir.'

'From what you saw of him, was there anything that reminded you of your son?'

The two men had come into the courtyard now, clearly unaware that Kathryn was there, standing just behind a tall flowering bush.

'It is impossible to tell,' Charles said with a heavy sigh. 'He could be Richard, but I do not recognise him.'

Kathryn moved towards them and saw the startled expression in both their faces. 'Will you let me see him?' she asked. 'I would know Dickon if I saw him, I am sure of it.'

'The scar you told us of…' Charles shook his head sadly. 'It would not help you to look for that, Kathryn. His wrists are so badly scarred and callused by the wearing of manacles and chains for all that time that any previous scar would have been obliterated.'

'Oh, the poor man—' Kathryn began but was interrupted.

'It would not be fitting for you to see him,' Lorenzo said. 'It caused your uncle much grief and a woman would find it too upsetting.'

'Have you such a low opinion of our sex, sir?' Kathryn's

head was up, her eyes flashing with pride. Why must he always imagine that she was foolish? 'Do you think I have not seen suffering before? My dear mother was ill some months before she died of a wasting sickness, and I have seen beggars with sores that were infected with maggots in the marketplace at home. If I saw this man, I might know if he is Dickon.'

'Kathryn knew my son better than anyone,' Charles said, looking at her uncertainly. 'She is a woman of some spirit, Signor Santorini. I think—with your permission— I should like her to see him. After all, what harm can it do for her to speak with him if someone is near by?'

Lorenzo's eyes flickered with what might have been anger, but it was controlled, not allowed to flare into life. 'Very well, I shall arrange it for tomorrow. But I warn you, Kathryn, he has suffered things that you cannot begin to contemplate. I fear your tender heart may sway your good sense.'

'I shall know if he is Dickon,' Kathryn said stubbornly, though in her heart she was not sure that she would truly know. For that one moment when her senses had betrayed her, she had thought that Lorenzo himself might be her lost love, though that was impossible, of course. There was no possibility that Dickon and this cold, arrogant Venetian could be the same man. He had clearly been born to priv-ilege and wealth and could never have suffered as this poor slave he would deny the chance of a new life.

'Very well, you may see him tomorrow. I shall have him brought here for you.' He inclined his head curtly, clearly not pleased to be overruled in this matter. 'I fear I have an appointment this evening. In my absence, I beg you to make yourselves free of my home. My servants will serve you supper and care for your needs. Do not hesitate to ask for whatever you want.'

'You are generous,' Charles said. 'I myself have a business meeting this evening, but Mary and Kathryn will be company for each other.'

'Yes, of course we shall,' Kathryn said and smiled at him. She did not look at Lorenzo, annoyed with him because he had tried to deny her the chance to identify Dickon. 'We have many little tasks that need our attention.'

'Then I shall wish you a pleasant evening.' Lorenzo inclined his head, turned and left them together.

Charles looked at her for a moment in silence, then said, 'It was a harrowing experience, my dear. Signor Santorini is probably right in thinking that it will upset you.'

'I do not expect otherwise,' Kathryn said. 'Who could remain unaffected by suffering such as he describes? But it was for this that I came with you, Uncle. I can only trust my instincts. If I do not feel it is Dickon, I shall tell you.' She looked thoughtful. 'You said that he hardly spoke to you—do you think he might tell me more?'

'Perhaps he does not remember,' Charles said. 'Signor Santorini believes that he has been a slave for many years, perhaps not always in the galleys. He might have been a house slave for a while and sent to the galleys for some misdemeanour. It is the way of things. Youths make amusing slaves for some men, but when they grow older and stronger they become too dangerous to keep in the house. I shall not tell you of the things these youths are forced to endure, for it is not fitting, but it may be that a man would prefer to forget rather than remember such abuses.'

Kathryn's eyes were wet with tears, for she could guess what he would not say. She brushed her cheek with the back of her hand. 'How can men be so cruel to one another?'

'I do not know, Kathryn,' Charles said with a deep sigh.

'How can anyone survive such terrible things?' Kathryn asked. 'It seems impossible. Yet this man has done so and deserves our kindness, if no more.'

'Yes, you are right,' Charles said, looking thoughtful. 'I must leave you now, Kathryn. Go into your aunt, my dear, and do not dwell on this too much. I think it unlikely the poor wretch I saw today is my son, but I should value your opinion.'

Kathryn kissed his cheek, doing as he bid her.

She spent the evening with Lady Mary, working on her sewing, for they had purchased many materials before they left England and had not had time to complete their wardrobes. One or other of the servants they had brought with them did much of the plain sewing, but they liked to finish the garments with embroidery and ribbons themselves.

Kathryn was not tired when she retired for the night. She felt a restless energy that would not let her sleep, and sat by the open window looking out over the courtyard. The sky was dark, but there were many stars, besides a crescent moon, and she found it fascinating to look at them, for it was possible to see far more here than at home where there was so often clouds to obscure them.

She became aware of someone in the sunken courtyard. A man just standing there alone, staring at the little fountain that played into a lily pool. He was so still that he might have been one of the beautiful statues that adorned his house and garden, and yet she knew him.

What was he thinking? Was he too unable to sleep? He was such a difficult man to understand, and sometimes she wanted to fly at him in a rage, though at others…she liked him. Yes, despite herself she had begun to like him.

Sighing, Kathryn turned from the window as the man moved towards the house. It was time she was in bed, even if she did not sleep, for Aunt Mary wished to go exploring again in the morning. They were to be taken in a gondola through the waterways so that they might see more of the city.

Lorenzo unbuckled his sword, dropping it on to one of the silken couches that he preferred about him, something he had learned to appreciate at the house of Ali Khayr. A wry smile touched his mouth, for his friend had tried hard to convert him to Islam, though as yet he resisted.

'You are more at home here with us than in the Christian world,' Ali Khayr had said to him once as they debated religion and culture. 'And no one hates the Inquisition more than you, Lorenzo—and yet you resist the true faith.'

'Perhaps there is good reason,' Lorenzo said and smiled as the other raised his brow. 'I do not believe in a god— neither yours, nor the Christian variety.'

'And yet it was by the will of Allah that you came to me and my son was saved,' Ali Khayr said. 'Why do you not accept the teachings of the Prophet? It might help to heal your soul and bring you happiness.'

'I think I am beyond redemption from your god or the

god the Inquisition uses as an excuse for torture and murder.'

'Hush, Lorenzo,' Ali Khayr told him. 'What a man may do in the name of religion may not be called murder, though it would not be our way. We use our slaves more kindly, and those that convert to Islam may rise to positions of importance and a life of ease.'

'You may choose that way,' Lorenzo said, a glint in his eyes, 'but others of your people are less tolerant.'

'You speak of pirates and thugs,' Ali Khayr said with a dismissive wave of his hand. 'There are men of all races in that fraternity, Lorenzo: Christians as well as Muslims. They say that Rachid, your enemy, was from the Western world, though I do not know if it be true.'

'It is true,' Lorenzo said. 'He wears the clothes of Islam and he speaks the language like a native, but a clever man may learn many languages. I have seen him close to, though he did not look at me, for I was beneath him—a beast of labour, no more.'

'You have good cause to hate him,' Ali Khayr said. 'And I do not condemn you for what you do—but I would bring ease to your soul, Lorenzo. If you put your faith in Allah, you might die a warrior's death safe in the knowledge that you would be born again in Paradise.'

'And what is Paradise?' Lorenzo smiled at him. 'You would have it a place of beautiful women, and wine such as you have never tasted? My business is fine wines and if I cared for it I could have a beautiful houri when I chose.'

Ali had laughed at his realism. 'You are stubborn, my friend, but I shall win you in the end.'

Now, alone in his private chamber, Lorenzo smiled

grimly as he removed the leather bracelets from his wrists, rubbing at the scars that sometimes irritated him beyond bearing—the badges of his endurance and his slavery. The three years he had served as a slave in Rachid's personal galley had almost ended his life. Had he been taken sick at sea he would no doubt have been thrown overboard, for there was no mercy for slaves who could not work aboard Rachid's galley. His good fortune had been that they were near the shores of Granada and he had been taken ashore when the men went to buy fruit and water from traders on the waterfront. He had been left where he fell on the beach, left to die because he was no longer strong enough to work.

It was luck, and only luck, that had brought the Venetian galley to that same shore later that day. He had no memory of how it happened, but he had been taken aboard the personal galley of Antonio Santorini and brought back to life by the devotion of that good man—a man who had also suffered pain and torture, but at the hands of the Inquisition.

Lorenzo recalled the time shortly after he was brought to his father's house. He had been broken in body, though not in spirit, and it was the gentleness, the kindness of a good man who had brought him back to life. Antonio had taken him in, treating him first as an honoured guest and then as a son, adopting him so that he had a name and a family. For Lorenzo did not know his own name. He had no memory of his life before the years he had spent as a galley slave.

This was the secret he so jealously guarded. No one but his father had known of his loss of a past life, and only

Michael amongst his friends knew that he had served in Rachid's galley, though some might guess. There was a look about him, a hardness that came from endurance. For, once he had regained his strength and health, Lorenzo had worked tirelessly to be the best swordsman, the best galley master, the best judge of fine wines. No softness was allowed into his life. On his galleys he lived as his men lived, worked and trained as hard as they did, and he treated them with decency, though never with softness. He was known as a hard man, ruthless in business, but fair. He had repaid Antonio Santorini for his kindness, taking the Venetian's small fortune and increasing it a thousandfold.

'God was kind to me when he sent me you,' Antonio had told him on his deathbed. 'I know that you have cause to hate Rachid and all his kind, my son—as I have cause to hate the Inquisition. I was tortured for what they said was blasphemy, though it was merely the debate of learned men who questioned the Bible in some aspects. They would have us all follow their word in blind obedience, my son. Yet the God I believe in is a gentle god and forgives us our sins. I pray that you will let Him into your heart one day, Lorenzo, for only then may you find happiness.'

It was strange, Lorenzo thought, as he prepared for bed, that two good men would convert him to their faith, though they believed in different gods. A wry smile touched his mouth as he buckled on his bracelets again. He wore them to guard his secret, for knowledge was power and he knew that some would use it against him.

As he lay on his couch, he thought for a moment of Kathryn. He had deliberately shut her out of his mind, for she was too dangerous. When he was with her he forgot to be on his guard, he forgot that he had sworn to dedicate his life to destroying evil.

To feel warmth and affection for a woman would weaken him, nibble away at his resolve so that he became soft, forgot his hatred, the hatred that fed his determination to destroy Rachid. He could not love. He had felt something approaching it for Antonio—but a man might feel that kind of affection for another man and remain a man. To love a woman… He could not afford to let her beneath his guard, though at times she tempted him sorely. Had she been a tavern wench he would have bedded her and no doubt forgotten her, but a woman like that was for marrying.

He smiled as he remembered the way her eyes flashed with temper when she was aroused. She gave the appearance of being modest and obedient until something made her betray her true self. The man she loved—her cousin, it seemed—would have been fortunate had pirates not taken him that day.

It was a sad story, but one that Lorenzo had heard often enough through the years. He thought of the poor creature she had insisted on seeing. If he was indeed the man they sought, she would probably devote the rest of her life to him—and that would be a shame.

Lorenzo glared at the ceiling as he lay sleepless, Kathryn invading his thoughts now though he had tried to keep her out. It would be a waste of all that beauty and spirit if she considered it her duty to care for a man who might never be a husband to her.

Kathryn had chosen to receive the former galley slave in the courtyard of Lorenzo's home. She thought that it might be easier for him than the splendid rooms of the palace, where he might be afraid of what was happening to him. Here in the garden, she could sit on one of the benches and wait in the warmth of the sunshine until he was brought to her.

'You do not mind if I join you?'

Looking up, she saw Lorenzo and frowned. 'I had hoped I might be allowed to see him alone, sir. He may be frightened of you and refuse to speak to me.'

'I have not harmed him, nor would I.'

'Yet he may fear you.' Kathryn hesitated. 'Your expression is sometimes harsh, sir. If I were a slave, I would fear you.'

'Do you fear me, Kathryn?'

'No, for I have no reason,' she replied with a smile. 'I find you…difficult, for you seem to be not always the same. At times—' She broke off, for she heard voices and then three men came into the courtyard. One of them was clearly the former galley slave—he was thin almost to the point of emaciation and his hair was grey, straggling about his face. His clothes hung on his body, though they were not rags, and some attempt had been made to keep him clean, his beard neatly trimmed.

Kathryn's throat closed and she could hardly keep from crying out in distress as she saw him, for pity stirred her and her eyes stung. She got up and moved towards him, a smile upon her lips.

'Will you not come and sit by me, sir?' she invited. 'I would like to hear your story if you will tell it to me.'

His eyes were deep blue, though not quite the colour of

Lorenzo's—or Dickon's. Kathryn felt the disappointment keenly. A man might change in many respects, but his eyes would surely not change their colour?

For a moment the man seemed confused, as if he feared to believe his eyes, and then he shuffled forward, sitting on the bench she indicated. He stared at her, seeming bewildered, not truly afraid, but wary.

Kathryn sat beside him. She saw that Lorenzo made a dismissive movement of his hand, causing his men to withdraw to a distance, though he still stood closer than she would have liked.

'There is no need to be afraid,' she said to the former slave. 'No one will hurt you. I promise you that, sir. I only wish to hear your story.'

'I am not afraid,' he replied. He spoke English, but hesitantly as though the words came hard to him. Yet that was not surprising, for he must have become accustomed to another language, the language of his cruel masters.

'What is your name?'

'I do not know,' he said. 'I am called dog. I am less than a dog.'

Kathryn swallowed hard, for the tears were close. 'Do you have no memory of what you were before…?'

'I am an infidel dog,' he repeated. 'I do not think, therefore I am not a man.'

'That is so wrong, so cruel,' Kathryn cried and saw him flinch as she put out a hand to touch him. 'No, no, I would not hurt you.'

'Am I yours now?' he asked. 'Have you bought me?'

'You are not to be sold.' Kathryn turned to Lorenzo

with a look of appeal in her eyes. 'Tell him that he is not a slave…please?'

Lorenzo hesitated, then inclined his head. 'If you recover your strength, you might work for me, but you are not a slave. If you wish to leave here, you are free to go when you wish.'

'Where would I go?' The man's blue eyes were so bewildered that Kathryn spoke without thinking.

'You may come to Cyprus with my uncle and me,' she said impulsively. 'Not as our slave, but as one of our people. When you are well, you may perhaps work in the gardens or some such thing, but you will be paid for what you do.'

'You would take me with you?'

'Yes,' Kathryn promised recklessly. 'You shall be my friend and help me when you can.' Her heart caught as she saw tears trickle from the corner of his eyes and she had to wipe away her own tears. She was shocked as the man fell to his knees before her and kissed the toes of her shoes that were peeping from beneath her gown. 'No, no, you must not do that. You are not a slave. I shall take care of you.'

'Get up,' Lorenzo commanded, his voice harsh. 'You are a man, not a dog. Since you understand English you shall be called William. You will return to the house where you have been cared for until Mistress Rowlands leaves for Cyprus with her uncle and aunt.' He signalled to his men, who came to help the newly named William to his feet.

Kathryn watched as the former galley slave shuffled off, helped by Lorenzo's men. She turned to look at him, her eyes bright with anger.

'Why were you so harsh to him?'

'He needed to be told, for you had unmanned him with your kindness. He is not used to that, Kathryn. You must give him time to become accustomed to his new life.'

She felt hurt by his accusation. 'He needs kindness, not harsh words.'

'I have dealt with many such victims. You do not know what you do, Kathryn. If you treat him too kindly he will become as your lapdog, a pet to beg at your feet for scraps. No man should feel that way. It is better that he hates, for hatred makes a man strong.'

Kathryn's eyes widened as she looked at him. 'Is that how you became so strong?' she asked. 'Do you hate so much that you cannot feel kindness, Lorenzo?'

It was the first time she had used his given name and she did not know what had prompted her to do it, and yet she felt that somehow she was closer to him, closer to knowing him than she had ever been.

'I learned from a master,' he said. 'What will you do if your uncle refuses to have the man as one of his people?'

Kathryn dropped her eyes, for she did not know. Lord Mountfitchet had come to find his son and she knew that William was not Dickon, felt it instinctively inside her. She had wanted it to be so, but it was not—and yet her heart was filled with pity for the former slave.

'I do not think he will refuse me,' she said. 'Lord Mountfitchet has always been kind and generous to me—especially since we lost Dickon.'

'You called him Lord Mountfitchet then—is he not your uncle?'

'We are not blood relations,' Kathryn said. 'My father

and Uncle Charles are lifelong friends and I would have married Richard Mountfitchet if…' She shook her head sadly. 'This man is not the one I loved. I would have known it—besides, his eyes are too pale a blue. Dickon had eyes like…' She looked up and found herself gazing into eyes so blue that they took her breath. 'He had your eyes, Lorenzo. If I did not know it was impossible, I would say that you were more likely to be Richard Mountfitchet than that poor creature.'

'I am not the man you seek!' Lorenzo's tone was harsh, even angry.

'I know that. Forgive me,' she apologised. 'How could you be a poor galley slave? You have too much pride, too much arrogance.'

To her surprise, Lorenzo threw back his head and laughed. She had not expected him to be amused and was at a loss for words.

'Nay, Madonna, do not look so bewildered. Should I be angry when you pay me a compliment?'

'It was not meant as one,' she came back swiftly.

'Perhaps not, but I take it as one,' he said. 'You think me a Venetian prince, perhaps, born to the life I lead?'

'Is that not the case?' she asked and for a moment as she looked deep into his eyes her heart raced. Something in his eyes made her think that he would take her in his arms and kiss her, and her heart leapt with sudden excitement. Her breath caught, her eyes opening wider as she looked up into his face.

'It might be—and then again it might not,' Lorenzo told her, a smile of mockery in his eyes now. His laughter had been genuine, but this was meant to put her in her place. 'You will not gain my secret so easily, Kathryn.'

'Why should I wish to know it?' she asked and turned on her heel, walking into the house, her back stiff with a mixture of anger and pride.

'Why indeed?' he called after her, and then, in a softer tone that she could not hear, 'Better that you should not know the devil you would rouse, sweet Kathryn. Better for you…and for me.'

Kathryn did not look back, but she was shivering with some strange emotion that she did not understand. When he had looked at her a moment or so earlier she had felt that she was drowning in the ocean of those blue eyes, and she had wanted him to kiss her.

'You will take him with us, won't you, sir?' Kathryn asked when her uncle came in from his business later that day. 'I know that I should have asked you before I gave my promise, but he looked so…desperate.'

'It was in my mind to ask Santorini what he wanted as a ransom,' Charles told her with a smile. 'I am not sorry that you do not think he is Dickon, for to see my son like that…' He drew a deep breath, a look of sadness in his eyes. 'The search for Dickon will go on, but I have room enough in my household for this poor wretch. He may never be able to do much for his keep, but I dare say we shall find him something to keep him out of mischief.'

'Oh, thank you, dearest Uncle,' Kathryn said and hugged him. She did not know whether to laugh or cry, but her smile won through. 'Lorenzo thought you might refuse to take him and then I should not have known what to do.'

'You might have taken him as your own servant,' her uncle said. 'Your father has provided money for anything you might need. This man may be your servant if you choose. If he knows how to write, he may be of some use as a scribe. We shall have to see how he goes on as he recovers his strength.'

'He speaks English and understands it, though he is hesitant,' Kathryn said. 'But he will learn once he is living with us.'

'I am certain that he will,' Charles said. 'And I am proud of your tender heart, my dear. I wish that we might find Dickon safe and well, but I would not have you live your life in expectation of it. If you should find yourself able to love another, I would rejoice in your happiness.'

'You are so good to me,' Kathryn said with a smile that lit up her whole face. 'But as yet I have not met anyone I would wish to marry.'

There was someone who could make her heart beat faster, but he could also rouse her to anger and despair and he was not at all the kind of man she would wish to marry. Nor, indeed, did she flatter herself that he would ever think of her as a woman he might take as a wife.

'My business here should be done within another week,' Charles told her. 'I advise you to make the most of your stay here, Kathryn, for I imagine the life on Cyprus will be very different. I do not believe you will find merchants there of the kind that are here, and we shall be reliant on ships that call at the island for much of our provisions, though I believe we may be self-sufficient for the food we eat and such things. However, any luxuries you need should be bought before we go.'

'Lady Mary has already suggested another shopping expedition,' she said. 'Perhaps you could send some of your servants with us, sir. I do not like to ask Signor Santorini for his escort again.'

'Yes, of course, my dear. I shall arrange it myself and there is no need for Santorini to know. He has been a considerate host and we should not take up more of his time.'

Kathryn tossed and turned restlessly. Her dream had been pleasant at the start for she had been walking in a beautiful garden and she had been happy. Someone was with her—a man. The man was Lorenzo Santorini, but not as she knew him. This man laughed and teased her, looking at her with eyes of love. He had taken her into his arms and kissed her, telling her that she was everything to him.

And then, just as she was about to answer him, a great tide of water had come rolling towards them, sweeping her up and carrying her away from him. She woke suddenly, shivering and frightened.

Why was she having these dreams? It was not as if she even liked Signor Santorini, and yet…when she was torn from his arms she had felt as if her heart was breaking.

Kathryn shook her head, clearing it of the troubling images that had caused her so much distress. She was being very foolish. She was confusing Dickon with the proud Venetian in her dreams, for it was her dearest friend who had been torn away from her. She must put all this nonsense from her mind and get ready for the shopping expedition later that day.

'Well, my dear, I think we have spent our time and our money profitably,' Lady Mary said as they turned their steps towards the gondola that was to take them back to the Santorini Palace. 'When our stores are delivered to Charles's ship we shall be ready to leave. I do not think we shall go short of anything we require for the next six months, and before then we may order what we need.'

'I am glad to have so many beautiful embroidery silks and such fine cloth—I dare say we shall find the life a little quiet after our time in Venice, Aunt Mary. At home I had my father's library whenever I needed something to fill my time, but Uncle Charles was unable to bring everything he might have wished for and I believe many of his books were left behind.'

'I shall mention it to him this evening at supper,' Lady Mary promised. 'It may well be that he has already thought to order books for himself and might do the same for us.'

They had reached the steps leading down to the lagoon where their gondola was waiting. Kathryn was a little ahead of Lady Mary and the two servants who had accompanied them. She ran down the steps, accepting the hand of a man who came forward to help her. As she stepped on board, she glanced back at the steps, expecting to see Lady Mary follow, but to her surprise she saw that she was being restrained by one man, while the servants were engaged in a battle with several burly rogues armed with cudgels.

'It is a trap, Kathryn,' Lady Mary cried. 'Come back!'

Kathryn gave a cry of alarm, trying to jump back to the steps, but it was too late. Already the gondolier was pushing off from the steps and someone grabbed her from behind, clasping her in a strong hold as she struggled to get free. She watched as the shore receded, seeing that her aunt seemed to have been released and was standing on the steps staring after her. She sensed Lady Mary's distress, realising too late that it was not her friend who had been in danger, but herself. Lady Mary and the servants, who had now joined her on the steps, had been diverted for long enough for the abduction to be carried out.

'Stop struggling, girl, and you will not be harmed,' a voice said and all at once she felt herself released. Turning, she saw a man of middle years. Heavily built, he had a small pointed beard in the Spanish fashion, his hair cut short and thinning at the temples.

'I beg your pardon for this inconvenience,' he said, speaking in English, but in an odd accent that told her he was unused to the language. 'Please believe me when I say that I mean you no harm. You are simply the means to an end, Mistress Rowlands.'

'Who are you?' Kathryn demanded. Her heart was racing, for she could not help but be afraid despite the words that were meant to calm her. 'And why have you abducted me?'

'My name is Don Pablo Dominicus,' he said. 'And you are my guest. I mean you no harm, mistress. Providing you are sensible and do not try anything foolish, you will be made comfortable aboard my ship.'

'Your ship?' Kathryn stared at him in horror. 'Where are you taking me?' It was like something out of one of her nightmares! She was being taken from her friends, just as in her dream.

'To my home in the hills of Granada,' he replied. 'It is a temporary arrangement, Mistress Rowlands. You are to be held until you can restore my younger daughter Maria to me.'

'But I do not understand,' Kathryn said. 'How can I help your daughter? I do not know her.'

'Maria is being held by a man called Rachid,' Don Pablo said, a look of anger in his eyes. 'His price for her release was that I should deliver his enemy to him—dead or alive. He would prefer to have him alive, for I believe he has a score to settle with Lorenzo Santorini.' He smiled cruelly as Kathryn gave a little gasp. 'Yes, I see that you begin to understand. I asked Signor Santorini for his help, but he would not give it, therefore I have taken you. We shall see what he is prepared to offer in exchange for you.'

Kathryn's head went up proudly. 'Why should he offer anything? Signor Santorini is merely a business acquaintance of my uncle. My father might be prepared to ransom me, but Signor Santorini will not be interested in your proposition. You have made a mistake if you believe that he will give into your blackmail on my behalf.'

'Then I shall offer you to Rachid in exchange for my daughter,' Don Pablo said. 'If Santorini will not come for you himself, you may be my only chance of regaining my daughter.'

A thrill of horror went through her. He could not mean it!

'Surely you would not…that man is a pirate of the worst kind…'

'I see that you have heard of him, from Santorini, I dare say.' An unpleasant smile curved Don Pablo's mouth. 'No, Mistress Rowlands, I do not believe that I have made a mistake. I think that Santorini will come for you and when he does…'

'You mean to trap him! It is his life for mine, is that not what you are saying?' Kathryn felt icy shivers all over her body. It was worse than any of her nightmares. This man was desperate for the return of his daughter. He would stop at nothing to get her back—and that meant he would kill Lorenzo if he could. No, she could not bear it if he were to sacrifice his life for hers. Lifting her head, her eyes glittering with angry pride, she said, 'You are a fool if you think he will come. I mean nothing to Lorenzo—nothing at all.' Yet, she was beginning to realise, it seemed that he meant something to her.

'How could she have been so foolish as to go without the proper escort?' Lorenzo's anger was fearful to see and Lady Mary felt quite faint. 'God only knows where she is now or who has taken her!'

'But we had our servants to protect us…'

'Little good they did you,' Lorenzo growled. 'Surely the attack on me in St Mark's Square was enough to warn you that it was dangerous for ladies to go out without sufficient protection?'

'I thought the attack was against you personally…' Lady Mary swallowed hard as she saw the flash of fire in his eyes. 'Forgive me. My brother believed that two servants should be enough.'

'No,' Lorenzo said, 'do not apologise, ma'am. This is my fault, as you so rightly say. I acknowledge it freely. Kathryn has been taken because my enemy believes she is important to me—this was done against me.'

'Against you?' Lady Mary fanned herself, for the heat and the shock of what had happened that day had overset her and she was feeling quite unwell. 'Then…what will they do with her?'

'I am not sure,' Lorenzo said. 'It depends who has taken her. She might be used as a hostage—in that case we shall receive a ransom demand for her, but…' If she had been abducted by his enemy she might pay with her life.

Lady Mary gave a cry of distress as she saw the look in his eyes. 'Mercy on us! You do not think that they will kill her?'

'If she should fall into the hands of Rachid, he would do so without a flicker of remorse,' Lorenzo said. 'However, I believe there may be more to this than meets the eye.' He frowned, taking a turn about the salon. 'For the moment there is little I can do but make some inquiries. I beg you to be patient, Lady Mary. Be assured that I shall do all I can to return Kathryn to you safely.'

'I can do no other than trust you,' Lady Mary replied. 'She is very dear to us, sir. It would break her father's heart if she were lost—and I believe my brother would be deeply distressed. It almost killed him to lose Richard. I do not think he could bear the responsibility of losing Kathryn too. And her father would be devastated.' She gave a little sob. 'This is terrible—terrible…'

'The responsibility for this is mine and mine alone,' Lorenzo said and something in his eyes shocked Lady Mary, for she suddenly understood something that she had not guessed before. 'I promise you that I shall do all in my power to find her. If she lives, she shall be restored to you, no matter what it costs.'

Lorenzo left her, for he had much to do. He was not a man to wait for news. He would make searches, discover what he could before his enemy could demand whatever it was he intended.

His mind was working furiously. This was the third unpleasant incident to occur since his trip to Rome—was it possible they were connected? He had suspected Don Pablo of some treachery, and it was unlikely that Rachid would have had the necessary contacts in Venice to make that attack on him in St Mark's Square.

It was more likely to be the Spaniard—but why? Why should Dominicus hate him that much? He could not think that they had met before that night in Rome. Was it only that he had refused to help him escort his daughter from Cyprus? Surely not.

He had been used to danger and hardship and could bear with them—but Kathryn had never faced the kind of danger that threatened her now. Lorenzo was consumed with a terrible anger, and fear—fear that he might not be able to help her.

Chapter Four

Kathryn made no attempt to escape as she was taken on board the Spanish galleon. She had considered jumping into the lagoon, but she could not swim and the weight of her clothes would soon drag her under. As yet she was not desperate enough to take her own life. Lorenzo would not walk into the trap that Don Pablo had set for him—why should he? But perhaps a ransom could be paid? Don Pablo had told her that in the last resort he would try to exchange her for his daughter Maria, and perhaps Rachid would accept a ransom for her.

It was very frightening, but she comforted herself as best she could. Perhaps Rachid would not be interested in exchanging the other girl for her and then Don Pablo might release her.

Once on board the ship, Kathryn was treated well. She was shown to a cabin, which clearly belonged either to Don Pablo himself or another important member of his crew. It was furnished with a heavily carved, ornate wooden box bed, on which was a mattress of feathers cov-

ered by a silken quilt and several pillows. There was also
a table, chair and two sea chests. Looking about her, she
noted the iron sconces that held lanthorns secured to the
wooden panelling, and when she glanced inside one of the
chests she discovered a quantity of women's clothing, also
silver items and ivory combs that she might need for her
toilette. There was, however, nothing that she might use
as a weapon to defend herself. It seemed that this abduction had been planned with some care.

The door to her cabin had been locked once she was inside and when she looked out of the small square window,
she saw that the cabin was situated at the stern of the ship,
and she realised that they were leaving the waters of the
Grand Lagoon far behind. They were heading out to the
open sea, on their way to Spain as her captor had promised.

She whirled around as the cabin door opened, half-ex-
pecting to see Don Pablo, but it was merely a sailor come
to bring her food and wine.

'Where is your captain?' she asked. 'Has a ransom demand been sent to my uncle?'

The sailor shook his head, saying something in Spanish that she took to mean he did not understand her. It was
useless to ask questions—he probably would not have
dared to tell her had he known what she was asking.

Kathryn sat down at the table where the tray awaited her.
She looked at the bread, meat and fruit provided warily, wondering if it might be drugged or even poisoned. The sailor
watched her for a moment, then picked up the wine cup and
took a sip as if to show her it was harmless. Afterwards, he
wiped the cup with his fingers and gave it back to her.

Kathryn took the cup. She realised that she was actually feeling hungry for she had not eaten since early that
morning and it was now late in the afternoon. It would do
no good to starve herself, she decided, and ate one of the
rich black grapes, the juice running down over her chin.
The fruit was crisp and delicious and she reached for a
peach as the sailor nodded his satisfaction and left her to
her meal.

Kathryn ate most of the fruit and some of the bread. Her
fear had begun to abate. It seemed that she was to be
treated as a guest as Don Pablo had promised, and, since
there was no possibility of her escaping while on board this
ship, she must accept the situation and wait as patiently as
she could.

Please come for me. The words were in her mind. She
knew that she was hoping Lorenzo would find some way
to rescue her, but why should he? He had no reason to care
what happened to her. Besides, she did not want him to risk
his life for hers.

Lorenzo took the letter his servant offered, breaking the
wax seal at once. He read the brief message it contained,
cursing aloud as it confirmed his fears. Ever since
Kathryn's abduction he had suspected something of the
sort.

'You have news of Kathryn?' asked Charles, his face
drawn with concern. 'Do they ask for a ransom?'

'Yes, but not the kind that you can supply, my friend.'
Lorenzo handed him the letter, but he stared at it blankly
and gave it back. 'Forgive me. You do not read Spanish. It
is from a man called Don Pablo Dominicus. He is holding

Kathryn hostage. He promises she is unharmed, and will be exchanged for his daughter Maria.'

'What does this mean? Do you have the girl of whom he writes?'

'No—but Rachid does.' Lorenzo frowned as he saw that Lord Mountfitchet was puzzled. 'Some weeks ago Don Pablo came to me with an offer I refused. He asked me to escort his elder daughter Immacula from Cyprus to Spain, but I believe he wanted me to commit myself to him so that I was at a certain place at a certain time.'

Charles stared at him in silence, then, understanding, finished, 'So that Rachid would know where to find you?'

'It has a certain logic. One thing that Rachid can never know is where I am at any given time or how many galleys will be with me. If I had agreed to commit three of my galleys and accompany the lady myself as he asked…' Lorenzo shrugged. 'At the time I was not sure. My instincts told me that Domincus was lying, hiding something, but I did not know why. Now I understand. Rachid has his younger daughter Maria and demands a ransom from him.'

'He was prepared to trap you for Rachid so that he might regain his daughter?'

'A fair exchange in his mind.' Lorenzo's face was set in stone. 'Would not any man be prepared for such a bargain?'

'Are you suggesting…?' Charles stared at him in horror. 'Good grief, sir! No, I cannot ask such a thing of you. Surely we can arrange a ransom for Kathryn? I know that most men have their price.'

'Rachid's price is my life,' Lorenzo said. 'It seems he would do anything to have me at his mercy. Only if I can return Don Pablo's daughter to him will he release Kathryn to you.'

'But that is hardly possible,' Charles objected. 'Even if you were willing to make such a sacrifice, how could you trust a man such as you have described to me? You do not know that the Spanish girl is still alive. Besides, what is to stop Rachid murdering you and retaining the girl?'

'Nothing at all,' Lorenzo agreed, a hard glint in his eyes. 'That is why I shall not walk tamely into his trap. At least I know that Don Pablo has taken Kathryn to his home not far from Granada. I have a friend living near there who may be able to help me.'

'So you will try to rescue her?' Charles looked at him with respect. 'You will be at risk, sir. Should you be discovered or captured…'

'I have survived Rachid's loving attentions once,' Lorenzo said with a wry smile. 'I am prepared to risk it again for Kathryn's good—but I prefer to believe that it will not be necessary. I may yet bring her out safely. If I fail…' He shrugged his shoulders.

'I shall pray that you do not, for Kathryn's sake and your own.'

'Perhaps your god will listen,' Lorenzo said, his eyes glinting with some deep emotion that he tried to suppress. 'For myself I have little faith in prayer, but for Kathryn's sake I shall hope that your prayers are answered.'

Inwardly, he shuddered as he imagined her fate if he should fail. She was beautiful and would fetch a huge price in the slave markets of Algiers.

'And what would you have me do?'

'Go on to Cyprus as you planned. Find your vineyard

and begin a new life. If I succeed, I shall bring Kathryn to you.' Lorenzo smiled oddly. 'If not, you must send her father my apologies.'

Charles nodded, guessing that the other's manner was deliberately reserved, hiding the swirling passion, the anger inside him. 'It shall be as you say—and may God protect and keep you, sir.'

Lorenzo inclined his head, his eyes dark with an emotion he could not hide, try as he might. 'May your god go with you, sir. Please excuse me, there are things I must do.'

Charles watched as Lorenzo strode from the room. He must put his trust in this man, for there was no other way. It was strange, but he felt a bond between them, an understanding that went beyond words. Perhaps only such a man as this could save Kathryn, a man who knew far more about the suffering of those who served in the Corsair galleys than he would ever tell.

Kathryn looked at the house to which she had been brought. Nestling on a plateau in the mountains overlooking the city, it was a substantial building of grey stone with small windows, most of which had iron grilles. Once within its walls she would truly be a prisoner. She shivered as Don Pablo came himself to help her down from the horse she was riding.

'Welcome to my home,' he said, smiling at her as he took her arm, steering her through the heavy iron gate, which enclosed the house and gardens and swung to behind them with an ominous clink. 'Think of yourself as my guest, *señorita*. You are at liberty to walk in the gardens and my home is yours for the duration of your stay.'

'You are gracious, Don Pablo.'

She held her anger inside. It would do no good to rage at him, for he would only keep her closer. She knew that she was a prisoner, for all his conciliatory words—he would not have allowed her the privilege unless he was sure she could not escape. The walls that enclosed his garden were too high for her to climb. Besides, she had no doubt that she would be watched whenever she was allowed to walk there, but at least it would be better than being kept a prisoner in her room the whole time.

Her good behaviour thus far had been accepted at face value by the Spaniard, who thought her suitably cowed by her situation. Indeed, she was helpless, because his hacienda was almost a fortress. For the moment she could do nothing, but she would remain watchful, waiting for her chance. One of these times her captors might grow careless and then…she would take her chance to escape if she could.

Kathryn would rather die in the attempt to escape than be sold to Rachid, for she knew what her fate would be, and it turned her stomach sour. Better to die than live as a harem slave.

Lorenzo stood in the prow of his galley looking out to sea. They were a day behind the galleon, but his men were pulling at attack speed for long periods. They would not catch the Spanish ship before it reached harbour, but they would not be far behind. With luck they could reach Granada long before they were expected and take Don Pablo off guard.

Lorenzo had not confided his plans to Lord Mountfitchet—they involved serious risk of injury to Kathryn. It was possible that she might be harmed in the attack on the Spaniard, but there was no real alternative. To give himself up in return for Kathryn's safety was no guarantee that she would be freed. His only true chance of getting her back was to storm the hacienda, hoping for the element of surprise. And the alternative was unthinkable. Better for her that she should die in the attempt to free her than be sold to Rachid.

Don Pablo would think himself safe for a few days, but in believing that he would have mistaken his enemy. Lorenzo's instincts had warned him of the reason for Kathryn's abduction. He had begun to make his plans from the moment he had learned she had been snatched.

Lorenzo motioned for the speed to be taken down. The men could only keep up the fast stroke for a certain length of time, but all his men would take their turn at the oar, including Lorenzo himself. He would not demand anything of others that he was not prepared to do himself.

These men were his most loyal, the strongest and the best. Every man aboard this galley was prepared to die if need be.

Kathryn had noticed that the main gates were kept locked at all times, opened only when a body of men went in or out. However, there was a small side gate that the servants used. She had seen an old man with a donkey bringing fruit and vegetables early in the morning. He had left the gate open for several minutes while he carried the produce into the house. From the window of her bedchamber she had watched carefully to see if it was locked after he left, but no one had come for some minutes afterwards.

If the old man came at the same time every day it was possible that she might be able to slip out of the side gate during the period that he was in the kitchens.

Kathryn did not know what she would do if she succeeded in escaping from her prison. She was alone in a foreign country and penniless. It might be that she would make her situation worse, for thus far Don Pablo had kept to his word to treat her as his guest. If she escaped and was mistaken for a woman of loose morals, which she might well be if she approached a stranger for help, her virtue might be in as much danger as her life.

Yet what was the alternative? If she did nothing, she might find herself being exchanged for Don Pablo's daughter. Kathryn thought that almost anything would be better than to become Rachid's slave. Lorenzo had spared her the details of the Corsair's cruelty, but she was not so innocent that she could not guess what her destiny might be once she was in his hands.

Even if Lorenzo were fool enough to come for her, to offer his life for hers, it was unlikely that she would be returned to her family. She would be sold to the highest bidder!

Lorenzo cursed the delay, for more than two days had passed since they landed on the shores of Spain. It had taken that long to contact his friend Ali Khayr and to buy horses for the small party of men he had chosen to accompany him inland. He would have preferred to attack at once, but Ali had counselled against it.

'I know the man of whom you speak,' he had told Lorenzo. 'If he has taken the girl hostage, she will not be harmed. Yet if you attack his hacienda with no plan you may fail. It is well defended and you would be seen before you could get near. Anything could happen to her then. She might be spirited away while you were kept busy at the gates. You would do better to take her by stealth.'

'Your words are wise as always,' Lorenzo said, controlling his impatience as best he could. 'But it would be dangerous—unless I could discover where Kathryn is being kept.'

'If you will wait in patience for a while, my friend, it may be that I can help you. My servants may go where you may not. Stay your hand for the moment, Lorenzo.'

Against his inclination, Lorenzo had waited, chafing at the bit at the enforced idleness. Some of his men were able to mingle with the townspeople and discover what they could about Don Pablo and his hacienda, but it seemed true that it was almost impregnable to a frontal attack.

Now, at last, Ali Khayr had news for him.

'There is a side gate,' Ali began. 'The main gate is kept locked and heavily guarded. There are armed men patrolling the garden all the time, though the girl you seek is allowed to spend some time there. Sometimes the men grow careless and forget their duty.'

'Do you think we could gain entrance through the side gate?'

'One man could do so,' Ali told him. 'There are two paths to it. One passes the main gate and would be impossible to negotiate without being seen. The other is difficult terrain, which is why it is undefended. If the girl you seek were near the gate at the right time it would be a simple thing, if she were brave enough, to bring her down to where you and your men were waiting.'

'I should be the one to go in and fetch her!'

'With your eyes? A blue-eyed Arab is very rare,' Ali said with a smile to ease his words. 'No, my friend, I think not. You would never get past the gate. However, every morning at a certain time an old man delivers fruit and vegetables. He is an Arab and they know him; they scarcely look at him.'

'Then who…?' Lorenzo cast his mind over his men. 'It must be someone who is willing to risk his life. Surely if I stained my face and kept my head down I might pass for a Moor?'

'Your eyes remain as blue. You need not concern yourself about who shall enter the hacienda,' Ali told him. 'Just be there ready at the foot of the descent. You may need to repel an attack—if they realise she has gone, they will try to take her back.'

'How will this man know where to find her?'

'I have not lived peacefully in Granada all these years under Spanish rule without knowing their ways. When Bobadil was driven weeping from the Alhambra most of my people left for other shores, but some of us stayed. We live quietly, peacefully, and we watch our backs. Even when Galera was under siege my people and I were left in peace, because we make no trouble for our Spanish masters. The Spanish hardly see us, for we do nothing to make them notice we are still here. We are nothing, of no importance, mere shadows in the night. Some of our people work for them and they take our service for granted. Money is a great persuader. Someone will make sure that the girl is near the gate and the guards are not. If Allah wills it, she will be with you tomorrow at the appointed time.'

'I shall owe you much if you can arrange this, Ali.'

'It will be repayment for the debt I owe you,' Ali Khayr said. 'Had you not acted so swiftly the day my son was attacked in the marketplace by a mad dog, he would have died. You put your life at risk, for to be bitten by such dogs is to die of the foaming disease. Without my son I should have had no reason to live. Therefore my life is yours.'

'It was instinctive,' Lorenzo said. 'And you have repaid the debt.'

'Gold alone cannot repay such a debt. But if I give you back this woman the debt is ended. We may meet then as friends.'

'We are friends now,' Lorenzo said. 'And I shall be for ever in your debt.'

Ali smiled and opened his hands. 'Allah will provide, my friend. Only if he wills it shall our plan succeed.'

Kathryn was unable to sleep. She had risen with the dawn, washing and dressing in the clothes provided for her use, which were Spanish and heavier than she was accustomed to wearing. She stood by the window, looking out at the garden, which was rich with lush greenery and exotic flowers. Soon now the old man would come with the fruit and vegetables and it was in her mind to go down to the garden and take her chance of escape.

'*Señorita…*'

Kathryn looked round as she heard the woman's voice. She had seen the old woman before when walking in the garden and believed she worked in the kitchens. Her skin was a dark olive tone and Kathryn thought that she might be of Moorish descent. Once the Moors had ruled the province of Granada until they were defeated and driven out by the Spanish king, but, though many had sought a life elsewhere, some had remained.

'What is it?' Kathryn asked, but the woman placed a finger to her lips, shaking her head. The Morisco woman put her hand on Kathryn's arm, seeming to want her to go with her and saying something that she could not understand.

Kathryn hesitated, but the woman pulled urgently at her, speaking rapidly, repeating the same instruction over and over. There was no point in resisting, for if she did Don Pablo would send his men to fetch her. She nodded to show that she would go with her, but when she attempted to speak to her the woman put her finger to her lips again and smiled.

Suddenly, Kathryn was alert. Something was happening. She had the strangest feeling that this woman was attempting to help her and that Don Pablo knew nothing of it. When the old woman led her down to the door that led out to the back of the garden and pointed to the far end, she knew that she must mean the gate. She smiled and gave Kathryn a little push, then waved her hands as if she were shooing a goose.

Kathryn smiled, but when she would have spoken the old woman shook her head and disappeared into the house. Feeling nervous and yet excited, Kathryn walked in the direction she had been shown, and as she did so the gate opened and an old man came in with his donkey. She hesitated, but he beckoned to her urgently and she ran the last few steps towards him.

'Go quickly,' he said, pulling her through the gate. 'Down that path. See where it curves to the right and follow. The way is steep and hard, but you will find what you seek there.'

Kathryn's heart was racing—he had spoken to her in English, though from his looks he was a Moor. She whispered her thanks and heard the gate shut behind him as she began to walk down the steep path he had indicated. It was not the road by which they had come and, as she paused to look back, she realised that only a couple of small windows at the back of the house looked out this way. Once she was past the place where the rock jutted at an angle, it would be impossible to see from the house. Perhaps the path was too narrow and steep to be thought a likely approach for any surprise attack. Indeed, it was not easy for Kathryn to negotiate the path, for some of the rock was loose and twice a shower of debris went hurtling from beneath her feet, tumbling down the side of the rocky crag. Her progress was slow and her heavy skirts made it difficult for her to keep her balance. Had she had a choice she would never have ventured down such a path as this, but she steeled her nerves, knowing that it was her only chance. The old man had promised she would find what she needed at the bottom, and therefore someone must be waiting there for her.

When she reached the place where the rock jutted out at an angle, she paused—the path was so narrow that she did not know if she dared to pass the protrusion. If she fell, she would surely go plunging down the side of the mountain to her death. As she took a deep breath she heard a slithering sound as some loose shingle went sliding down into the valley and then a muffled curse, and then, as she held her breath, a man came round the path and beckoned to her.

'Come, Kathryn,' he commanded. 'Take my hand and I shall help you.'

'Lorenzo…' she breathed, her heart leaping. She moved towards him, and somehow she was not surprised that he should be there. Ever since the woman had taken her to the garden she had believed that only one person could have arranged to have her freed.

He frowned as she came towards him, his eyes going over her with disapproval. 'What is the matter?'

'Take off those wide skirts,' he told her. 'You will never be able to negotiate this path in that gown, Kathryn.'

Kathryn did not hesitate. Untying the strings that held her overskirt, she let it fall to the ground. At once she felt so much easier in the petticoat that fitted to her body more closely than the cumbersome panniers she had donned that morning. She went to him with new confidence, taking the hand he offered. His fingers closed about it tightly and he smiled at her in a way that set her spirit soaring.

'You are a good, brave girl,' he told her. 'Trust me, for this next bit is difficult, but I shall not let you fall.'

'Thank you.' She nodded at him bravely, trusting him, confident that he would not let her slip.

He smiled but said nothing, and, looking down, Kathryn saw that the brownish-grey rock jutted out to an alarming degree over what was a sheer fall. The path around it was no more than a ledge and could never have been intended as a path at all. It looked as if at some time a part of the rock had fallen away, leaving this overhanging ledge dangling precariously. It was hardly surprising that the Don had not considered it necessary to guard this side of his mountain home, for a party of men could not pass this way, and the only other approach was past the main gate.

She could never have done it alone! Her heart was in her mouth as she took a tentative step on to the narrow ledge, and only the firm grip of Lorenzo's hand on her arm kept her steady. They had their backs to the rock, which pressed into Kathryn's flesh, scraping her as she pushed back against it, edging one tiny step at a time, moving sideways, inch by inch, not daring to look down. Only the firm pressure of Lorenzo's hand kept her from falling as her eyes closed against the dizziness that seemed to take her mind and for a moment she felt that she could not go on.

'Not much further,' Lorenzo said. 'We are almost there, Kathryn.'

She could not answer—she was too terrified. She breathed slowly, deeply, hanging on to her nerve by the merest of threads, and then, all at once, she found that her feet were on more solid ground and she was suddenly swept into a crushing embrace. Lorenzo held her so fiercely that she almost swooned from the surging emotion that possessed her body and mind. She held on to him, her breath coming in great sobbing gasps as she clung to his strong body and felt the relief wash over her. She wanted to weep, but the feel of his body warmed her, giving her courage.

'You are safe now, Madonna,' Lorenzo said. 'Come, my brave one. My men and the horses are waiting. We have no time to waste—once they know you are missing they will come after us.'

As she looked up at him, he bent his head, his lips brushing hers in the lightest of kisses, so light that she hardly felt it, yet it was enough to set her heart fluttering wildly.

Kathryn blinked as he let her go. She longed to be back in his arms, for she had felt so warm and safe there, but he was already hurrying her down further to where a small party of men and horses were waiting. From there the way was a gentle slope, widening out into the valley, and in the distance the grandeur of the sleeping city lay shimmering in the first rays of the morning sun.

'Once we reach the galleys we are safe,' he told her. 'We shall talk then, Kathryn. But first we have some hard riding ahead.'

She nodded at him, recovering her breath now as he lifted her on to the back of one of the horses and then mounted his own. There was a sense of urgency about him that made Kathryn realise they were not yet safe and she did not need to be told to urge her horse first to a canter, and then, as they left the steep roads behind, to a gallop.

The pursuit did not begin until they had almost reached the shore. One of Lorenzo's men gave a shout and pointed to a party of horsemen outlined against the sky. The alarm must have been given soon after Kathryn's disappearance, for the Don's men were not that far behind them. Lorenzo's party were urged to make a final effort, and then they were within sight of the cove.

The horses were abandoned to one of the party, who rode off with them in another direction as Lorenzo, Kathryn and half a dozen men began the scramble down to the sandy beach where the boat was ready to take them out to the galley moored in the bay. From above them they could hear shouting and, as she paused to look up, she saw that some of Don Pablo's men were preparing to fire at them with their deadly mosquettes, a superior weapon of Spanish invention.

Lorenzo pushed her into the boat and climbed in himself, though two of his men had fired their matchlocks at the Spaniards above; however, they were useless at such a distance and did nothing to deter the pursuers from beginning to scramble down the rocky incline to the beach below.

Now they were all in the boat and pushing off from the shore. Don Pablo's men had reached the beach and were racing to the water's edge, some of them wading out to take aim at the rowers. One found his mark and an oarsman fell wounded. Lorenzo took his place while Kathryn bent over him, distressed to see that he was bleeding from a shoulder wound.

She tore strips from her petticoat, making a wedge and then binding him as best she could, her attention given to her task as the shots of the men on the beach began to fall short of their target. By the time she had finished her work they had reached the galley and many hands reached out to take both her and the wounded man aboard. She heard Lorenzo giving orders and then a cannon boomed out and she looked towards the shore, seeing that the men there had fled back to the cliffs and were scrambling up them.

'Kathryn.' Lorenzo came to her as she stood shivering and at a loss to know what to do. Around her the men were preparing to put some distance between them and the shores of Spain. She alone could do nothing and she suddenly felt lost and terribly alone. 'Come, you must go to my cabin and rest. This has been a harrowing experience for you. Forgive me, but there was no other way.'

'There is nothing to forgive,' she said in a trembling tone. 'I must thank you for my life.'

'I did very little. The friend I told you of—Ali Khayr— it was he who risked his life to come to you at the hacienda. I pray that he was not taken, for it will go ill with him. He lives in Granada only because his neighbours tolerate him. He says that money buys him freedom, but it was a great risk he took for our sakes.'

'Then I shall pray for his safety,' Kathryn said. She raised her head to look at Lorenzo, seeing the customary hard line of his mouth, his eyes giving no hint of his feelings. 'I have had time to think of and to regret my own folly. Had I not ignored your advice, this would not have happened. I hope that you will forgive me for causing you so much trouble?'

A faint smile curved his lips. 'Would that I could believe it will be the last time, Madonna.'

'What do you mean?' Her eyes sparked with indignation.

Lorenzo merely shook his head. 'Forgive me, I have work to do. I must stay on deck in case we are followed and attacked. I do not think it, for Don Pablo does not have galleys swift enough to match ours. However, I must be here to direct the men. Michael will take you below.' He nodded to a man standing nearby, who smiled at her as he approached.

'I hope you will permit me to say how pleased I am to

see you safe, Mistress Rowlands. Please, follow me and I will show you where you can rest.'

Kathryn thanked him. When she glanced back she saw that Lorenzo was bending over the man who had been wounded while rowing them back to the galley. She felt a little hurt—clearly she was less important to him than his men. He had saved her and for that she must be grateful but, for a few moments on that mountainside, he had seemed so different. When he held her in his arms, when he had kissed her so softly, she had believed that he truly cared for her, that she was more than an errant girl he had rescued, perhaps for a price.

But she would be foolish to imagine that she was anything more than another captive he had rescued, no more than a galley slave he might snatch from a watery grave. She wondered how much her uncle had promised to pay him for her safe return, and the thought made her heart ache.

She could not but be grateful to him for what he had done, but she did wish that he had done it because he cared for her and not for money.

Following Michael into the cabin, she saw that it was sparsely furnished, unlike the cabin in Don Pablo's galleon. There was a plain wooden cot with a straw mattress and one thin blanket, a sea chest and a table with maps spread upon it, but nothing else. Clearly the master of this galley lived much as his men did with no concessions to comfort. His home might be the height of luxury, but here there was no softness of any kind.

'Forgive us, Mistress Rowlands,' Michael apologised. 'There was no time to make provision for your comfort.

We did not dare delay for we could not be sure what Don Pablo intended. Had he decided to sell you to Rachid in exchange for his daughter, we might have been too late. Taking you from the Spanish merchant was an easier task, for Rachid's fortress is guarded day and night. No one who is taken there comes out alive unless Rachid wishes it.'

Kathryn shivered as she realised how great had been the danger of her being lost for ever in some harem. 'Do not apologise,' she said. 'I am grateful for all that you and the others have done, sir. If this is how Lorenzo lives on board ship, then it is good enough for me.'

'Captain Santorini claims no privileges that are not given to the rest of us,' Michael said. 'But I know he would not have chosen that you should travel in this way.'

'Please, no more apologies,' Kathryn told him, lifting her head proudly. 'I shall be perfectly comfortable here. I dare say it is more than I should have been given had I been sold to Rachid.'

'You may thank God for it that you were not,' Michael said and made the sign of the cross over his breast. 'Please rest as best you can and food will be brought to you once we are underway.'

Kathryn nodded. After he had gone she went to look out of the tiny porthole at the sea, which seemed wide and empty, then returned to sit on the edge of the bed. Now that she was alone she was beginning to feel the effects of her desperate escape and to realise how close to death she had been on that mountainside. She closed her eyes, shutting out the memory. It was over. She was here on Lorenzo's galley and safe.

Tears stung her eyes but she would not release them.

There was no sense in giving way to her emotions now. She was safe because Lorenzo had risked his life and others to rescue her. He must be angry with her for causing him so much trouble. As yet, he had not chided her for her foolishness, but no doubt that was to come.

Kathryn lay down for a while. She was tired and hungry, and, waking after a fretful sleep that had not refreshed her, she discovered that Michael seemed to have forgotten his promise to bring her food. She got to her feet and pushed a strand of hair back from her face, feeling dirty and crumpled, and also a little cold in her torn petticoat. When Michael returned she would ask him if there was anything she could wear instead of the clothes that had been given her in Don Pablo's home.

She had just decided that she would go up on deck when she heard a loud boom and the galley shook from stern to prow. Startled, she rushed to the porthole and looked out. It seemed that two galleys were attacking them, and from the flag they were flying, looked as if they might be Corsairs. The pennant had a white background and bore the sign of the crescent and the letter R in a blood-red colour. Something about the bold statement of the Corsair's flag made her shiver.

It must be some of Rachid's men! Kathryn felt chilled as she looked out and saw that the shot Lorenzo's galley had fired had gone home. One of the galleys had been holed and was clearly in some difficulty. The other galley had fired at them and as their vessel rocked, she knew that they had taken a hit, but then several of Lorenzo's guns roared at once and the second galley, which was very close, was holed. It went down so fast that she could hardly believe her eyes. One moment it was there, firing at them, and she could see fierce-looking men on deck preparing to board and fight. And now it had gone—but there were some men in the water.

The second galley was retreating, leaving their comrades in the water. She could see them screaming, calling out to the men who had deserted them, but as Lorenzo's guns roared once more she knew that the second Corsair galley dared not stop to pick them up. Surely they would not leave the men to die?

Kathryn went to the door of her cabin, opening it and going to stand on the little deck that was directly above the rows of oarsmen. For a moment she thought that Lorenzo's crew were going to ignore the men in the water, for they were cheering as they saw that they had routed their enemy. But then she saw that some of the men were at the rails as if to snatch those they could from a watery grave.

'You should go below, Mistress Rowlands,' Michael said, coming to her. 'It is not fitting for you to be here— and like that.'

She glanced down at herself, realising that she must look as if she were in her nightgown. 'May I not help with the wounded?'

'We have our own surgeon to do that,' he told her. 'Please go below.'

'But those men in the water…'

'We shall do what we can. Please go!'

Kathryn retreated, feeling angry and disturbed. She could hear shouting on deck and men moving about, also the movement of oars that told her they were going on.

Looking out of the porthole, she saw that there were several bodies floating in the water, but could not tell whether any of them were still alive. She felt the sting of tears, because she knew that those left behind would surely die.

How could Lorenzo abandon them? She had thought he had more compassion. Yet she was foolish to believe in a softer side. For a moment she had glimpsed another man on that mountainside, but in truth he was ruthless. A hard, cold man who saved only those he believed would bring him a profit.

Kathryn felt chilled. She had believed herself to be falling in love with him—but how could she love such a man?

Chapter Five

'Forgive us,' Michael said when he brought food and wine to her later. 'We were attacked by two of Rachid's galleys, as no doubt you saw, and there was no time for anyone to eat.'

'Those men in the water…' Kathryn said. She felt sick to her stomach, revolted by the sight of food. 'Why did you not stop to pick them up?'

'We rescued a few, most of them galley slaves,' Michael said, but she noticed that he would not look at her as he set down the tray of food. 'Do not concern yourself for the others. Most were already dead and, besides, they were not worth your pity, mistress.'

'Is not any man worthy of help?' she asked, a catch in her voice. 'In God's eyes even a sparrow is worthy of notice.'

'Thank you, Michael,' Lorenzo said, his voice harsh. 'You will leave us now if you please.'

Kathryn turned her accusing gaze on Lorenzo as he stood aside for his captain to leave the cabin. 'There were so many,' she said, a choke in her voice. 'Surely they were not all dead?'

Lorenzo's face showed no emotion as he answered her. 'They were Rachid's men—ruthless pirates. They take no prisoners. Can you imagine what would have happened if they had been the victors? Save your tears for those that deserve it.'

'But they were beaten…' Her words died as she saw that he was angry. He was arrogant and ruthless. He would not listen to her. She was merely a foolish girl who had caused him enough trouble.

'Has it not occurred to you that there might have been more of his galleys waiting for us? If we had spent too much time trying to rescue men, most of whom were already dead—or likely to be hung for their crimes if we had rescued them—we might have been attacked again. I do not think that Lord Mountfitchet would have been pleased if you had escaped from Don Pablo to fall into the hands of Corsairs, Kathryn.'

'Are you saying that it was for my sake that you did not stop?'

'Does that grieve your tender heart, Kathryn? Do not take my guilt upon your shoulders, Madonna. I saw no profit in saving men I would have to either hang or kill another day if I set them free.'

'Is everything a matter of profit?' Kathryn said angrily. 'Tell me, how much did Lord Mountfitchet pay you to rescue me?' She saw him flinch and regretted the words as soon as she had said them, but her pride would not allow her to take them back. Raising her head proudly, she looked into his eyes. 'Perhaps you should know that I am an heiress and my true worth is what my father will give to have me back.'

'I shall bear that in mind,' Lorenzo said, his eyes glinting. 'Perhaps I shall not take your uncle's ransom after all, Madonna. It might be that you would fetch a higher price elsewhere.' He moved towards her, towering above her so that she felt shivers run down her spine. For a moment she thought he meant to take her into his arms, and his expression frightened her, but then he shook his head and stepped back. 'You are a troublesome girl and I have better things to do! Be careful or I may find it easier to be rid of you.'

Kathryn stared as he turned and walked from the cabin. He could not mean that! Surely he was merely punishing her for what she had said to him? He could not seriously mean to sell her to the highest bidder?

No, of course he didn't. He would hand her back to Lord Mountfitchet and take the agreed price—wouldn't he? And yet what did she really know of this man? He guarded his feelings so well that anything might be going on inside his head.

Kathryn sat on the edge of the bed, hugging herself as she tried to come to terms with her feelings. For a moment as she gazed into his eyes she had wanted him to kiss her. How foolish she was! He was a hard, cruel, dangerous man and the sooner she was with Charles and Lady Mary the better.

Lorenzo stood staring out to sea. It was a dark night with only a few stars to guide them, but within hours they would enter the Grand Lagoon. He had decided to return to Venice before setting out to Cyprus. His galley had received some

serious damage and was not fit to fight again without repairs. It would be sensible to send Kathryn with another
of his ships. She might travel on one of his merchant galleys with an escort of fighting ships to protect her. She had
found a way to get beneath his guard, and it would be madness to keep her near him—and yet he was reluctant to let
her go.

What was it about this woman that had got through to
that secret part of him he had kept so well hidden these past
years? He had known other beautiful women, sophisti-
cated lovers, who had given him the pleasure of their company and their bodies, but none of them had touched him.
There was something about Kathryn that tugged at his
heartstrings, making him feel things that he did not wish
to feel.

For so long he had kept all his emotions under rigid control, feeding only on his hatred of the man who had en-
slaved him. Lorenzo had no memory of being captured. His
first memory was of being chained to an oar and the lash
of a whip on his shoulders to make him pull harder. He
could remember the pain of the cuts on his back, which had
been tended by another, older slave during the hours of
darkness, and the constant chafing of the manacles on his
wrists. The memory made the rough skin beneath his wristbands itch, but he resisted the urge to take them off. To ease
them he needed a salve that he kept in his cabin, and he
would not expose his one weakness to the eyes of the
woman who already had too much power over his emotions.

'Kathryn…' he said the words without realising he was
speaking. 'Kathy…sweet little Kathy…'

For a moment there was a roaring in his ears and his mind whirled as the stars disappeared and there was only blackness, deep, deep blackness, and then terrible pain. He made a moaning sound as for one moment he saw something—a girl's face and blood...

'Did you speak, sir?'

Lorenzo's mind cleared as his captain approached him. He frowned, for he was not quite sure what had happened to him. It was as if a curtain had lifted in his mind, revealing some incident from the past, which had never happened before. The time prior to his enslavement had been a complete blank, but just for a moment he had seemed to remember.

'No, I merely cleared my throat,' he said, banishing the images that would sap his strength. He must banish her from his mind! He could not allow himself the luxury of caring for a woman like that. 'We were fortunate today, Michael. Somehow Rachid must have known that we were unaccompanied. It was a mistake. When you deal with wolves you should hunt as they do, in a pack.'

'There was no time to waste if you were to rescue her,' Michael said and frowned. 'I fear she does not understand the law of the sea, Lorenzo. It seems cruel to her to leave men in the sea, but she cannot know what they are capable of or that we were in no position to rescue them.'

'Women and war do not mix,' Lorenzo said; he had recovered his usual calm. A little smile touched his mouth, though it did not reach the icy blue of his eyes. 'Do not allow her to make you feel guilt, my friend. The men we killed today served a cruel master because they wished it and we should feel no pity for them. They would have killed us and used her for their pleasure.'

'Some did not serve willingly.'

Lorenzo saw the doubts in the other's face. 'We pulled three alive from the water,' he said. 'The others had no chance, chained to their oars—they went down with the galley. We did not make them slaves, Michael. If we are to rid the seas of such men as Rachid, there will be innocent men who must die. We too may die for our beliefs. Only if we accept this can we carry on our chosen path.'

'Of course.' Michael smiled wryly. He should not have allowed himself to weaken because of the accusation in a woman's eyes. 'She is very beautiful, Lorenzo, and I am a fool. Forgive me.'

Lorenzo smiled. 'If we let them, women may make fools of us all, my friend.'

Kathryn saw the deep blue waters of the lagoon and felt a sense of relief to know that she would soon be back with Aunt Mary and Uncle Charles. They had been forced to delay their departure for Cyprus and would no doubt be impatient to leave. They could be no more impatient than she, for then she would not have to see Lorenzo Santorini again.

A part of her knew that she was being both ungrateful and wrong-headed in her judgement of him, but she could not help her feelings of irritation. He was such an arrogant man, so sure of himself. So many men must have died when that galley sunk so quickly, and he had saved only a few of them. How would he feel if he were one of those poor creatures chained to an oar and doomed to die unless someone rescued them? He could know nothing of their suffering or their pain.

She remembered his harshness towards the man he had named William. Was there no softness in him, no compassion? For a moment as he held her on the mountainside she had felt such…warmth, love…desire.

Kathryn's cheeks flamed as she admitted to herself the mixture of emotions that had swirled through her in those brief moments in his arms. No, it was imagination, she could not have felt anything like that! It would be impossible to love such a cold man. What she had felt had mercly been relief.

She turned as the door to her cabin was opened and saw Lorenzo standing there, watching her with those deep blue eyes that stirred such feeling in her.

'My gondola will take you to my home,' he told her. 'Please feel free to do as you please within the house and garden—but do not leave it without my escort.'

'I shall be only too pleased to be with my aunt again, sir.'

'Lady Mary and Lord Mountfitchet have gone ahead of us to Cyprus,' he told her. 'My galley needs urgent repairs and so I returned to Venice for that purpose.'

'But…' Kathryn stared at him in dismay. 'How am I to… It is not fitting that I stay in your house without Aunt Mary, sir.'

His eyes mocked her. 'You have lately been a prisoner of Don Pablo, Kathryn. Your reputation must have suffered. If, however, you worry for your virtue, you should know that you are quite safe from me. I have no interest in foolish children.'

Her cheeks burned as she saw the mocking light in his eyes. 'I did not mean—but my reputation…' She faltered as she realised that in truth she could no longer claim to have one. She had been Don Pablo's captive, living on board his ship and in his house for several days. Anything might have happened to her during that time, and some might believe it had. 'I dare say it is too late to worry what others may think of me…'

Lorenzo's laughter was low and husky. 'Let them think what they will, Kathryn,' he said. 'The man who weds you will know your innocence is untouched and the others are as nothing.'

'Yes, you are right, sir.' She lifted her head proudly, though she was sorely troubled. Reputation was everything to an unmarried girl and hers had been tarnished through no fault of her own.

'We took three galley slaves from the wreck,' Lorenzo said. 'None of them have blue eyes, but when they are well enough they will be questioned for any information concerning Richard Mountfitchet that they may have.'

'I always called him Dickon,' Kathryn said, her eyes sad and slightly dreamy. 'And he called me Kathy…his sweet Kathy. We were but children, but we loved each other well.'

Lorenzo's gaze narrowed intently. A little nerve was flicking at his temple as he said, 'If you think of any other information that may be relevant, you may tell me. It should take no more than a week to repair my galley and then I shall escort you to your uncle. I believe he took William with him as you asked.'

'Thank you…' She looked into his eyes despite her determination to keep her distance, and her heart caught. Oh, no! She was being foolish. She could not be attracted to this man. It was impossible—wrong! Her heart belonged to Dickon and she would never marry someone who could do the things this man had done. 'I shall be glad to be with my friends again.'

'Yes, of course,' he said. 'Now, if you please, the gondola is waiting.'

Kathryn paced the floor of her chamber, feeling restless. They had been in Venice for two days now and she had hardly seen Lorenzo at all. Her meals were served to her wherever she wished, but she ate them in solitary state, which only made her feel more alone than ever. It seemed that in being rescued from Don Pablo she had merely exchanged one prison for another.

She was so tired of being in the house! She decided to go down to the courtyard and walk in the garden, but as she went down the stairs and into the main hall, she heard voices and saw that Lorenzo had that moment come in with Michael dei Ignacio. They both turned to look at her. Michael smiled warmly as he saw her, but Lorenzo's eyes were as cool as ever.

'I was about to go into the garden,' she said, feeling it necessary to explain. 'It is warmer today and the house seems too confining.'

'You must be tired of being shut in the house,' Michael told her. 'I fear we have been too busy to entertain you, mistress. However, this evening there is a masque being held in the open air—perhaps you would care to attend? I shall be going and I dare say Lorenzo may be persuaded to spend a little time with us. And I shall take several of our men to protect you, though I think it unlikely that Don Pablo will try another such trick.'

'I should like to go with you, sir.' Kathryn looked at Lorenzo. 'Have I your permission to go?'

His mouth seemed hard and censorious as he said, 'You are not my prisoner, Kathryn. I am sure that Michael will take good care of you, though I have business that will prevent me from attending. You will need clothes for the masque, which is said to be very entertaining, I believe. I shall instruct my servants to bring you gowns and masks that you may like to wear for the occasion.'

'Thank you.' She sensed his disapproval, which was almost anger that she had agreed so willingly. 'I shall look forward to it, Signor Ignacio.'

'I shall be here at the hour of seven to collect you,' he said and bowed to her. 'And now, if you will excuse me, I have some business I must attend.'

Kathryn turned away as he left, but Lorenzo followed her into the courtyard. She waited, wondering what more he had to say to her.

'I shall do nothing foolish,' she told him before he could speak.

'Michael will make sure that you are well protected. Besides, I do not think that Don Pablo will try another abduction. I have sent him a message and I believe you are safe from him in future, Kathryn.'

'What kind of a message?'

'It is not necessary for you to know that,' he replied, a wintry expression in his eyes. 'I wanted to tell you that we shall be ready to leave for Cyprus the day after tomorrow.'

'Oh.' Kathryn did not know why her spirits had suddenly fallen so low. 'Thank you, sir. I shall be pleased to be with my friends again.'

'Once there you will have the freedom that has been denied you here.'

'Yes…' She felt her throat closing and was suddenly emotional though she did not know why. 'Lorenzo…' She swayed towards him, wanting him to take her in his arms, to hold her as he had for that brief moment on the mountainside. She saw something in his eyes, a glow deep down that made her tremble with anticipation, with a strange longing that she could not name. For a brief moment she thought she saw that longing reflected in his eyes and believed that he was struggling with some fierce emotion, but then he moved back and it was as if a barrier had sprung up between them.

'Excuse me, I have business,' he said in a curt tone that brought her swiftly back to reality. 'You should rest, for you will find our Venetian festivals somewhat riotous.'

He inclined his head, turned on his heel and left her. Kathryn's cheeks flamed. Had she given herself away? Had he seen that longing in her eyes? Oh, what a fool she was! She did not like what he was or what he did—so how could she feel such tempestuous emotions when he looked at her?

Kathryn chose a gown of white silk trimmed with black ribbons. Her mask was a pretty thing of white, silver and black that fitted over the top half of her face and fastened with ribbons. Her cloak was fashioned of fine soft velvet that felt so comforting to wear, for, though the sun had been warm during the day, the night air was much cooler.

She was waiting downstairs in one of the salons when Michael came to collect her. He wore a harlequin costume in the colours of black and white, which complemented her gown perfectly, and looked the picture of a courtier. He was a handsome man, his dark hair and eyes enough to set the hearts of most ladies fluttering. Kathryn wondered why she could not feel something more for him, for he was much kinder and more courteous than his commander.

'We make a pretty pair, sir,' she said and curtsied to him.

'You are beautiful, Mistress Rowlands,' he told her. 'I am but a simple sea captain, but you are a lady and far beyond me.'

Kathryn did not know how to answer him, for she was surprised by his words, which seemed to hint at something much deeper and stronger than mere friendship. She smiled and gave him her hand, blushing as he held it to his lips before leading her out to the front of the palace and down the steps to the waiting gondola.

'I thought that you might like to see the sights before we join the revellers in St Mark's Square,' he said. 'For this evening is a celebration.'

Kathryn allowed him to hand her into the gondola. Their oarsman took them through the narrow waterways of the city, which was lit with many tiny lanterns and torches, and bedecked with ribbons, flowers and flags.

When they reached the square it was already crowded. Music was playing and people were dancing, everyone dressed in beautiful clothes and carrying or wearing masks. Some were very exotic, resembling the heads of animals or mythical beasts, others were sad or comic, though most were very simple, like hers.

She danced with Michael three times, and then stood to one side to watch the others dancing while he fetched her a cool drink mixed with fruits that tasted sweet. She sipped it and then set the glass down, just as someone caught her arm and she was suddenly whirled back into the throng of dancers. Her heart raced for a moment as she thought it might be an attempt at abduction, and then, as she looked up at the masked man, she knew him.

'Are you enjoying yourself, Madonna?'

'Yes, very much,' she said. 'I thought you were too busy to come with us?'

'My business was finished sooner than I thought,' Lorenzo said and smiled. His mask, like hers, was plain and fitted over the top half of his face, but he was dressed all in black, though the sash at his waist was of silver. 'I thought I would discover for myself what happens on this night of mystery and feasting.'

'Why mystery?'

'Do you not know the legend of the Seventh Moon?'

Kathryn shook her head, her eyes wide with curiosity. 'What is the Seventh Moon?'

'It is said that if a virgin looks at the full moon in a bowl of water for seven nights without fail, on the last night she will see the face of her lover—and by morning she will no longer be a virgin.' There was a wicked, teasing note in his voice that made her want to laugh. 'Have you looked to see the face of your lover, Madonna? And whose is the face you see, I wonder?'

'Oh!' Kathryn felt her cheeks grow warm. She looked away hastily for she did not know how to interpret his teasing. 'But why is the feast held on this night?'

'That I cannot tell you,' he said and she knew that he was laughing at her. 'Perhaps to celebrate the beginning of the legend—who knows?'

'I think you invented your story, sir,' Kathryn said and her heart beat faster as she heard his laughter.

'Did I, Kathryn?' he asked. 'Now, why should I do that?'

She shook her head. Her heart was beating so fast that she felt a little faint, as if she were swept away with some emotion that thrilled and yet terrified her. He seemed so different from the cold, hard man she had become accustomed to thinking him, reminding her of someone she had known long ago. Dickon had told her stories, making them up on the spur of the moment to tease her and make her laugh.

The music had ended for the moment and people were moving away to find food and refreshment. Kathryn stood looking up at him, caught by some strange sensation that gripped her, sweeping her back through the years so that she seemed to be a child again.

'Who are you?' she asked, her eyes seeming to be locked with his.

'I do not know who I am, Kathryn,' he said, and then, as her breath caught in her throat, he bent his head and kissed her on the lips very softly. 'Since you came I do not know anything…'

'Lorenzo.' Her mouth seemed to tingle from his kiss though it had been sweet and gentle, and her heart was racing wildly. 'What do you mean?'

'Who knows what words mean?' he asked, an odd smile touching his mouth. 'Did I not tell you this was a night of mystery? Michael is looking for you. I shall take you back to him, Kathryn.'

She wanted to stay with him, to be back in his arms, but

she knew that the moment had passed as he took her arm, steering her back to where Michael awaited her. Then, before she could say or do anything, he turned and disappeared through the throngs of people crowding the square.

'I have never known Lorenzo to attend the masque before,' Michael said, watching him go. 'Nor have I known him to dance.'

'Not ever—with anyone?' Kathryn's heart jerked as he shook his head. How strange that was! 'He said that his business had finished early.'

'Even so…' Michael looked thoughtful. 'Will you eat something, Mistress Rowlands?'

'I am not very hungry,' Kathryn confessed. 'Would you mind very much if I asked you to take me home?'

'No, of course not,' he said and smiled at her. 'I am here to serve you.'

'You were very kind to bring me this evening. I have enjoyed myself.'

'Lorenzo asked me to bring you. He said that you had been confined to the house too long. I asked him why he did not bring you himself, and he said that you would be safer with me. I did not understand him.' Michael frowned. 'I would give my life for Lorenzo Santorini, but…' He paused, then rushed on. 'I do not think he is a man who would make a woman such as you happy, Kathryn. There are things in his past that he can never forget.'

'What do you mean?' She looked at him, her eyes wide, feeling coldness at the nape of her neck. 'What kind of things?'

'Forgive me, I may not tell you. I have perhaps said too much. It is not my business to interfere—but I have a deep regard for you, Kathryn. Forgive me if I use your name without permission.' She shook her head. 'You are as brave and generous as you are beautiful. I do not know what Lorenzo intends towards you, but I would not have you hurt.'

'Thank you for your concern, sir. But I do not think he intends anything towards me—other than to deliver me safely to Lord Mountfitchet and collect the ransom.'

'What ransom?' Michael stared at her. 'If you imagine that he snatched you from that Spaniard for a ransom, you are much mistaken. You do not understand him, Kathryn. Yes, sometimes he takes money for restoring a man to his family. Most are only too eager to pay it and he puts that money to good use. For every man that can be restored to his family there are a hundred that cannot; some can never work and without help would simply starve.'

Kathryn felt very strange, her throat tight with emotion. 'Are you telling me that the money…?' Her voice caught on a sob as she realised how badly she had misjudged Lorenzo. 'He helps the men he rescues if they are not strong enough to work?'

'Did you imagine that he cast them out to fend for themselves? Better that they should die quickly than starve, Kathryn. Lorenzo is rich, but he cares little for money for its own sake. His purpose in life is to destroy those evil men who prey on others, enslaving them and using them like beasts. That is why I warned you not to love him, for there is such pain in him…' He shook his head as her eyes begged the question. 'No, I may not tell you more. I have already said too much and I beg that you will not speak of this to Lorenzo. He would be angry. He makes no apology for what he does to any man—or woman.'

'I shall never tell him what you have said this night,' Kathryn said. 'But I do thank you for telling me. I did not understand.'

She had had no idea what lay behind that mask of coldness, the apparent ruthlessness of his business, the way he saved or took life seemingly at will. Even now she could not think of the men left behind in the water without shuddering, but she could begin to understand.

Lorenzo removed the leather wristbands, rubbing at the ridge of dark purplish-red flesh beneath. The badge of his slavery, a constant reminder that would never let him forget those years of pain and humiliation or the hatred that had festered inside him. At Antonio Santorini's deathbed, he had sworn that he would not rest until he had brought Rachid down and freed all those he held prisoner. That purpose had driven him from this day until now, and he could not let anything change that—not even the enticing lips of a woman who filled his senses as no other ever had.

She had felt so good as he'd held her in his arms during their dance that the temptation to kiss her had been overwhelming. She filled his mind even now, making him burn with desire such as he had never known. Only the strength of his will was keeping him from going to her now and making her his own. He wanted to feel her soft skin as she lay beside him, to touch her, kiss her, know her fully. To make love to her, to love her, have her always…

No! That way lay madness! He could not lie with Kathryn without letting down his guard. He could not seduce her without offering her his home and his name—but what was his name?

A shiver went through him as he recalled the moment she had looked into his eyes and asked him who he was, and his answer had surprised even himself. He was Lorenzo Santorini, a man dedicated to destroying his enemy. Of course he knew who he was! To let himself dwell on the past—on things that could never be proved— would be to invite confusion.

He rubbed at his left wrist. It was always this one that irritated the most. The flesh was swollen now for he did not use the healing salve as often as he should. Getting out of bed, he took the pot of lotion that had been given him by Ali Khayr, rubbing it into the ridges of tortured flesh. He frowned as he traced the thin line, which extended from beneath the welt of scarred skin. It looked darker than the other scars, older and in some way different. He had not really noticed it until lately. His finger traced it absently, sliding down over the welt of disfigured flesh, making the sign of a letter.

Kathryn! She was too often in his mind. If he allowed her to take over she would destroy him. He had begun to imagine things, impossible dreams that were not for a man such as he—and there were the images that came to him now. Flashes of memory, perhaps? He could not be sure. For so many years he had remembered nothing, had wanted to remember nothing beyond the moment he had seen the face of his enemy and known that he lived only to kill him.

Rachid was not of Arab descent, nor was he a Turk. His skin was sunburned and his eyes were grey, but he was from the Western world—something that had made Lorenzo despise him more. How could he, a man raised to Christian values, use and torture other men so cruelly? He was evil, a disciple of Satan—and Lorenzo could not rest until he was dead.

Nothing must deflect him from his purpose. He must not allow himself to be softened by a woman's smile—nor must he let those disturbing flashes of memory rob him of his identity. It did not matter who he had been. He was Lorenzo Santorini. A man with no mercy for his enemy.

The sooner he could return Kathryn to her friends the better. If he were sensible, he would send her with Michael as her escort, finish it now. The longer she stayed with him the more enmeshed in her web he might become.

Kathryn looked around the cabin to which she had been shown. It was much more luxuriously appointed than the one she had used on board Lorenzo's war galley. This was the largest and finest of his merchant ships. It was carrying a cargo of goods to the island, which would be sold to the merchants there in return for another cargo of fine wines and citrus fruits. These fruits were much valued by those who spent their lives at sea, for they were believed to help prevent the dreaded disease that some called scurvy.

She turned as she heard someone behind her, and, looking towards the door, saw that Lorenzo stood there. His eyes were thoughtful as they looked at her, almost brooding. She felt herself tremble inside and knew a longing to be in his arms as she had been on the night of the Seventh Moon.

'I hope you will be comfortable here, Kathryn. My own cabin was not fitting for you, but we have made more provision this time.'

'I was happy enough to live as you do,' she said. 'Do you travel with me on this ship, sir?' Her heart was fluttering as she waited for his response, for though she feared what he did to her with those devastating eyes, she also longed for it.

'No, on my personal galley,' Lorenzo replied. 'You will be safe enough for we shall escort you to Cyprus. I have some business there with Lord Mountfitchet.'

'Yes, of course,' she said, though she sensed that he was not telling her the whole truth. 'It is good of you to go to so much trouble for my sake.'

'But I do not want to lose my ransom,' he said, an odd smile on his lips. 'Surely you must know that, Kathryn?'

'You shame me, sir,' she said, blushing. 'I was wrong to say such things to you.'

'Were you?' His eyes narrowed, intent on her face. 'I am not ashamed of what I do.'

'Why should you be?' She flushed deeper as he looked at her more closely, clearly wondering why she had changed her mind, and knew that she must be careful or she would betray Michael's confidence. 'Any man is worthy of his hire. If you do someone a service, they should expect to pay for it.'

Lorenzo inclined his head. 'I have questioned the men we took from Rachid's galley. No one knows anything of a youth taken from Cornwall all those years ago. It was not likely that they would. I believe that you will never find the man you seek, Kathryn. And if you did…he would not be the same man.'

'I know…' She sighed. 'I have begun to think that it may be best if Dickon is never found. Sometimes I hope that he died long ago. I had heard stories of men being put to the galleys as slaves, but I did not understand what it meant until now. It must be the most soul-destroying thing that a man can suffer, to be forced to work so hard and to know that he is a slave…'

'Dickon is dead,' Lorenzo said, his eyes violet dark. 'The youth you once loved would not have survived without becoming someone very different, believe me.'

'Yes, I know,' she said and her voice caught with tears. 'I know that his father will go on searching for him, but I shall try to remember him as a friend that died.'

'It would be a waste if you were to spend your life waiting for a man who will never come back to you,' Lorenzo told her. 'You should marry, Kathryn. I dare say you would not look at Michael Ignacio, though I know he cares for you. And I can vouch for him as a man of good family and honest values. You could do much worse than to marry a man such as he, for I dare say he would give up the sea for your sake.'

'If I felt that way for him, I should be pleased to wed him,' she replied, her eyes stinging with the tears she held back. He was doing his best to persuade her to think of Michael as a husband. Why should he do that? It could only mean that he was telling her not to think of him. She looked at him proudly, coldly. 'Perhaps I may marry one day—when I return to England. But I am not sure that I could be happy with any other man than Dickon. It may be that I shall never marry.'

Lorenzo nodded and frowned, silent for a moment, then he said, 'When do you plan to return home?'

'I do not know,' Kathryn said. 'I shall stay with Lady Mary and Lord Mountfitchet for some months and then…' She could not go on, for her heart felt as if it were breaking, and she wanted to say that she would stay for ever if only he cared for her. His eyes seemed dark with some hidden emotion as he looked at her, but he said nothing that could give her encouragement, nothing to indicate that she meant anything to him. She must put her foolish notions from her head. She could not love a man such as Lorenzo Santorini.

But of course she didn't! He had called her a foolish child enough times, and she knew that he must despise her for the trouble she had caused him.

'I believe there will be a campaign in a few months,' Lorenzo told her, changing the subject abruptly. 'His Holiness the Pope has gathered a great alliance to try and wipe the scourge of the Turkish invaders from our seas, and, with the demise of their power, much of the piracy that takes place under their flag. I have pledged my support, but if you waited until the following spring I should be happy to escort you to your home.'

'Thank you, sir,' Kathryn said. She lifted her head proudly, blinking back her tears. 'I think my father or brother may come to fetch me—but if I should need your help, I shall ask for it.'

'As you wish,' he said and smiled. 'We shall meet again on Cyprus. Excuse me, I have work to do.'

Kathryn felt the tears she could no longer restrain trickle down her face as he walked from the cabin. He was so withdrawn, so distant. How could she have been so foolish as to fall in love with him?

No, no, of course she wasn't in love with him. It was just that he had saved her from a terrible fate, and she was grateful to him. Yes, that was it. She was grateful to him, and she liked him. It was reasonable to like him for she owed him a great deal. But she did not love him. She must remember who and what he was, a cold, harsh man who lived by the sword.

No, she could never love such a man.

Chapter Six

Why had the ship stopped moving? Kathryn went to the porthole and looked out, her heart beating wildly as she wondered if they were being attacked. She was relieved as she saw that they had halted so that Lorenzo could come aboard. It was a tricky manoeuvre, but she saw him swing himself over the rigging with an ease she could only admire. He had an air of authority, seeming so strong and sure, a natural ability to lead that was apparent in the way his men greeted him. For a moment she was lost in admiration, her pulses racing.

Kathryn sat down to wait, her heart beating faster than normal. Several minutes passed before he knocked at her cabin door and then entered. She was shocked by the gravity of his expression. Her knees felt like jelly and she was trembling from head to foot. What had made him look like that?

'Kathryn...' She thought that she had never heard him speak with such emotion, except perhaps for one moment on that Spanish mountainside. 'I fear I have received bad news. The Turks have invaded Cyprus. It is believed that Nicosia has fallen.'

'Invaded?' Kathryn looked at him in dismay. 'But Lady Mary, Lord Mountfitchet—what will happen to them?' She had risen as he entered, but now sat down on the edge of the bed, overcome by her concern.

'We must hope that they have somehow escaped,' Lorenzo said. 'Or that a ransom may be paid for their safe return. Sometimes that is the case, especially for those who might not be worthwhile as slaves.'

'Because they are not young and beautiful—or strong enough to work in the galleys?' Kathryn's throat tightened and she felt the sting of tears as she thought of the people she loved become prisoners of the Turks. 'This is so terrible. How could such a thing have happened? I thought Cyprus belonged to Venice?'

'As it does,' Lorenzo said, looking angry. 'We refused their demands to surrender the island to them, but it seems that the invasion has gone ahead. This means the Pope must marshal the forces of the Holy League. I must go to Rome, Kathryn, and you must come with me. You will wait there for me until I know how things stand.'

Kathryn was silent. Had she been with Lady Mary and Lord Mountfitchet, she would have been on Cyprus when the invasion happened. She might even now be dead or a captive of the Turks, perhaps destined for a harem. She felt shocked by the news, unable to come to terms with the loss of her friends.

'I have been nothing but trouble to you,' she said, on the verge of tears. 'I must accept your offer, sir, for I do not know what else to do.'

'There is nothing you can do,' he told her, his words and manner seeming harsh to her. 'It seems that fate has delivered you into my care, and we must both make the best of it. Now I must ask you to transfer to my galley, for this ship will return to Venice. I must muster my war captains and a ship like this is little use for the task that awaits us now.'

'Would it not be better if I were to return with this ship?'

'No, I think not. I cannot afford to send an escort with it and in these uncertain times anything might happen. Besides, I shall not be returning to Venice for some months. I shall leave you with a friend in Rome. You will be safer there until I can decide what best to do with you.'

Kathryn was too subdued to answer him. The possible loss of two people who had been dear to her was heartbreaking and she could not fight Lorenzo this time. Without him she would have been even more vulnerable, for she had little money of her own and could not return to England without help. She was, in fact, completely dependent on him, even for the clothes she wore and the food she ate. It was a humiliating feeling and she hardly knew how to face him.

'Come, Kathryn,' Lorenzo demanded. 'Do not despair. Lord Mountfitchet was warned that invasion was a possibility. It may be that he changed his mind at the last minute.'

She knew that he was trying to comfort her, but her heart was heavy. Despite Lorenzo's words, she doubted that Lord Mountfitchet would have changed his plans without good cause. All she could hope was that he and Lady Mary had somehow escaped with their lives.

* * *

Kathryn looked around the room she had been given at the home of Lorenzo's friend. The Contessa Rosa dei Corleone had welcomed him with a smile and the warmth of old acquaintance. Kathryn was not certain that she was so pleased to have a stranger as her guest, though she had accepted her graciously.

'Of course Mistress Rowlands may stay with me, Lorenzo,' she said, her dark eyes sparkling as she looked at him. 'You know that I would do anything you asked of me.'

Why, she was flirting with him! Kathryn realised it and felt a spurt of disgust. The Contessa was years older than him!

'You are generous, Contessa,' Lorenzo said, an amused glint in his eyes. 'I shall return as soon as possible. In the meantime, I shall make some provision for Kathryn. Should I not return from the coming encounter, there will be sufficient money to see her safely back to England.'

'As you wish, my friend.'

The dark eyes were speculative as the Contessa looked at Kathryn.

'My servant will take you to your room. I am sure you must wish to tidy yourself after so long at sea.'

Kathryn sent Lorenzo a look of appeal. Now that he was about to leave her, she felt as if she were being abandoned. She wanted to cling to him, to beg him not to leave her, but knew that she must not let him see how she felt.

'I shall see you again before we leave,' he said, smiling at her reassuringly. 'There are preparations to be made and I have much to do. It may be three or four days before the rest of my fleet can join me, and another two before we put to sea.'

Kathryn nodded. She fought her tears. Her heart felt as if it were being ripped in two, but she must not weep.

'You must not think of me. You have your duty—but I would have news of my uncle and aunt...'

'I shall not abandon you,' he said and smiled. For a moment her heart lifted as she saw something in his eyes—a look that she had seen only once before. 'Go with the Contessa's woman now. She will take you to your chamber. You should rest for a while.'

Kathryn had obeyed him. There was so much she wished to say and could not. Now, alone in this room, the guest of a woman she instinctively knew disliked her, Kathryn admitted to herself that she was in love with Lorenzo Santorini. She did not know how it could have happened, for she had been determined to dislike him. Now she knew that she would find it unbearable if she were never to see him again. If he should be killed... She could not think about it. It was too painful.

'The Contessa asks that you will come down to her salon as soon as you are ready.'

Kathryn turned, her heart sinking as she looked into the hostile eyes of the Contessa's servant. She was not welcome here in this house—but what could she do? Lorenzo had brought her here and there was nowhere else for her. Her abduction had taught her how vulnerable she was. She was dependent on Lorenzo's generosity, at least until there was some news of her friends.

She followed the servant down to the grand salon where the Contessa was waiting for her, and her heart sank as she saw the expression in the older woman's eyes. She had pretended to be welcoming while Lorenzo was here, but there was no mistaking her hostility now.

'So,' the Contessa said. 'I must make you welcome since Lorenzo asks it of me. In return I demand that you behave with proper modesty while in my house, Mistress Rowlands. I would not have you disgrace me before my friends.'

'In what way do you fear I shall disgrace you?' Kathryn lifted her head, eyes flashing with pride. She felt humiliated and was angry. What was this woman implying?

'You have been travelling alone with Lorenzo Santorini. You stayed with him at the Santorini Palace in Venice. What do you imagine people will think of you if they discover your shame?'

'I have done nothing to be ashamed of—and I had my maid with me at the palace, and on the journey from Venice to Rome.' Kathryn did not tell her of the time she had spent alone on Lorenzo's galley after her abduction, for it could only make her situation worse. 'This awkwardness is not of my making.'

'A servant is not a chaperon. You have forfeited your reputation, girl,' the Contessa said harshly, her mouth twisting with spite. 'What you choose to do is your own affair, but do not shame me by speaking of it in public, if you please.'

Kathryn's cheeks flamed. Her anger at being spoken to so unfairly banished the tears that had been hovering. Had there been any other alternative she would have left this woman's house at once, but there was no way out for her. She must endure the Contessa's spite, at least until Lorenzo was ready to escort her to her home.

'I shall behave as befits an English gentlewoman,' she said with dignity. She lifted her head high, refusing to be cowed by the woman's hostility. 'I cannot change your opinion of me, Contessa. For both our sakes, I hope that Lorenzo will remove me from your house very soon.'

'Very well. This has been distasteful to me, Mistress Rowlands. This evening I attend a private supper at a friend's house. Tomorrow evening there is a grand reception, which you will attend with me. I hope you have suitable clothes?' Her tone suggested that she thought it unlikely, stinging Kathryn on the raw.

'My trunks are on the ship. Once they are delivered, I believe I shall not disgrace you.'

'See that you do not.' The Contessa waved her hand. 'You may go. I shall tell you when I require your presence. If you wish, you may use the gardens and the salons at the back of the house.'

Kathryn left the room, her back very straight. She was humiliated and upset, but anger made her keep her spirits up. How could Lorenzo have brought her to the house of such a woman?

Kathryn dressed in a gown of dark green silk the following evening. She wore a small ruff of gauze that was stiffened with wire and stood up at the back of her neck. Her hair was swept up on her head and covered by a green velvet hood trimmed with silver and brilliants. It was the most matronly of her gowns and chosen to make her look as ordinary and respectable as possible.

The Contessa looked her over as she went down to join her in the salon. 'Yes, that is well enough,' she said, her mouth sour with disapproval, for even in this plain apparel Kathryn was beautiful, young and desirable. 'Do not forget what I have told you.'

'I shall not forget.'

Kathryn would have preferred not to accompany the Contessa to the reception that evening, but she had little choice. She must do as she was told while she lived under this woman's roof.

The reception was being held in a large villa built in the hills overlooking the city. Kathryn joined the other guests, smiling but saying very little as she was introduced to the Contessa's friends as the ward of a dear friend. She was in public a very different woman, smiling and calling Kathryn a sweet child, which made Kathryn want to run away and hide.

However, she stood obediently at the Contessa's side, speaking only when addressed and wishing that the evening might be over. She liked none of these people and remembered how kind Aunt Mary's friends had been to her in London, something that made her heart ache as she wondered if her friend was still alive. Would she ever see her kind friends again? Would she ever be able to return to her home?

Seeing that the Contessa appeared to have forgotten her, Kathryn moved towards the marble arches that opened out into the huge gardens, needing suddenly to be alone. She felt lost and alone and so unhappy that she was having to fight very hard to hold back her tears. She went out into the cool of the night air, looking at the stars. Somehow she must find a way to bear this time of unhappiness.

'Why are you out here?' Lorenzo's voice close behind

her made her jump for she had not been aware of him. 'The Contessa was anxious about you.'

Kathryn turned to look at him. Was he angry with her too? She felt a tear slip down her cheek and turned aside, not wanting him to see. She walked away, wanting to escape deeper into the gardens.

He came after her, catching her arm, swinging her round to face him. 'What is wrong? Why are you crying?'

'I'm not crying,' Kathryn sniffed, brushing her face with the back of her hand.

'Something has upset you. Tell me, Kathryn!' She shook her head. 'Are you crying for your uncle and aunt?' She shook her head again. 'Then it is the Contessa…'

'She hates me!' The words burst from her.

'Do not be foolish, Kathryn. Why should she hate you?'

'She says that I have lost my reputation, that people will think I am your—' She broke off and turned away from him once more.

'Ah.' Lorenzo looked at her thoughtfully, seeing the pride and anger, and the despair. 'I understand. There was always the risk that this would happen, but the damage is done, Kathryn.'

'I know. There is nothing anyone can do.'

'No…unless you become my wife.' He smiled oddly as she whirled round, her eyes wide with shock. 'Forgive me. I know the idea cannot please you, but it would stop the vicious tongues before they can start.'

'But you do not want to marry me!'

'It is a matter of indifference to me,' Lorenzo said with a shrug of his shoulders. 'I have no wish for a wife, but it would be a marriage of convenience only. You have told me that though you may marry one day, your heart belongs to the man you lost so many years ago. Therefore it can make no difference who you marry. As well me as another. Indeed, I may be the only chance of marriage you will have.'

'That is no reason for marriage!' Kathryn did not know whether to rage at him or weep. 'Why should you want me? How does this benefit you?'

'Did you not tell me you were an heiress? This war is likely to cost me a small fortune. A wealthy wife would be no bad thing.'

Was he teasing her? There was a glint in his eyes, though he was not smiling.

'It is not a huge fortune…' She stared at him uncertainly. A part of her wanted to refuse his offer, for it was almost insulting in the manner of its making, and yet she could not help feeling that as Lorenzo's wife she would be safe. 'You cannot want me?'

Kathryn could not know how vulnerable and uncertain she looked or that the appeal in her eyes touched something in Lorenzo that he had thought long dead.

'Believe me when I say I have my reasons,' he told her, a smile upon his lips now. Surely he was teasing her! 'You know that I never do anything without profit, Kathryn—believe that I want you. You are beautiful and a man should have a wife, after all.' He had her fast so that she could not escape. As she gazed into his eyes her heart raced and she longed for him to kiss her, to tell her that he was marrying her because he cared for her.

'Then…if you truly mean it, I shall accept,' she said, finding it difficult to breathe. Surely this was but another of the dreams that came to plague her when she slept? 'I shall try to be what you would have me be.'

'Do not worry about what I would have of you,' Lorenzo told her, a faint smile on his lips. 'We shall be married and then I shall leave you. Only He that they call God—whether he be Christian or Muslim—knows whether I shall return. If I do not, you shall be a rich widow, Kathryn. Choose your next husband with more care, I beg you.' Again his eyes were bright with mockery and she did not know what to make of him.

'Lorenzo…' Kathryn looked at him wordlessly. How could she tell him that she did not care for his wealth, that she wanted him to return to her? He said that he had his reasons for marrying her, but she could think of none—unless she had led him to believe that her father was richer than he really was?

'I told you not to worry,' he said, and then, moving towards her, he touched her face, lowering his head to kiss her softly on the lips. A wave of desire coursed through her, making her feel as if she would melt into him, become a part of his very body, though his next words brought her back to her senses. 'We did not choose this, Kathryn, but it seems that it is our fate. Let fate take its course and we shall see.'

Kathryn wore the gown she had borrowed for the night of the masque, which had been packed in her trunk with the rest of her things. She did not know why she chose it, except that that night Lorenzo had seemed so different, and she wanted him to be the man she had glimpsed then. She wanted him to laugh and tease her, to love her—but of course he did not. She looked at her reflection in her hand mirror, and then decided to let her hair flow on her shoulders, wearing only a small cap of silver threads on the back of her head.

She was still at the Contessa's house, for Lorenzo had begged her to be patient until he could arrange for the wedding and her removal to a villa he had taken for her stay in Rome. When she went downstairs the Contessa was waiting. She looked at Kathryn with dislike, her eyes moving over her with disapproval.

'Do not imagine that he loves you,' she said coldly. 'No one woman would ever be enough for a man like that. He is marrying you because he feels pity for you—and he will be unfaithful within a year.'

Kathryn held her tongue, for what could she say in answer? The Contessa might be speaking the truth for all she knew. Lorenzo was marrying her for reasons of his own, reasons that he had not chosen to divulge to her. She did not think that he was in love with her, but perhaps he might want her in his bed. She had been told many times that she was beautiful, and she believed that she was comely enough. Perhaps that odd look she had seen in his eyes sometimes meant that he wanted to make love to her.

It was evident that the Contessa was angry as she almost ordered Kathryn from the house, and she suspected that the older woman wanted him for herself. She thought that perhaps they had been lovers in the past and that the Contessa had hoped he might marry her now that she was a widow. Her husband had been dead for six months, and it must have seemed to her when Lorenzo first came that he had come for her, which made it easy to understand why in her disappointment she had felt so hostile towards the girl he had brought with him.

Lorenzo was waiting for them at the small church. Michael was to give her away, and a man she did not know stood up with Lorenzo as his witness. The Contessa was Kathryn's only attendant, and she left immediately after the ceremony, refusing to attend the small wedding feast. Kathryn could only be pleased.

Michael and the stranger, who told her that his name was Paolo Casciano, and that Lorenzo was a friend of many years, accompanied her and Lorenzo to a villa in the hills overlooking the city. It was not as large as the Contessa's home, but pleasant with lovely gardens.

'This will be your home until we can return to Venice,' Lorenzo told her. 'I have engaged servants to care for your needs and a lady who will bear you company while I am away.' He beckoned to an elderly woman with a sweet face, who came forward to curtsy to Kathryn. 'This lady is Madame Veronique de Bologna. She was born in France, but has lived in Italy since her marriage, and is now a widow.'

'May I welcome you to your new home, my lady,' the widow said and smiled. 'I was so happy to be of service to you when Signor Santorini asked me to come and bear you company.'

'And I am very grateful for your presence, *madame.*'

'I beg you to call me Veronique,' she said, 'for I hope we shall be friends.'

'Yes, of course. I hope so too.'

'Come,' Lorenzo commanded, 'our guests are waiting to see the bride.'

'Our guests?' Kathryn looked at him in surprise.

'Did you imagine I had no friends?' Lorenzo's violet-blue eyes were laughing at her as he drew her out into the garden where a feast had been laid out on boards over trestles, covered with white cloths and laden with platters of wonderful food.

Several ladies and gentlemen were gathered there and they burst into a spontaneous round of applause as Lorenzo drew her forward.

'My friends, I give you the lady who has been brave—or foolish—enough to become my bride this day.'

His introduction brought laughter and then the guests gathered round, giving her kisses and smiles, presents of money, silver, jewellery and objects of art. Kathryn was overwhelmed by this unexpected kindness—she had not expected anything of the sort.

She looked at them shyly, her throat caught with emotion. 'I do not know what to say…you are all so very kind.'

'They are curious,' Lorenzo said, a sparkle of amusement in his eyes, 'for they wonder that any woman would wed such as I.'

'No, I do not believe that,' she said. 'You are not so very terrible, Lorenzo.'

Her remark brought much laughter and she found herself swept away by a group of smiling women who chattered away to her in a mixture of Italian and English, wanting to know all manner of things about her.

'How did you meet Lorenzo?'

'Where do you live?'

'How did you come here?'

'I lived in Cornwall and journeyed to Venice with friends.'

'Cornwall? I have never heard of such a place!' one rather pretty woman with a lively manner cried.

'Do not show your ignorance, Elizabeta. It is in England!'

The questions came so thick and fast that Kathryn's head was spinning by the time Lorenzo came to rescue her. The laughter continued throughout the feast and the traditional toast to the bride and groom, and then music began to play and everyone demanded that they should dance.

Kathryn trembled as he took her into his arms, but found that it was easy to follow his steps as they danced on the tiled patio. Glancing up, she saw that he was smiling and her heart fluttered. Surely he did care for her a little or he would not look at her that way.

The merriment continued throughout the afternoon, but as the sun started to dip over the sea in a flash of fiery orange, their friends began to take their leave. The ladies kissed Kathryn and promised to call on her soon, and the men clapped Lorenzo on the back and told him he was a fortunate man.

At last only Lorenzo, Veronique and Kathryn were left. They went into the house and the servants came out to begin the task of clearing up the debris.

'If you have no need of me, my lady, I shall leave you alone.' Veronique smiled at Kathryn and curtsied to Lorenzo. 'Good evening, *signor*.'

'Goodnight, *madame*.'

Kathryn felt a little shiver run down her spine at the sound of his voice. They were alone at last and she was nervous, because she did not know the man she had married. She did not know what he expected of her. Her heart told her that there was nothing to fear, but still she could not help the trembling she felt inside.

'Let us take a cup of wine together,' Lorenzo said, pouring some of the sweet white wine she liked into a glass and handing it to her. He poured another for himself and sipped it, before setting the glass down. 'Did you like my friends, Kathryn?'

'Yes, of course. How could I not when they were so kind to me?'

'You were surprised to find so many here to welcome you?'

'I did not know what to expect.'

'That is hardly surprising, for we know nothing of each other's lives,' he said, looking thoughtful. 'Perhaps that will change when I return, Kathryn. I have never considered marriage, but a man may acquire new ideas. Now that you are my wife, I would have you content. However, should you be unhappy, I would consider taking you back to your father.'

Kathryn did not know how to answer him. 'I shall try to please you, Lorenzo.'

'You mistake my meaning,' he said. 'My life will be much as it has been, for I shall be often away. However, when I am at home I shall do what I can to make you happy.'

'Thank you. You have already done so much for me.' He had given her back her reputation and her pride. She could ask nothing more of him—unless he wished to give it.

'You must try not to worry too much about your

friends,' Lorenzo said. 'If you wish to write a letter to your father, Paolo will see it on its way for you. I shall leave money with him, for you will need to run the house and to buy things for your own use. You may address any accounts to him and he will pay them for you. And when I return we shall talk again.'

Kathryn felt the emotion rising inside her. She swallowed hard, determined not to let him see that she was so affected. She wished that he did not have to leave her, but he had made his position clear. He had married her to keep her safe and would try to be a kind, considerate husband, but he had no use for a wife. She meant nothing to him.

She took a deep breath, controlling her voice as she said, 'When must you leave?'

'We put to sea in the morning. I have business that I must attend this night. I am sorry to leave you so soon, Kathryn, but we are at war.'

'Yes, I know.' Was she to spend her wedding night alone? 'Shall I see you again before you leave?'

Lorenzo hesitated, then shook his head. 'I think there will not be time. Besides, I shall make no demands of you this night, Kathryn. You must learn to think of me as your husband, and then, perhaps…but we shall see if we suit each other.'

Kathryn felt as if he had slapped her. She knew that he did not love her, but she had imagined that he would claim his right as a husband to sleep in her bed that night. Surely any man would do as much? It could only mean that he did not find her desirable enough. She swallowed her hurt pride, refusing to show him how she felt at being so summarily abandoned.

'As you wish. I pray that you have a safe journey, Lorenzo.'

He hesitated for a moment, then took two steps towards her and stopped, looking down at her with such a strange expression. She thought that he would take her in his arms and kiss her and her heart beat wildly, but then he seemed to change his mind. He moved away from her, as if deliberately putting distance between them.

'If anything should happen to me, you will be taken care of, Kathryn. You have nothing to fear. And now, forgive me, I must leave.'

Kathryn nodded, feeling miserable as he walked from the room. He did not find her desirable enough to want to lie with her. She was a bride, but not a wife, and the pain of humiliation at his rejection twisted inside her like the blade of a knife. She had longed for him to kiss her and make her his own, but he did not want her.

Tears stung her eyes, but she refused to let them fall. She would never, never let him see that she was fool enough to love him.

Lorenzo found the endless meetings and discussions tedious beyond bearing. It was now early autumn and the Sicilian squadron had gathered at Oranto. Many of the galleys were neither as well equipped nor manned as adequately as his own, including those of his countrymen. Venice had boasted that they had the finest fleet of all, but it was seen to be a hollow boast, for many of the galleys had lain idle for too long and were in need of repair. The papal fleet itself was weak, which meant that the Spanish had most of the power. A man called Marcantonio Colonna had overall command of the fleet, but, despite his skill at diplomacy and his personal courage, it was proving almost impossible to hold the different factions together. Colonna wanted to go after the enemy at once, but another commander, Gianandrea Doria, had so far resisted. As one of the principal galley owners, he was concerned for the fate of his ships.

'We are not yet strong enough,' Doria said at one of the eternal meetings. 'We must wait.'

'I believe they will argue for ever,' Lorenzo said to Michael, his patience exhausted when he learned that the decision to disperse for the winter had been taken late in September. 'What of our people on Cyprus? Are we to abandon them to their fate?'

Doria had decided to take his ships to Sicily for the winter, but Lorenzo would take his fleet to Rome.

'I see no point in wasting months in idleness when we might be more profitably employed,' he said. 'There are repairs to be made and they will be better done in Rome than Sicily.'

'So we return to Rome at once?'

'Yes, to Rome.' Lorenzo's eyes were distant, his thoughts clearly far away.

Michael returned to his own command to give the orders. Lorenzo frowned as he stood staring out to sea. Would he have chosen to winter in Sicily if it were not for Kathryn?

His thoughts had been with her these past weeks, and he felt a deep, instinctive pleasure at the prospect of her waiting for him, a sharp desire forming in his loins as he anticipated their meeting. He had not forced her to submit on their wedding night for it would not have been right. She had married him because she had no choice, but he would teach her not to fear his lovemaking. In time he believed that she would welcome him to her bed.

A shout from one of his men alerted him. 'Six galleys to the leeward, sir!'

Lorenzo looked in the direction the man was pointing. As yet there was some distance between them, but he could see that the oarsmen were pulling hard as they tried to catch up to him. He needed no one to tell him that they were the galleys of his enemy. He had been thwarted in his desire to beard the Turks in their den, but at least the chance of revenge was in sight. Rachid meant to attack them. His personal galley was at the forefront of the small fleet. It was the first time that Lorenzo and his enemy had met like this and they were evenly matched, for Lorenzo had five galleys with him. What Rachid did not know was that another six were not more than half an hour behind him.

He felt a sense of exhilaration, of destiny. It was the confrontation that he had always known must come one day, and it seemed that luck was on his side.

The battle lasted for two hours or more, but the Corsairs were outnumbered when the rest of Lorenzo's fleet caught up with them, and now, at last, it was over. Two of Lorenzo's galleys were damaged, but still afloat and able to limp home. Two of Rachid's galleys had been sunk, another three were crippled. Rachid's own galley had left when the battle was at its hottest, abandoning the rest of the galleys because it was clear that the Venetian was winning.

'Shall we take prisoners?' Michael asked as they saw that the flags on the Corsair ships had been hauled down and the men had surrendered their weapons.

'One of the galleys—that most of need in repair—may be left to those who wish to continue in Rachid's service,' Lorenzo said. 'They may save themselves if they can and we shall not hinder them. We shall take the other two as our prize. Any men aboard any of the galleys who wish to serve with me may transfer to the ships we take with us. Any who resist will be killed.'

'Yes, sir.' Michael was about to leave to see that his commands were carried out when they became aware of a commotion on board one of the captured galleys.

'See what that is about,' Lorenzo instructed, frowning.

Michael shouted to their own men who had boarded the stricken pirate galleys and then came back to report. 'It seems that Rachid's oldest son Hassan has been taken prisoner. What shall we do with him?'

'Bring him to me.'

Lorenzo felt a strange excitement. At last he had the means to punish his enemy for all that he had suffered at his hands. He could repay Rachid for his cruelty a thousand times over by taking the life of his son. Coming on top of the loss of five of his best galleys, it might be a blow from which the Corsair would never recover.

He had his back turned when they brought the prisoner. Lorenzo tensed, then swung round to look at the son of the man he hated, his eyes moving over the youth. He let his eyes dwell on Hassan's face for some minutes, discovering to his surprise that his overriding emotion was pity rather than hatred. The youth could be no more than sixteen and was plainly terrified.

'Down on your knees, dog!' one of Lorenzo's men growled.

'No,' Lorenzo said. 'Let him stand. He is a man, not a dog, whoever his father may be.'

'Kill me,' the youth said, trying to act bravely, though he was shaking with fear. 'Let death come quickly, that is all I ask.'

'I shall not take your life, for it would not profit me,' Lorenzo said, his eyes narrowed, cold. 'Your father is my enemy. I do not make war on boys or innocents. You shall be ransomed.' He turned to Michael, giving him his instructions.

Michael looked surprised and then nodded. 'It shall be as you command, Captain.'

Lorenzo glanced at the youth again, for he had spoken to Michael in Italian and the Corsair did not understand. 'You are to be exchanged for the captive woman Maria, daughter of Don Pablo Dominicus. My captain Michael dei Ignacio will rendezvous with your father off Sicily and the exchange will take place at a given time. If Rachid brings more than one galley to escort him, you will die.' He nodded to Michael. 'Take him with you.'

'And the girl?'

'Bring her to me in Rome. Her father owes me for Kathryn's abduction. He shall pay a ransom to have his daughter back.'

Michael smiled, understanding the cleverness of his captain's mind. 'It is good,' he said. 'A life for a life and still we have our prize.'

'We need more galleys,' Lorenzo said. 'This war with the Turks has been delayed but it will come—and it will cost us much.'

He watched as the men took Rachid's son away. Many

of them would have killed him without a second thought, but they would not disobey their captain, and when they learned of the ransom they would smile and see the logic of their commander's thinking. There was no profit to be had from a dead Corsair.

Despite the damage to his own fleet, this had been a good day, Lorenzo thought grimly. He would repair one of the captured galleys and paint it with his own colours. The other would be sold and the money shared between his men. The captive slaves would be given the choice of serving as free men or, in some cases, questioned before being either ransomed by their families or given their freedom. Any who betrayed their surrender terms would be killed at once. The first thing that Lorenzo demanded of any man was loyalty.

However, he had not forgotten his promise to Kathryn. He would continue to question all those who were taken, seeking information about the long-lost Richard Mountfitchet. It was possible that Lord Mountfitchet had been killed on Cyprus, but Kathryn was still alive and he would keep his word no matter what.

As for the dreams that had begun to haunt his sleep of late, he would dismiss them as nonsense. It mattered little who he had once been. He was Lorenzo Santorini and his purpose in life was… He frowned as he realised that he was no longer certain of his purpose.

He had spared the son of his enemy out of pity for a youth who surely did not deserve a cruel death. Yet that did not ease the hatred he felt for Rachid or the bitterness that had burned inside him like a candle flame for so long, driving him on. It would be foolish to let softer dreams rob him of his purpose in life, for he could not change all that had been, all that he was. He had taken life ruthlessly in pursuit of his enemy, and though he acted for good reason it did not wash away the blood.

How could a man such as he love a woman like Kathryn? He knew himself unworthy and yet his body burned for her, his soul thirsted for the sweetness of a life spent at her side.

But he was what life had made him, and surely there was no changing what fate had decreed.

Chapter Seven

Kathryn laughed at something her companions were saying. Her grasp of the language had improved gradually during the months she had lived in Rome. Almost four months had passed since her wedding day. She had had no word from Lorenzo in all that time and did not know what had been happening, for there had been very little news.

'Elizabeta!' Adriana Botticelli cried. 'You are the most wicked flirt. If I were your husband, I should beat you.'

'If Marco were not so dull, Elizabeta would not need to flirt with Caius Antonio,' Isabella Rinaldi giggled. She was the youngest of the ladies present, and unmarried. 'If my father chooses an old fat merchant as my husband, I shall take a lover too.' She fluttered her fan artlessly, her face alive with mischief. 'I hope that he chooses someone like your husband, Kathryn. If I were you, I should die of happiness.'

'But poor Kathryn was married only a few hours before her husband left her,' Elizabeta said. 'Have you heard nothing from him, Kathryn?'

'Nothing. Lorenzo is always so busy. He will come

when he is ready.' She looked up as her companion came into the salon where they were sitting. 'Is your head better, Veronique?'

'Much better, thank you, Kathryn.' She sat down by the window and picked up her embroidery and then, seeing someone approaching, said, 'Oh, I believe we have company... Why, it is Signor Santorini. Kathryn, your husband is here!'

'Lorenzo is here?' Kathryn's heart missed a beat. 'You are sure it is he, Veronique?'

'Yes, quite sure.'

Kathryn's impulse was to run to meet him, but she fought her desire, pretending to go on with her sewing. She must not betray herself. Lorenzo would not wish her to show too much emotion at his return. He had married her out of pity. He did not want a wife who demanded love.

'We should go,' Elizabeta said, sensing the emotion she struggled to hide. 'Your husband will want to be alone with you, Kathryn.'

Kathryn shook her head, but all the ladies had followed Elizabeta's example. They trooped out of the room with Veronique in their wake. Kathryn stayed where she was, her heart thumping painfully. She could hear her friends chattering and laughing amongst themselves and then the deeper tones of a man's voice.

Her heart jerked as Lorenzo came into the salon. His eyes went over her, seeming to search for something, some sign, though she knew not what he wanted from her.

'Are you well, Kathryn?'

'Yes, sir. I am happy to see you back. I was anxious for your safe return. We have heard little news of the war.'

'That may be because there is little to tell. The Turks have taken Famagusta and Nicosia. The League talked of blockading Rhodes, but once Cyprus had fallen the plan was abandoned. Doria has decided to winter at Sicily. I preferred to return to Rome, for there are galleys to be repaired and provisioned and I can do that better here.'

'I am glad that you did.'

'Are you, Kathryn?' His expression was serious, intent on her face.

'Yes. You must know that.'

'It will be good to be here with you for a while. We shall be a long time at sea once we leave again in the spring.'

She stood up and went over to the table where a tray with glasses and jugs of wine and fruit drinks had been set out for her guests. She took a deep breath to steady her fluttering nerves, then turned to look at him.

'May I serve you some wine?'

'Yes, thank you.' He stood watching her as she poured the wine and brought it to him. 'What have you been doing while I was gone?'

'I have made friends with the ladies you saw here. They take me shopping with them and invite me to their homes.'

'So you have not been unhappy?'

She had missed him dreadfully, spending many lonely hours in the villa and gardens, crying herself to sleep for several nights after he left, but she would not tell him that. He did not want a wife who clung and wept for love of him.

'No, I have not been unhappy.'

'I am glad of it, for I have some news for you, Kathryn.'

'Of Lady Mary and Lord Mountfitchet?'

'No, I am sorry to tell you that as yet no news of them

has come my way, though I have heard that some did escape the onslaught and reached other islands, before and since the invasion. Even if your friends are still alive, Kathryn, it will take time for letters to reach us. My news was of a possible sighting of Richard—one of the prisoners we took told us of a blue-eyed slave who works in the gardens of a wealthy merchant in Algiers. He was a youth when taken and, though he is apparently physically strong, has the mind of a child.'

'That is very sad,' Kathryn said. Once that news would have devastated her, but now she could feel only sadness and regret. Another love had replaced that childish one she had felt for Dickon. 'Is there any way we can discover more?'

'I have arranged to make further inquiries. I thought you would want me to continue the search.'

'I know that Uncle Charles would wish it to go on,' Kathryn said. 'And I should feel happier if Richard could be rescued from slavery. If his father is dead, he is the heir to the Mountfitchet estate in England.'

'He would need to prove his identity, I think?'

'Yes—and that might be difficult if his father is dead. There will be other claimants, and those who matter would not listen to the claims of a slave who behaves like a child. If I believe he is Richard, my father will help him, but as for the rest…'

'Do not concern yourself,' Lorenzo told her. 'Something will be done. You have my word.'

'Thank you.' Kathryn looked at him shyly. 'Will you dine with me this evening, husband?'

'Yes, certainly. It is my hope that now I am home we

may spend some time together—learn to know one another, Kathryn.'

'That would be very pleasant.'

How could she speak so calmly when her heart was hammering against her ribs? Kathryn fought her desire to be close to him. When he looked at her that way she felt as if she were melting and wanted only to be in his arms.

'Pleasant…' A wry smile touched his mouth. 'Yes, it will be pleasant, Kathryn.'

'If you will excuse me, I shall go to make sure that everything is in readiness.'

She had no need to bother, for the house ran perfectly and the servants would already have done all that was necessary, but if she stayed she might disgrace herself by falling into his arms. She might have begged him to kiss her, to love her.

What had he expected? Lorenzo frowned as he cleansed himself of the dirt of his months at sea. It was good to bathe after weeks when only the most basic of cleanliness was available. A douche in seawater every now and then was all that any of the men could expect. A man got used to the stench of the galleys, but he had been too eager to see her to delay even for that little time. Small wonder that she had kept her distance.

Yet was it only that he had come to her with the dirt of his journey still upon him? She knew what life was like on board ship and had not flinched from it when she was forced to travel with few comforts. Was she keeping her distance because she did not wish to become his wife in truth?

He had thought of this homecoming for weeks, dreaming of what she would smell like, how she would feel lying next to him in bed. Had he been mad to let himself imagine that she might welcome him once she had accustomed herself to the idea?

Most women he had wanted had been eager enough to fall into his arms, but he had never wanted one this badly before. All too often it had been he who had refused the offer of a lady's company, too busy and too caught up in his quest to want the bother of a love affair. His chosen companions had been ladies who understood that he would go sooner rather than later.

Dressing in black Venetian breeches and hose and a doublet of black slashed with silver, the hanging sleeves attached by silver buckles at the shoulders, Lorenzo looked a true aristocrat. His hair was longer than usual for it had not been trimmed in months, curling to his shoulders, his skin a deep bronze. He glanced at his reflection in the glass, wondering as he had so often who he really was. For a moment his fingers strayed towards the leather wristbands, feeling the accustomed discomfort. All he knew for certain was that he had been captured by the Corsair Rachid and kept as a slave, chained to the oar until he was abandoned for dead. Yet he must have had a life before that day, a family, friends…perhaps a lover.

There had been no more flashes of memory recently. It seemed that the curtain was back in place, shutting out the past. Yet it did not matter—he knew that he was Lorenzo Santorini, owner of a fleet of galleys, his mission in life to destroy his enemy and others of his ilk.

Yet was his purpose as firm as it had been? Lorenzo

frowned as he tried to understand the change that had come over him as he looked into the frightened eyes of that youth. Had it been Rachid himself he would not have hesitated to kill him—or would he?

He cursed softly as he realised that he was not sure. He had fed on hatred for so long. It was necessary to him, for without it what would he have?

The answer was so shocking, so alien to all that he had been and believed that he could not accept it. Dreams of a wife and family were not for him. He would grow soft, forget what had made him the man he was—become someone else.

Surely that was not what he wanted? He realised that he did not know. He did not know who he truly was any more.

Kathryn had dressed in an emerald green gown that set off the colour of her hair and made her eyes glow like jewels. She had only a small strand of pearls that her father had given her as a present for her birthday just before she left England, but she wore them with pride, never guessing that beauty such as hers needed no artifice.

'You look lovely, Kathryn,' Lorenzo said when he saw her. She was standing in the open arches that led out into a paved courtyard, her face pensive, a little sad perhaps. 'Of what are you thinking, Madonna?'

'It is such a lovely night. I was thinking of my home and my father.'

'Have you written to him?'

Kathryn turned to face him. 'I wrote to him when we reached Venice, but thought it best not to write again for the moment. Until we have more certain news of our friends I would not worry him.'

'Do you not think you should tell him that you are married?'

'Perhaps.' Kathryn took a step towards him. 'Lorenzo…'

She hesitated as a servant came to tell them that a meal had been served.

'You must be hungry?'

'Yes,' he agreed. 'Let us eat, Kathryn. We have all the evening to talk.'

Her heart began to race as she saw the look in his eyes. All these weeks she had convinced herself that he did not want her, but the way he looked at her now made her think that perhaps she had been mistaken. Perhaps he had left her on their wedding night because there was no time, just as he'd told her. And now he was home and there was plenty of time before he must put to sea again…

'Tell me what you like to do with your days, Kathryn,' Lorenzo invited as they sat down to enjoy their meal.

'Oh, I walk in the garden. I shop with friends and visit their homes. Sometimes they visit me—but there is one thing I miss here, Lorenzo.'

'And what is that, Madonna?'

'Books,' she said. 'My father has a library at home and he allows me to read his books. Here there are no books.'

'Why did you not buy some for yourself? I left money enough for your needs.'

'I did not like to spend too much,' Kathryn said. 'And I did not know if you would approve of such purchases.'

Lorenzo smiled. 'I must show you my library when we go home, Kathryn.'

'When shall we return to Venice?'

'Not for some months,' he said. 'I have made arrangements to winter here—and you have friends, Kathryn. You would have to begin again in Venice. I thought it would be better to wait until we can return together.'

'Yes, you are right,' she said. 'I have not been bored, Lorenzo—but you asked what I like to do.'

'We shall buy you books,' he told her. 'But now I would hear about your life in England, Kathryn. Tell me what you did there.'

She told him of her home overlooking the sea, and the long walks she liked to take when the weather permitted, and then, somehow, she found herself telling him of the day Dickon was stolen by Corsairs.

'You say it was your idea that you should go down to the cove to investigate?' He was looking at her thoughtfully. 'And you have felt guilt because of it ever since?'

'Had I not suggested it, he would not have gone.'

'Can you be so sure of that? Most men would be curious and you were so much younger.'

'But Dickon always tried to please me. He was so kind, so generous—always laughing and teasing me…' Her eyes grew dark with remembered grief.

'Is that why you still love him?'

'I…am not sure that I do,' she confessed, not daring to look at him. 'We were but children. How do I know that we would still have loved each other when we grew up? Besides…' Her voice tailed away. 'I am your wife now, Lorenzo. And…and I would be a good wife to you…'

'What do you mean by that?'

Kathryn looked at him, her breath catching in her throat.

How could she answer, how could she tell him what she meant without betraying her feelings? If only he would give her some sign, show that he at least desired her, wanted her in his bed.

She was saved from answering by the arrival of a servant.

'*Signor,*' the woman said, 'Captain dei Ignacio is here to see you. He has brought someone with him—a woman.'

'Michael is here?' Lorenzo got to his feet. 'Excuse me, Kathryn. I must attend to this.'

She stared after him as he walked from the room. She had come so close to confessing her love, but the interruption had saved her. She wondered why it was so important that Lorenzo must speak with his captain immediately— and who was the woman Michael had brought with him?

Lorenzo's eyes went over the woman standing at Michael's side. She was wrapped in his cloak, and from the slippers on her feet and a glimpse of the harem pants she wore beneath it, he understood why.

'Donna Maria,' he said, speaking kindly, for he understood that she must be bewildered and perhaps frightened by all that had happened to her since she was taken from her father's ship. 'Welcome to my house. I trust that Michael has told you—you are to be restored to your father on payment of a ransom?'

'Please…' Maria looked at him with tear-drenched eyes. 'Do not tell my father where I have been…' Tears fell from her eyes and trickled down her cheeks. 'He would disown me—send me to the nuns.'

Lorenzo glanced at his captain. 'Perhaps you should tell me the whole?'

'Stay here, Donna Maria,' Michael said and moved a little aside with him. 'She has been kept in Rachid's harem. I am not sure whether she was sent to his bed, but she has been with his women.'

'And she believes that her father would disown her if he knew?'

'It is what she says.' Michael frowned. 'I brought her to you as you bid me—and now I ask leave to return to Venice for a while. I have had news of my father. He is unwell and asks for me.'

'Yes, of course you must go to him,' Lorenzo said at once. 'I hope you will return to me here as soon as you can?'

'You have my loyalty as always,' Michael said. 'But for the moment there is little here that cannot be done by others.'

'Go then with my blessing,' Lorenzo said and frowned. 'But the girl—how did she seem to you? Has she been mistreated? You understand my meaning—has she been subjected to rape?'

'I am not certain what to think,' Michael told him. 'It is true that she has been kept in the harem, but I do not think she was ill treated there. She asked me several times to let her return to her friends.'

Lorenzo nodded. 'I shall keep her with us for a while, and then we shall decide what to do about her father.'

'If you will excuse me, I would leave at once.'

'Of course. May your god go with you, my friend.'

'And with you. Give Kathryn my good wishes.'

Lorenzo inclined his head. His eyes moved to the Spanish girl. She was very beautiful, her hair black and thick, her eyes dark and her mouth soft and sensuous. Something in the way she looked at him made him vaguely uncomfortable, a knowing, calculating expression that he disliked and thought immodest in an unmarried girl.

'I am sorry for what has happened to you, Donna Maria,' he said. 'I shall ask my wife to take care of you. I am not sure what to do about you—though in the end you must be returned to your father. However, it may be that you would prefer to stay with us for a time?'

'Yes, please.' She came quickly towards him, catching at his hand, her eyes pleading. 'I do not want to go home.'

'Lorenzo…' Kathryn came into the hall at that moment, in time to see the girl clutching at his hand. She stopped, frowning and uncertain. Who was this girl? 'Has Michael left already?'

'He brought Donna Maria Dominicus to us,' Lorenzo said. 'We have managed to ransom her from Rachid, and she will stay with us until we can restore her to her family. Will you look after her, Kathryn?'

'Yes, certainly,' Kathryn said, feeling remorse for her suspicions and pity for the girl, who she knew must have suffered dreadfully. 'How did you manage this, Lorenzo?'

'I shall tell you later,' he said. 'Donna Maria needs clothes. You may have something that she can wear until we can have something made for her.'

'I think we are much of a size,' Kathryn said readily. 'If you will come with me, Donna Maria, I shall take you to the room that will be yours. I think you must want to bathe and rest, for you have had a terrible time.'

'You are so kind.' The girl's tears fell readily. 'I have been so very unhappy…'

'You are safe now,' Kathryn said, her heart touched by the girl's plight. 'Come, we shall go upstairs where we can talk and you may ask me for anything you need.'

Maria glanced at Lorenzo, but, finding no softness in his face, she clung to the hand Kathryn offered, her head bent as she allowed herself to be led away.

Lorenzo watched them leave. His instinct told him that the Spanish girl was not as upset as she seemed. There was something about her that he could not like, but, having ransomed her, he was honour bound to look after her until she could be restored to her family.

'I was made to wear these things,' Maria told Kathryn when they were alone and she had shed Michael's cloak, revealing the flimsy harem pants and tunic. 'I feel so ashamed.'

'It is not your shame,' Kathryn told her, angry that the girl had been subjected to such humiliation. 'You were a captive and had to do as your cruel masters bid you. I have heard that Rachid is one of the worst of the Corsair captains, a ruthless man. We must thank God that you have been rescued before it was too late.'

'They told me I was to be sold to the Sultan,' Maria told her, her eyes lowered. She wiped her hand across her face. 'Perhaps I was fortunate that Rachid did not want me for himself.'

'Yes, I am sure that you were,' Kathryn said. 'It must have been a terrible ordeal for you.'

'I wish that I had died rather than become a slave. My father will disown me or send me to a nunnery.'

'Surely not, Maria? He will be glad to have you home.'

'I do not think so. I have disgraced him.' She turned her luminous eyes on Kathryn. 'Could I not stay with you— as your companion? I promise I would be no trouble to you.'

'It is my husband who makes these decisions,' Kathryn said, her heart wrung with pity. 'But I believe you worry too much, Maria. Your father was desperate to have you back.' She explained what Don Pablo had done to try and trap Lorenzo. 'That must make you realise that he loves you?'

'Perhaps.' Maria drew a sobbing breath. 'But he did not know that I had been kept in a harem with…' She shook her head. 'You cannot know what they did to me to make sure that I was…'

'Do not distress yourself, Maria,' Kathryn said. 'I shall speak to my husband and see if he will keep you with us, at least until we can be sure what your father feels. I promise you that, if he says you have disgraced him, I shall not let you go back to him.'

'Oh, you are so kind!' Maria seized her hand and kissed it. 'I would do anything you asked of me, my lady.'

'No, no, you must call me Kathryn as my friends do. I promise you that you shall not be ill treated for something that was not your fault.' She smiled at the girl. 'Our servants will bring you water to bathe in and clothes, also food. You will want to rest this evening, but in the morning we shall talk again. The clothes you are wearing shall be burned.'

'May I not keep them to remind me?' Maria said. 'I must keep them to remind me of my modesty and that it was once lost. Please do not make me give them up.'

'Surely you do not want them?'

'Please!'

'As you wish, but you must not think of what happened to you as your shame.'

Kathryn left the girl to the ministrations of the servants and went downstairs to join Lorenzo. He gave her a look of inquiry.

'She is going to bathe, eat and rest. We shall see her in the morning.'

'I am sorry that I brought her here,' Lorenzo said. 'It was not my intention that she should stay with us, Kathryn. I had intended to send her to her father almost at once.'

'She is so distressed. Would it not be kinder to keep her with us for a while? At least until she can become accustomed to what has happened to her? She feels ashamed and it must have been awful for a young girl.'

'There is something I cannot like about her.'

'Lorenzo! You are too harsh,' Kathryn said. 'She has been through a terrible ordeal.'

'It would seem so and yet…' He frowned, uncertain why he felt that it would be best to be rid of the girl at once.

'Please, I ask you to be kind to her—for my sake.'

'For your sake?' Lorenzo's eyes narrowed. He moved towards her, gazing down into her eyes. 'I might do much for your sake, Kathryn.'

Her eyes widened as she saw the hot glow in his, and she swayed towards him, wanting him to take her in his arms, to kiss her.

'Why…' she asked, 'why do you say that?'

'Because you are my wife—because I care for you. Surely you know that, Madonna?'

'I thought that you left me because you did not want me. I thought you did not find me attractive enough to want to lie with me on our wedding night.' Kathryn gazed up at him, her eyes filled with an innocent appeal. 'Was that not so?'

Lorenzo laughed, the sound of it making her heart race as he reached out, drawing her into his arms, his eyes dark with some deeply felt emotion.

'Can you be so foolish, my love?' he asked. 'How could you think it was for my sake that I did not stay that night?'

'Was it not?'

'You married me because you had no choice. I would not force you to lie with me, Kathryn. I wanted you to become accustomed to the idea of a husband before you were forced to your duty. I want you warm and willing in my arms—not out of wifely duty.'

'I do not think I should mind my wifely duty so very much,' she said, her cheeks pink as she saw the laughter in his eyes. 'I think it might be pleasant...'

'Pleasant?' Lorenzo shook his head at her, wickedness in every line of his face. He seemed to her then a man she had never seen before, the man he might have been had life been kinder to him. 'It may be wonderful, exciting and passionate, but I do not think pleasant is a word I would use concerning my feelings for you, Madonna.'

'Then would you please kiss me?'

'Sweet Kathy,' Lorenzo said and pulled her into his arms, his mouth taking hungry possession of hers. The kiss was long and sweet and demanding, and it left her breathless. She stared at him in wonder as she began to understand what loving a man might mean. 'Shall I come to you tonight?' She nodded wordlessly, and he smiled at her, touching her hair. 'My red-haired witch. I never meant to let you beneath my skin, Kathryn. You have taken root inside me and I find I cannot live without you.'

'Oh, Lorenzo,' she breathed. 'I am so glad you have come home.'

Kathryn turned in the arms of her husband, lifting her face for his kiss. She had never expected to discover such pleasure in loving as he had given her and she curled into his strong, lean body, compliant as a sleepy kitten.

'Are you happy, Madonna?'

'You know that I am.' Her cheeks were warm, for she knew that she had behaved with shameless abandon as he loved her, crying his name aloud. Her hands moved on his shoulders and encountered the thick welts of old scars. She had been aware of them during their loving, but now she traced them with her fingers.

'Do they distress you, Kathryn—the scars?'

'Only because I know you must have suffered.' She leaned up on one elbow to look down into his face. 'Who did this to you, Lorenzo? Was it Rachid? Is that why you hate him?'

'I was a slave in his galley for three years.'

'Oh, my love,' Kathryn cried, not caring that she betrayed herself. 'How you must have suffered—but you never told me. No one told me.'

'Only Michael and my father ever knew,' he said, his voice husky with emotion. 'It is not something I care to have told, Kathryn.'

'I shall never speak of it without your permission—but how did you escape?'

'I was left for dead on the shores of southern Spain. A sick galley slave is worthless. They left me on the beach, threw me into the shallows, and I should undoubtedly have died if Antonio Santorini, a merchant of Venice, had not chanced to come ashore that day to provision his ship. He found me, took me aboard his ship and brought me to Venice.'

'You are not his son?'

'He was childless; his beloved wife dead some years before. He gave me his name, adopted me and made me his legal heir. As much as I was able I loved him, for he was a truly good man. He had suffered at the hands of the Inquisition himself; because of it, he devoted his life to helping others. I helped to restore his fortune, much of which he had given away to those who needed it. And when he died I mourned him.'

'You were lucky that day, Lorenzo.' She kissed his shoulder, which tasted salty with sweat after their loving. 'I am so sorry for what happened to you.'

'Do not be,' he said. 'For years I lived on hatred and that sustained me, giving me strength. It was only my hope of revenge that made me determined to live.'

'Lorenzo…' She bent over him, her hair brushing his face as she kissed him on the lips. 'I love you.'

'My sweet Kathy.'

He rolled her beneath him in the bed, his mouth plundering hers as the desire flamed between them once more. His hands stroked and caressed her, making her moan and move beneath him, her body arching up to meet him as he thrust deep inside her. Deep, deeper, into the inviting moistness of her femininity, her legs curling over his hips as they reached the heights of pleasure together. She screamed his name as he buried his face in the intoxicating softness of her hair.

'No other woman has pleased me as you do, Kathryn,' he murmured huskily against her throat. 'If you ever left me...'

'Hush, my love,' she said and there were tears on her cheeks. 'I shall never leave you. I want only your love.'

'My love, Kathryn?' His voice was harsh, his body suddenly stiff with tension. 'I am not sure that I know how to love—but all that I have I give to you.'

Kathryn clung to him in the darkness, her heart aching. She had begun to understand the man she loved. He had suffered things that no man should and the scars had gone deep, much deeper than those he bore on his shoulders and back. All the natural feelings, the softness and pleasures that others knew had been denied to him, and it had taken its toll. Perhaps he would never love her as she loved him, but he desired her and she pleased him—and for the moment she must be content with that.

It was only later, when Lorenzo lay sleeping beside her, that she realised he had not told her who he really was. If he was not the natural son of Antonio Santorini, then who was he?

Was it possible that her senses had told her truly the first time they met, when she had looked into his eyes and believed she knew him? He had strongly denied it once, when she had told him that he might more likely be Richard Mountfitchet than the man he had named William.

Surely he would have told her if there was any possibility that he could be the man they had been searching for? Of course he would. She was being foolish. Kathryn dismissed the idea as she drifted into sleep, curled into the body of her husband, warm and safe, protected by his strength.

Lorenzo had told her much this night. When he was ready he would tell her anything else he wished her to know.

When he was sure that Kathryn slept, Lorenzo left her bed and removed his clothes to the adjoining room, dressing before he went downstairs. He had feigned sleep so that she might rest; he could not sleep beside her for fear that the dream might disturb her. Although it had not happened of late, when he woke, screaming a name, his body covered in a fine sweat, he sometimes struck out with his fists or feet. Better that he should not risk injuring his wife. Besides, he would not have her see him that way.

His fingers sought out the leather wristbands, rubbing at the old injuries. Sometimes the irritation was almost more than he could bear. He wondered if a part of it was caused by the wristbands themselves, but he could not bring himself to remove them, to reveal to the whole world the badge of his shame. Kathryn had not recoiled from the scars on his back, but he hated them, hated what they stood for. He hated the memory of his slavery, of the humiliation of knowing that he must obey his masters, of the sharp stinging pain of a whip lash.

How long would it be before Kathryn asked him who he really was? He could give her no answer, for his past was still a mystery to him, though since the dreams had begun again he had wondered.

Was it merely his imagination playing tricks on him—
or could he truly remember being taken by Corsairs when
he was a youth of barely fifteen? If that were so, he must
be six and twenty now, and yet he knew that he looked
older. His years of slavery and the hardships at sea had
taken a toll of him as it must of any man.

No, it was madness to let his thoughts take him down
that road. Already, he had let Kathryn inside his head and
that had changed him. Because of her he had let Rachid's
son live and exchanged him for a girl who was like to cause
them trouble, if his instincts proved true.

He frowned as he thought of the girl sleeping in his
guest room. She was young and he ought to feel pity for
her, but somehow he could not. She had looked at him in
the same way as the harlots who plied the streets for their
trade and he did not trust her.

Maria claimed that she had been kept in the harem and
was to be sold to the Sultan's harem, but Lorenzo had seen
something in her eyes—a knowledge that was not often in
the eyes of an innocent virgin. Perhaps he wronged her, but
he suspected that she had been one of Rachid's concu-
bines—and that she had liked the experience. He suspected
that she had resented being taken from him, and that was
the reason for her distress.

She had pleaded with them to keep her in their home.
She said that her father would send her to a nunnery because she had shamed her family. She could not be blamed
for what had befallen her, unless… If she had enjoyed the
position of favourite in Rachid's harem, that would explain
her fear of being rejected by her family.

He would have to watch her carefully, Lorenzo decided

as he left the house. And he would find another home for her before he put to sea again—either with her father or someone else.

Chapter Eight

'I do not like that girl,' Elizabeta told Kathryn when they were walking together a few days later. 'There is something about her—a slyness in the way she looks at you and Lorenzo, particularly Lorenzo. Be careful of her and trust nothing she tells you.'

'Oh, you are too hard on her,' Kathryn said with a smile to soften the words, for Elizabeta was perhaps the friend she liked to be with the most. She could not explain what had happened to Maria for she did not wish to ruin the girl's chances of making friends and she might be looked down upon if people knew that she had spent some time in a harem. 'She has been…ill. We are looking after her for a while, but she will go home to her family soon.'

'The sooner the better,' Elizabeta said. She took hold of Kathryn's arm as they approached the silk merchant's shop they had planned to visit that morning. 'Do look at that lovely green material! It would look so well on you, Kathryn.'

'Yes, it is very lovely,' Kathryn said. She turned and

beckoned to Maria, who was walking behind with Isabella Rinaldi. 'Come and look at these silks, Maria. We shall buy material for you today; you must be tired of wearing my old gowns.'

'Oh, no,' Maria said, her eyes downcast. 'You have been so kind to me, Kathryn. How could I be so ungrateful as to resent wearing your things?'

'Well, you shall have a new gown,' Kathryn said. 'Come, look, and choose the silk you prefer.'

'Oh, I do not know what to choose,' Maria said, her hands fluttering over the bales of beautiful silks that the merchant had spread on trestles before his shop. 'There are so many…that blue is lovely, and yet so is the green.'

'Kathryn was thinking of buying the green for herself,' Elizabeta said, her dark eyes narrowed and hostile as she looked at Maria. 'The blue would suit you much better—or that grey.'

'I do not like dull colours,' Maria said and for a moment her eyes met Elizabeta's in an expression of such hatred that the older woman gasped. 'I shall have the blue if Kathryn prefers the green for herself.'

'No, indeed, I do not need any more gowns for the moment,' Kathryn said. 'We shall take both the green and the blue, Maria. You shall have two new gowns and then you need not wear my old ones at all.'

'You are too generous,' Elizabeta said. 'That green was perfect for you.'

'It does not matter. There will be other silks,' Kathryn said. She turned away, speaking to the merchant and directing him to send both bales of silk to her at the villa. 'Shall we have something to drink at the inn or go back to my home?'

'We are nearer to my house,' Elizabeta said. 'Come, we shall go home once I have ordered the silk I want for myself, and my servants will bring us refreshments. It is too warm to shop any more today.' She smiled and linked arms with Kathryn.

Kathryn agreed that the sun was very warm and they all returned to Elizabeta's house, which was situated not far from the Campo de' Fiori, one of the streets of beautiful Renaissance buildings begun by Pope Nicholas in the fifteenth century.

The house was large, almost a palace, for Elizabeta's husband was wealthy, though some years older than she. She took her guests through the echoing rooms, which were cool after the heat of the sun, into the courtyard garden, then left them to talk while she went to order the refreshments served to them.

Kathryn and Isabella sat down on one of the small stone seats, which had been set with cushions and placed in a shady spot, but Maria wandered off alone to explore the garden, which she had not seen before.

'She is a strange girl, is she not?' Isabella said, frowning a little. 'She boasted to me that she has a lover and that he has promised to wed her. I thought you told me she had been ill?'

'Yes, she has,' Kathryn said. 'I think she meant that she will be betrothed to someone when she goes home.' She thought Maria foolish to talk of such things, for it would do her reputation no good.

'She asked me if I had a lover,' Isabella said. 'I am sure she meant that she had…well, you know…'

Kathryn shook her head at her as Elizabeta came back

to them, her servants carrying out extra chairs so that they might all be comfortable. Maria joined them as they sat down and the drinks were served.

For à while they sat talking about the things they had seen while they were out shopping, and Isabella told them that her father had said he was taking her to Venice in the spring.

'He says that there is a family he wishes me to meet,' she said. 'I think he means to make a marriage contract for me. I hope the man he has chosen to be my husband is as handsome as yours, Kathryn.'

'That is unlikely,' Maria said, having been silent for some time. 'There are not many men who look like Lorenzo Santorini. He is more likely to choose a rich man than a handsome one, for that is the way of fathers.'

'Kathryn's husband is very handsome,' Isabella agreed with a little secret smile. 'But I like his friend, Michael dei Ignacio. I would be happy if my father chose him.'

Maria pulled a face and then reached for her drink, knocking Elizabeta's into her lap so that she jumped up, brushing at her skirts as the liquid soaked through the material.

'Oh, forgive me,' Maria apologised. 'I am so clumsy.'

'Yes, you are,' Elizabeta said crossly. 'You should take more care. This silk was expensive and it is ruined.'

'I dare say your husband will buy you another,' Maria said with a little shrug of her shoulders. 'He must be very rich to own a house like this. One gown means nothing.'

Kathryn saw that Elizabeta was really angry, and poured her another drink from the jug on the table. 'Let me dry it for you,' she said. 'Come inside, Elizabeta.'

'No, no, it does not matter,' Elizabeta said and shook her head at her. 'I am sorry. It was an accident, of course. Do not worry, Maria. I have plenty more gowns—but this was a favourite.'

Maria lowered her head, her hands working in distress. 'I did not do it on purpose,' she said, but somehow not one of the other ladies present believed her. Her action had been quite deliberate and was meant to punish Elizabeta for some of her remarks earlier that day. It was a small spiteful thing, but somehow it made the other ladies join ranks against her. She was not one of them and they all thought it would be better when she went home to her family.

Kathryn was disturbed by the small incident at her friend's house. The ruin of an expensive gown was not so important, for it could be replaced, but if it was done out of spite it was quite another thing. She felt uncomfortable as they returned to the house, for if Maria was capable of doing something like that, what more might she do?

She tried not to let it make a difference to her manner towards the Spanish girl. Maria was in a difficult position and she felt sympathy for her, but as the days passed, she could not but be aware of something in Maria that she did not quite like.

The girl had a way of looking at Lorenzo that Kathryn found disturbing. She seemed to hang on his every word, and to follow him about the house and gardens. It was almost impossible for Kathryn to be alone with her husband, other than when they were in their bed.

The time they spent in bed together was very special.

Lorenzo's loving made Kathryn so happy that insignificant things could not really upset her. She wished that he might love her, but there was still a strange reserve in him at times, and she had woken twice to find the bed cold and empty. It seemed that he left her once she was asleep, and that caused a small hurt inside her, for she wanted to wake and find him still beside her. Yet it was but a small thing, for he did everything he could to make her happy, giving her costly presents and encouraging her to spend money when she went shopping with her friends.

'I want you to be happy, Kathryn,' he had told her several times. 'You must tell me if there is anything you want.'

'I have all I need,' she said, for how could she ask for the one thing he was incapable of giving her? She loved him, but he could not return that love—something inside him had created a barrier between them. He was good to her and she knew that he wanted her with a fierce, needy passion, but she did not have his heart.

Even so, she was content with her life. They entertained their friends, visited them at home and were seldom without company.

Lorenzo was often busy, for the galleys were being cleaned and made ready for the next spring when it was thought that a new and much larger campaign would begin. Lorenzo had mentioned a man called Don John of Austria who would lead the enlarged fleet in the fight against the Turks, a man respected by all the factions of the League.

'There was too much argument and indecision last time,' Lorenzo told her once when they lay thigh to thigh in their bed, his hand idly tracing the silken arch of her back. 'If we are to strike a blow that will break the power of Selim, we must bind together and put our differences aside. I have no love of the Spanish, Kathryn, but I will fight with them if it defeats our common enemy. The Turks have become too predatory, too greedy, and we must stop them before it is too late.'

He had made love to her with such sweetness that night that she felt her inner self reach out to him and it seemed that they were one, their hearts, minds and bodies joined so sweetly that they could never more be separate beings. And yet still he had not told her he loved her.

Kathryn saw them walking together in the gardens that morning, her husband and the Spanish girl. It had happened before, but this time Lorenzo was laughing at something Maria had said to him, and she looked up at him as they walked, her smile inviting.

Maria was wearing the new gown of green silk that Kathryn had commissioned for her. She looked very beautiful and for a moment Kathryn was jealous. She felt the pain of it strike her. Lorenzo was not in love with her, his wife, and a man might desire many women. Was he becoming interested in the Spanish girl? Would she lose him to her rival? For she sensed that Maria was trying to arouse his interest in her.

Elizabeta had warned her against trusting Maria, and later that day there had been the incident of the spilled drink. Kathryn had never thought it an accident, because she had seen the look of triumph in Maria's eyes before she lowered them, pretending to be distressed. And what was it Isabella had said—something about Maria having had a lover who had promised to marry her?

It was not true as far as Kathryn knew, which meant the Spanish girl had lied. And now she was doing her best to capture Lorenzo's attention...

But this was mere foolishness, an irritation of the nerves. She would not let jealousy poison her thoughts, against her husband or the other girl!

Kathryn lifted her head and went outside to meet them. Immediately, Maria let go of Lorenzo's arm and moved away from him, pretending to be interested in one of the shrubs in the garden.

'Kathryn, my love,' Lorenzo said. 'Maria was telling me how happy she is here with us—and how kind you have been to her. I think we should give a dinner for our friends to celebrate the coming of Christ's birthday. It will be expected of us and it will be our farewell to Maria—I have written to Don Pablo and he asks that Maria may be taken to him in Granada.'

'You are sending me home?' Maria whirled round, looking at him. Her dark eyes blazed with anger. 'But you promised—Kathryn promised that I should stay with you.'

'For a while, until you had recovered your spirits,' he told her. 'I think you will find that your father is only too pleased to have you home, Maria. There is no need to be afraid that he will send you to a nunnery.'

'Kathryn...' Maria looked at her, eyes wild with such a mixture of emotions that it was hard to tell which was uppermost—fear or anger. 'Do not let him do this to me, I beg you.'

'My husband does what is right for you, Maria,' Kathryn said, hardening her heart against the girl. Elizabeta was right. Maria was sly and deceitful and it would be best for all of them if she returned to her father. 'I am sorry if you are distressed, but I am sure that it must be best for you. Perhaps your father will arrange a marriage for you—'

'No! I will not be sent back to him,' Maria cried and her eyes blazed with anger. 'You will be sorry for this—both of you!'

She ran from the courtyard, leaving Kathryn and Lorenzo alone.

'Do not judge me unkind,' Lorenzo said, misjudging Kathryn's silence. 'She is no true friend to you, Kathryn. Another man might have found her tempting, but she wasted her wiles on me. She might cajole many a man for she is comely enough, but I have never trusted her. Nor do I desire her.'

'She has been through so much,' Kathryn said, ashamed now that she had been jealous even for a moment. 'Who knows what such an ordeal may do to anyone? How can we know what she has suffered?'

'Be careful of her, Kathryn,' Lorenzo said. 'I warn you because I must leave you for two days. When I come back we shall arrange our special dinner—but until then do not trust Maria. If my business were not important I would not leave you, but I think she cannot harm you if you give her no chance. You have Veronique and your friends to keep you company while I am gone.'

'I shall miss you,' Kathryn said, 'but do not worry for my sake, Lorenzo. Maria may be capable of small acts of spite, but I do not think she would seek to harm me. Why should she? I have been kind to her.'

'For some people that means nothing,' Lorenzo said.

'Indeed, she may despise you for your weakness. It is a pity that I did not send her to her father immediately. However, the arrangements are made for two weeks hence. We shall have our party and then she shall go.'

'It must be as you say,' Kathryn agreed. 'But I shall still be kind to her while she is with us, for she has suffered much.'

He nodded, drawing her to him, gazing down into her face. 'I would expect nothing else from you, Kathryn, but be careful. I would not have harm come to you while I am away.'

She smiled, lifting her face for his kiss. 'Do not worry, Lorenzo. I promise you I shall be careful. Besides, what harm could she do in such a short time?'

'What is the matter, Veronique?' Kathryn asked as her companion came to her in the little salon where she had chosen to sit and read her book later that morning. 'You look upset.'

'A letter has just been brought to me,' Veronique said. 'My sister has been taken ill and wishes to see me. It will be a day's journey for me and I would be away at least three days.'

'You are anxious about her, are you not?'

'Yes—but I do not like to leave you, Kathryn. I know that Signor Santorini will be away for two days...' Veronique was clearly uncertain and anxious, worried by the letter she had received.

'You must go,' Kathryn said. 'Do not fear that I shall be lonely. I have Maria for company—and Elizabeta has promised that she will come this afternoon.'

'Are you sure that you do not mind?'

'You must go,' Kathryn insisted with a smile. 'Tell me, have you money for your journey?'

'Yes—Signor Santorini has been more than generous. I shall return as soon as I am able, Kathryn.' Veronique was upset, clearly torn between her sister and her duty to Kathryn.

'Take a few days to stay with your sister,' Kathryn said and kissed her cheek. 'Go now, and do not feel guilty. I shall be perfectly all right.'

She smiled as the older woman hurried away. She liked the kindly Frenchwoman, but she would not be lonely. Maria and Elizabeta would keep her company until Lorenzo returned. Besides, she had many new books to read and she enjoyed walking in her garden.

Kathryn was sitting alone in the salon that looked out to the garden when Maria came to her a little later that day. She looked at her awkwardly, standing with her hands clasped in front of her, an expression of contrition on her lovely face.

'I have come to beg your pardon,' Maria said. 'What I said to you earlier was unforgivable. You must know I did not mean it.'

'I know that you did not,' Kathryn said with a smile of forgiveness. She understood what it was to be unhappy and could feel Maria's distress. 'Sometimes we all say things that we do not mean. I am sorry that you must return to Spain, Maria, but I am sure that once you are home you will be much happier. Your father will not be ashamed of you—why should he?'

Maria looked down at her shoes. 'He is so strict and not always kind to me, Kathryn. I have never been as happy as I am here with you. Please do not send me away. If you asked it of him, Lorenzo would not make me go home.'

'My husband is right,' Kathryn said, knowing that she must be firm. Maria could not stay with them for ever. 'It would not be kind to keep you with us for always. If you return home you will find a husband to—'

'I do not wish to marry!' Maria's head came up and for a moment her eyes blazed with anger. 'But if you say I must go, then I have no choice.' Her eyes filled with tears. 'Only let me stay with you until after Christ's birthday, I beg you.'

'I shall ask Lorenzo if you may stay a little longer,' Kathryn said, 'though I cannot promise that he will relent. Now, sit with me and I shall order refreshments for us both. It is a lovely day and we should not waste it in argument.'

'Let me order them for you,' Maria said. 'If I try harder to please, perhaps you will allow me to stay.'

Kathryn frowned over the book she had been reading as Maria went into the house. Was she being unkind to let Lorenzo send the girl home to her father? If he was very strict, he might make her life miserable if he considered that she had disgraced him. And yet, would he have gone to so much trouble to get her back, only to shut her in a nunnery? It did not seem likely and Kathryn could not truly understand why Maria did not want to go home. Had she been in her position she would have wanted to be restored to her family.

For a moment she thought about Lady Mary and Lord

Mountfitchet. As yet there was no news of them and she could not help worrying that they might have been killed when the Turks invaded the island of Cyprus. Surely if they were alive they would have found a way to let Lorenzo know? Yet she would cling to hope for a little longer, for, as Lorenzo said, it took so long for letters to be delivered in these dangerous times.

She looked up as Maria returned, carrying a tray of drinks and the little almond cakes that Kathryn was so partial to and which their cook made so well. Maria set the tray down and then poured a drink for herself and Kathryn, offering her the plates of sweetmeats.

'I love these sweetmeats,' she said, taking two for herself and popping one in her mouth. 'We had them in the harem, or very similar ones, and they were always so delicious.'

Kathryn took the cake nearest to her and bit into it. It was very sweet, but the whole almond on top seemed to be bitter. She placed it on the table and took another, which was much nicer.

'Was something wrong with that one?' Maria asked.

'The almond was bitter,' Kathryn told her.

'Oh, yes, it does happen sometimes,' Maria said. 'But do have another, Kathryn. They are so delicious—try this sort, they are softer and very sweet.'

Kathryn tried the one she indicated, biting into the soft sweetmeat and chewing it with some pleasure. Just as she swallowed it she tasted a little bitterness and took a long drink of her wine to wash it down. She pushed the plate of cakes away from her. Something must be wrong with the almonds the cook had used for these cakes.

Maria's hand hovered over the cakes, choosing with care. She ate three more with every evidence of enjoying them and finished her wine.

'Would you mind if I went to Isabella's house this afternoon?' she said. 'She asked me to visit her yesterday and I said that I would if you did not need me.'

'Of course you may go,' Kathryn said. 'Elizabeta said that she might call so I shall stay here—but you should take one of the servants with you. It is safer if you do not walk alone, Maria.'

'Yes, of course,' the Spanish girl said. 'You must not worry about me, Kathryn. I shall be perfectly all right.' Her face was pale but proud, as if she were struggling to be brave.

'And you must not worry, Maria,' Kathryn said. 'I am sure your father loves you and he will be only too pleased to have you home.'

'Perhaps you are right,' Maria said and lowered her eyes. She stood up, keeping her head downcast. 'If you will excuse me, I believe I shall go up and get ready for my visit with Isabella.'

'Yes, of course,' Kathryn said, watching as the girl walked away, her head still downcast. Was she being unkind to let Lorenzo send her home?

It was when she was sitting with Elizabeta that afternoon that Kathryn felt the pain in her stomach. At first it was slight and caused her to flinch, but then, as it struck again, she gave a cry and doubled over.

'What is wrong?' Elizabeta asked. 'Are you ill, Kathryn?'

'Pain…' Kathryn gasped. 'I feel terrible…' She got to her feet, hurrying to the shrubbery where she vomited. Her head was spinning and she swayed as the ground seemed to come rushing up to meet her. She might have fainted if Elizabeta had not come to her, steadying her as she vomited twice more. 'I am so sorry…'

'There is no need to apologise,' Elizabeta said, looking at her anxiously. 'Have you been feeling ill long?'

'I felt well first thing this morning, but it has been building up since then—not pain, just an uncomfortable feeling in my stomach.'

'What have you eaten?' Elizabeta asked as Kathryn moaned and clutched at her stomach again. 'I think we should send for the physician at once. Where is Lorenzo?'

'He had to leave for two days on business,' Kathryn replied as Elizabeta helped her back to her seat. 'I do feel very ill—perhaps I should go up to my room?'

'I shall help you,' Elizabeta said, looking at her anxiously. 'And the physician must be summoned. I do not like this, Kathryn. I think you must have eaten something that disagreed with you.'

'I have eaten very little today other than bread, cheese and fruit,' Kathryn said. 'Oh, there were also the little cakes that Maria brought out for us as we sat in the garden this morning. One of them tasted quite bitter.'

'Did she eat any of them?' Elizabeta asked, eyes narrowing with suspicion.

'Yes, most of them,' Kathryn said. 'I hope she is not ill, for if they were the cause she would be much worse than I am.'

'Where is she this afternoon?'

'She went to visit Isabella.'

'That is strange. I am sure that Adriana told me Isabella and her father were invited to their house for the day.'

Kathryn was feeling too ill to argue. Perhaps she had made a mistake? Her head was spinning and she could hardly put one foot in front of the other as Elizabeta helped her to her room. Once there, she vomited into a basin, and then collapsed on the bed, feeling too weak and ill to know what was happening around her. She lay with her eyes closed, unaware of the anxious faces of the servants or that Elizabeta sat with her, bathing her forehead until the physician arrived.

She told him what she feared and he examined Kathryn carefully, checking for signs of poison, and then, after careful consideration, giving his verdict.

'She may have eaten something that made her ill,' he said. 'But I do not think it was poison. Had it been, she would probably have been dead by now—and some poisons leave a smell on the breath and a blueness about the mouth. I believe she has taken a small dose of something that might in larger doses be dangerous, but I think she will be well enough when whatever upset her has passed through. It may be that something she ate was not quite fresh.'

'Kathryn told me that she ate only cheese, bread and fruit.'

'It must have been the cheese,' he said. 'It was most unpleasant for her, but I have given her something to settle her stomach and I think you will find that she will sleep now.'

Elizabeta thanked him, but she was not satisfied with

his explanation. The vomiting had been violent and she suspected that something had been put into the cakes to cause Kathryn to be ill. Perhaps she had not eaten enough to make her ill enough to die, but the results were harmful. Maria was spiteful enough to play such a trick; she had proved that when she knocked Elizabeta's drink into her lap—but had she meant to kill Kathryn?

The poison must have been something she had taken from the garden, for it was unlikely she could have access to the poisons sometimes used by physicians and apothecaries in their work. And that, of course, would make it more difficult to judge the amount needed to kill, if it had been her intention. She might only have wished to make Kathryn ill out of a spiteful impulse.

Kathryn was resting for the moment. Elizabeta got up from the chair beside the bed and went out into the hall. She knew that Maria's room was at the far end, and she hesitated only a moment before making her way there. Perhaps it was wrong of her, but she needed proof before she could accuse the Spanish girl of trying to kill her hostess, and she might find what she sought amongst Maria's things. It was wrong of her to go through the Spanish girl's private things, but Elizabeta quashed her scruples and began to search the various chests and cupboards.

Her search took only a few minutes, and at the end she found nothing incriminating. What puzzled her was the flimsy harem costume hidden at the bottom of one of the chests, and a beautiful necklet that looked like a huge ruby surrounded by pearls. She turned it in her hand, wondering if it opened somehow for the gold backing was thick and might hold a secret. Then, as she heard a sound behind her, she turned to find that Maria had come in.

'What are you doing with that?' Maria came towards her, snatching the necklet from her hands. 'That is mine! You have no right to touch it. You have no right to be in my room.'

'Kathryn has been ill,' Elizabeta said. 'The physician says that something she ate must have made her so—but perhaps something in the food should not have been there.'

'You are accusing me of poisoning her!' Maria cried, her dark eyes flashing with temper. 'You have always hated me! You tried to turn Kathryn against me!'

'I do not hate you,' Elizabeta said calmly. 'But neither do I trust you. You made eyes at Lorenzo from the start—and if you could get rid of Kathryn, you think he might turn to you.'

'That is all you know!' Maria cried. 'I have a lover who wants me—he gave me this.' She was smiling now, her eyes bright with triumph. 'If Kathryn has been ill, perhaps it was you who poisoned her. I was not here—besides, if I wanted her dead, she would be dead.'

'But you made her ill,' Elizabeta said. 'I know that you did it, Maria. If anything happens to her—if she dies of a mysterious illness—I shall see that you are hung for murder.'

'Get out of my room,' Maria cried. 'You are a liar. I did nothing to harm Kathryn. She is my friend. You can prove nothing. Besides, I shall be leaving very soon now.'

'The sooner the better,' Elizabeta said. She did not believe in Maria's protests of innocence. 'I intend to stay with Kathryn while she is ill. If I find you in her room I shall have you confined to yours—and if anything happens to her, I shall make sure that you are punished for it. Kathryn may be deceived in you, but I know you for the evil wretch you are.'

'One day you will be sorry for your unkindness to me,' Maria said, her eyes flashing with anger. 'The man I love is very powerful. You will suffer for this, believe me.'

'I do not fear you or your threats, whore,' Elizabeta said. 'I do not know where you got that ruby or the harem costume you hide in your chest—but I know you for what you are. And when Lorenzo returns, I shall tell him to be rid of you at once.'

Kathryn's head was aching terribly when she woke to find Elizabeta sitting by her side the next morning. She stared at her in bewilderment for a moment as she tried to remember, and then, as the memory of her illness returned, she said, 'Have you been here all night?'

'I was worried about you,' Elizabeta said and squeezed her hand. 'You were so very ill that I was anxious—and I would not leave you while Lorenzo is away. I do not trust that Spanish girl.'

Kathryn pushed herself up against the pillows. Her stomach ached, as did her head, but she was feeling much better now the sickness had gone.

'You should not have sat up with me all night,' she said. 'I am sure Maria was not the cause of my sickness. How could she be?'

'Perhaps she put something into the almond cakes—or your drink,' Elizabeta said. 'I do not know, Kathryn, but I am sure that she had something to do with what happened to you. I am not sure if it was just a spiteful trick to make you ill—or something more sinister.'

'Perhaps.' Kathryn sighed. She did not feel well enough to think about Maria. 'Lorenzo had told her that morning that she was soon to go home. She begged me to persuade him to let her stay—but to tell you the truth, I do not really want her here.'

'And why should you? There is something sly about her—and she tells lies.'

'Yes, I think she does.' Kathryn hesitated. She could not tell Elizabeta that the Spanish girl had been imprisoned in a harem for some months, for that would be unfair. 'You may be right about her being spiteful enough to make me ill, but surely she would not try to poison me?'

'It was not a deadly poison or you would have died,' Elizabeta said. 'Yet I think she intended to make you very ill. Be careful of her, Kathryn. She might be capable of anything.'

'Yes, I shall,' she promised. 'And now you must go home, for your husband will worry about you.'

'But then you will be alone…'

Kathryn shook her head. 'I am glad that you were here when I became ill, and that you called the physician—but I do not think Maria intends to kill me. As you said, if she had wanted me dead I would be already. Besides, I shall not eat anything she brings me in future.'

'If you are sure?' Elizabeta looked at her doubtfully.

'I have a house full of servants, who will come if I call,' Kathryn said and smiled at her. 'I shall be perfectly all right. I promise you.'

'Very well, if it is your wish that I go.' Her friend

smiled ruefully. 'I dare say my husband will be imagining that I have left him. It is foolish of him to think it, for he is kind and generous, and my little flirtations mean nothing. I have never been unfaithful, though I believe he fears it.'

'Please tell him that I am very grateful for what you did for me.'

After Elizabeta had finally been persuaded to leave, Kathryn rang for her maid and asked for water to be brought so that she could bathe. She had sweated a great deal while she was ill and she felt in need of a bath. The hip-bath was brought to her chamber and filled with warm, scented water. Kathryn's maid helped her to disrobe and to step into the water.

'Do you wish me to wash your back, my lady?'

'Not just for the moment,' Kathryn said. 'I am feeling very tired and I would like to relax in the water for a while—but stay within call, for I shall need you in a little while.'

'I shall be in the next chamber, my lady,' the girl replied. 'I am going though your gowns to see if any of them are in need of the services of the seamstress.'

'Thank you, Lisa,' Kathryn said. 'I shall feel better if I know that you are near by.'

She did not think that Maria would do anything to harm her, and she had only Elizabeta's suspicions to make her believe that her illness had been caused by the other girl's spite. Yet for the moment she would be very careful.

She lay back in the warm water, closing her eyes and feeling sleepy. Whatever had made her ill was most unpleasant, for her whole body had begun to ache and she felt drained. She would not want to go through an experience like that again.

Kathryn wondered where Lorenzo was and if he was thinking of her. She wished that he was with her—she would have liked to tell him what was on her mind, and she would feel much safer if he were with her. She was on the verge of sleep when she heard the slight sound behind her.

'Is that you, Lisa?' she asked and then something struck her on the back of her head. Just before she lost consciousness she smelled the heavy perfume that Maria had been wearing the day she first came to the house.

Lorenzo ran into the house, feeling that odd sense of anxiety that had hung over him throughout the night. It was his unease that had prompted him to cut short his business and return a day sooner than he had anticipated. It was foolish, of course, but he had the feeling that Kathryn was in danger.

As he entered the villa, he heard a cry from the direction of Kathryn's room and ran towards it, his heart racing. Entering, he saw that the maid Lisa was struggling with someone—Maria! As he hesitated, he saw that Maria had a heavy iron candlestick in her hand, which Lisa was trying to take from her. He rushed in, capturing Maria from behind, holding her as she struggled uselessly against him.

Glancing towards the hip-bath, he saw that Lisa had rushed to drag her mistress upright and was now set on pulling her from the bath. Kathryn had a slight wound to the back of her head, but even as he pushed Maria away from him with a cry of anguish, he heard a faint moaning sound from Kathryn and went to help Lisa lower her to the ground.

'Who did this to her?' he demanded.

'It was her!' Maria screamed. 'The maid. I came in and found her. I was trying to help Kathryn.'

'No…' Kathryn's lips moved with difficulty. 'Maria…'

'Call for more servants,' Lorenzo said. 'She is not to leave this house! I shall deal with her later.'

Maria backed away from him, then turned and ran from the room. Lorenzo let her go. If she succeeded in leaving the house, she would be found. For the moment all that mattered to him was his wife.

He lifted her gently in his arms, carrying her towards the bed and laying her down. Bending over her, he smoothed the hair from her face.

'The physician shall be called,' he said. 'I should never have left you alone with her. I knew she was not to be trusted.'

Several servants had responded to Lisa's call. Lorenzo asked for towels and dried Kathryn's body himself, turning her carefully to look at the wound to her head, which was slight.

'There is only a small cut,' he said. 'She could not have hit you hard.'

'I moved and the blow was deflected,' Kathryn said and caught back a sob. 'But it hurts, Lorenzo.'

'Yes, my love,' he said. 'I am sure that it is painful. She shall be punished for what she has done.' He glanced around the room. 'Where is Veronique? Is she not here?'

'She had a letter to tell her that her sister was very ill

just after you left, Lorenzo. She asked if she might go to her and of course I told her that she had my permission…'

'And that wretched girl took advantage of her absence and mine.' Lorenzo looked furious. 'She will be very sorry when I have finished with her, Kathryn.'

'Send her away,' Kathryn said. 'I do not want her punished—but she cannot stay here any longer. I think that she tried to poison me yesterday, but she did not know enough about the substance she used and it served only to make me sick.'

'She tried to poison you?' His face darkened. 'The evil bitch! I should kill her—but it will serve well enough if we send her back to her father.'

'Yes.' Kathryn smiled at him. 'I think she fears he will discover the truth—that she has been Rachid's woman. I think she must have loved him, for she has spoken of having a lover who would marry her.'

'You suspected that too?' Lorenzo nodded. 'It must be the reason she tried to kill you. I think she was angry because he exchanged her for his son—and she wanted to punish us. It is strange, but some women do fall in love with their masters, despite their captivity. She resented being sent away from him and took her spite out on you.'

Kathryn nodded, too exhausted to say more for the moment. She thought that Maria's plan might go deeper—that she might have been following someone else's orders. It might be that Rachid had promised to marry her if she could find some way of destroying his enemy. She would tell Lorenzo about it later, but for the moment all she wanted to do was sleep.

'Yes, sleep, my dearest,' Lorenzo said in a voice that she had never heard from him. 'I shall stay by your side. I shall not leave you until that evil woman has been taken…'

Chapter Nine

A week had passed and there was no sign of Maria, though Lorenzo had men out searching. Kathryn was now recovered both from the stomach upset and the blow to her head, which had not been serious even though it had rendered her unconscious for a moment.

'Had Lisa not been there, she might have drowned you,' Lorenzo said, his face dark with anger. 'She hoped to make it look like an accident, for she wished to deceive us all.'

'It seems that she did want me dead.' Kathryn sighed. 'It grieves me to think that she would act in such a way, Lorenzo. We were not her enemies. You had rescued her from Rachid…'

'Evidently she did not wish to be rescued,' Lorenzo said, frowning. 'If he had chosen her as his favourite…it might be that she enjoyed her position in the harem.'

'She is very beautiful and what you say may be true,' Kathryn agreed. 'When I offered to burn the clothes she was wearing when she arrived, she begged to keep them. And if she did not want to leave the harem, it may be that she hoped to return if…' She hesitated, for it seemed unlikely that Rachid would use a woman against his enemy.

'If I were dead or captured?' Lorenzo nodded. 'Yes, I had thought of that as a possibility. Had I been attracted to her, she might have managed to lure me into a trap. And yet she attacked you—why? You had shown her nothing but kindness.'

Kathryn was thoughtful. 'Perhaps she was jealous because I had the man I loved while she had nothing? She must have known that you had no interest in her, and she may have thought it would grieve you if I died.'

'Yes, perhaps,' he agreed. 'We shall forget her, Kathryn. She is not worth wasting our breath or our thoughts on. When she is found, she will be dealt with appropriately.'

'You will not be too severe?' Kathryn looked at him anxiously. 'She has done terrible things, but I would not have her punished beyond what is right.'

'Her punishment according to the law would at the least be imprisonment, and perhaps a flogging.'

'No! That is too harsh,' Kathryn said. 'Can you not simply return her to her father?'

'Is that what you want?'

'Yes, I think so. I know what she did was wrong, but I am well again, and I could not live with her death on my conscience.'

'Very well,' Lorenzo said. 'It seems that I must give way, my love, though against my better judgement. Yet she shall be returned to her father and he shall be her judge, for I shall tell him of her behaviour while our guest. And now we shall talk of her no more. She is not important.'

'Tell me where we are going this evening?' Kathryn

said. It was the first time that she had been out in a week and he had not told her where they were going, only that it was to be a surprise.

'You must wait in patience, Madonna,' he told her and bent to kiss her lightly on the mouth. 'You will see in a few hours and until then it shall be a secret.'

The secret turned out to be a huge masque ball, given in her honour and attended by all their friends. When Kathryn prepared for the evening she was given a new gown in a beautiful green silk; it had full panniers over a petticoat of a pale ivory silk, which was embroidered with appliqué and brilliants. Her cloak was of matching velvet, her mask a delicate silver thing that made her mouth look soft and kissable.

Lorenzo was wearing his customary black, though the sleeves were slashed with green silk to match her gown. He kissed her before they left, giving her a necklet of beautiful emeralds that sat like a little collar on her slender throat.

'It is lovely, Lorenzo. You spoil me.' She gazed up at him and he thought that the shine in her eyes put the jewels to shame.

'You have become very precious to me,' he told her in a voice that made her tremble inside. 'When I thought that I might lose you I realised that my life would be empty without you. I have not wanted to care for you so much, Kathryn, but I believe that I do…perhaps more than I had thought.'

'My love…' Kathryn's eyes were bright with tears, though she blinked them away. She had never thought to hear such words from him and they filled her with emotion. She had been content enough to be his wife and love him, but to have his love would be wonderful.

He smiled at her, kissing her hand, and then leading her out into the warm night. 'Come, Kathryn, our friends will be waiting for us.'

It was a perfect evening. Everyone was so kind to her, kissing her and telling her how much they loved her and how distressed they had been by what had happened to her. It seemed that none of them had truly liked Maria, and most had not trusted her.

'Lorenzo should never have let her stay,' Elizabeta said. It was at her house the party was being held, and she made a great fuss of Kathryn. 'I hope we shall remain friends when you return to Venice,' she told her. 'Perhaps you will invite me to stay with you sometimes.'

'I should like that very much,' Kathryn told her. 'I do not think Lorenzo can spare the time to take me home yet, but of course we shall go one day.' She thought she would miss the friends she had made in Rome, but she would make more in Venice and Lorenzo was talking of buying a summer villa in Rome so that they might spend some time here each year.

It seemed to Kathryn that night that she had never been as happy as she was then. She danced every dance, and most of them with Lorenzo. He seemed a different person, the grave looks and cold eyes banished as if they had never been. Indeed, several of his friends remarked on it to Kathryn, telling her that marriage must suit him for he had never been as relaxed and apparently happy as he now was.

'I think that you have worked a miracle, Kathryn,' Paolo told her. 'Or perhaps it is love?'

Perhaps it was love. Kathryn could not have wished for a more attentive or generous husband, and the evening passed in a haze of pleasure. It seemed that she had everything that she had ever dreamed of, her happiness complete.

It was very late when they left the celebrations. The torches had burned low in their sconces and there was very little light for clouds obscured the moon. As they emerged into the street, they met a man who was about to knock at the door and Lorenzo gave a cry of pleasure.

'Michael! It is good to see you back, my friend. How is your father?'

'Much better,' Michael said, smiling oddly. 'He lectured me about finding myself a wife—and that means he is well again.'

Lorenzo laughed. 'We have missed you. Will you not return to the house with us? We have much to discuss.'

'It was for this purpose that I came here tonight,' Michael said and he looked at Kathryn, smiling at her. 'I have good news, Kathryn. A letter from Lord Mountfitchet.'

'From Uncle Charles?' Kathryn felt the sting of tears behind her eyes. She had thought her happiness could not be bettered, but this news was wonderful. 'Oh, that is good news indeed. Is he well—and Lady Mary?'

'Yes, they are well. I thought it best to open the letter, though it was addressed to you, Lorenzo. It seems that Lady Mary was taken ill on the journey and Lord Mountfitchet ordered his ship to put into Sicily. They never got as far as Cyprus. When they heard of the invasion they decided to stay where they were for the time being. Because of the war, it was difficult to send letters, and Lady Mary was quite ill for a while. When Lord Mountfitchet was able to send a letter, he was not sure where you would be, so he sent it to Venice.'

'That is truly good news,' Lorenzo said. 'I am so pleased to—'

'My God!' Michael cried and suddenly gave him a great shove to one side. 'What do you think you are doing?'

Kathryn screamed as she realised that Michael had seen what neither she nor Lorenzo had noticed. A woman had come up upon them out of the shadows and she had a knife with a long thin blade, which she had attempted to plunge into Lorenzo's back. Because of Michael's swift action she had missed her target, but she was screaming wildly, out of control as she turned her vicious blade on the man who had thwarted her evil intent.

'I shall kill him!' Maria screamed. 'He took me from the man I loved. I was to have been Rachid's wife. When he is dead, Rachid will take me back again.'

Michael struggled with her, but somehow her blade struck him in the chest and he gave a cry of pain, staggering back as the blood spurted. Lorenzo caught Maria's arm as she attempted to strike again, twisting it back so that she screamed with pain this time and the knife fell to the floor. He kicked it away, jerking her arm up so that she was unable to fight him, and she went limp in his grasp.

Kathryn was bending over Michael as he clutched at his chest, and now people were spilling out of Elizabeta's house, alarmed by the noise and Maria's screaming.

'Take the bitch,' Lorenzo commanded as some of his men came running out of the shadows. 'We shall deal with her later. How is he, Kathryn?' He looked down at Michael as she cradled him in her arms.

'I fear he is in a bad way,' Kathryn said, her cheeks pale from shock. 'The wound went deep and he is bleeding badly.'

'Bring him into the house,' Elizabeta's voice commanded. 'My servants shall go for the physician at once and we shall do what we can for him.'

Kathryn watched as Michael was lifted and carried into the house. Lorenzo followed as she did, feeling bewildered amongst all the consternation. Everyone was shocked. It had been such a lovely evening and now a man was wounded, perhaps fatally.

How could it have happened? Kathryn heard the shocked whispers, for Michael was popular with many of the assembled company. People were saying that Maria must be punished, that she deserved to hang for her crime—and there were some who suggested burning, for she must surely be in league with the devil to have done such wicked things. Her attempt to murder Kathryn, and then Lorenzo—who would have been her victim if Michael had not acted so swiftly.

Kathryn followed Elizabeta as they carried Michael up the stairs to one of the many guest chambers. Together they prepared the bed for him, and made him as comfortable as was possible. He was still living, though he had lost consciousness as he was carried in, the blood soaking through his shirt and doublet.

'Help me remove his things,' Elizabeta instructed. 'We

must try to staunch the flow of blood until the surgeon can tend him.'

Kathryn obeyed her, for it was obvious that she knew what she was about. Between them they cut away his doublet and shirt, leaving only his hose. Servants had brought linen and water, and Elizabeta cleansed the wound. Kathryn helped her to bind it tightly. In all this time Michael had not opened his eyes.

'That bitch will pay for this,' Lorenzo said when they had finished their task. Grief was working in his face. 'Damn her to hell for this night's work! She has killed one of the best men that ever lived.'

'No, no, my love,' Kathryn said. 'Michael is strong. He has every chance of recovery.'

'You have not seen men die,' he said his voice harsh. 'I do not believe in miracles. If Michael dies, so shall she!'

'Lorenzo...' Kathryn's throat caught, for she knew that beneath the anger was a terrible grief. Michael was as a brother to him, his closest friend. 'Please do not...' She meant only to comfort him, but his eyes glittered with anger.

'Do not plead for her life, Kathryn,' he said coldly. 'She is an evil woman and she deserves her fate. I would see her dead for what she has done this night.'

'Where are you going?' she asked as he turned to leave the room.

'Stay here, Kathryn,' he said. 'Elizabeta may need your help. I shall return later.'

Kathryn stared after him. How could such a terrible thing have happened? It had been such a lovely evening. Lorenzo had been so pleased to have his friend back, and

Michael had brought her good news—and now it looked as if it might all end in tragedy.

Why had he ever traded Rachid's son for the Spanish girl? Lorenzo cursed himself as he left the house. It would have been better to have given Hassan the swift death he had pleaded for and left the girl to her fate. It was his fault for allowing himself to feel compassion. He had always known that to become soft was to invite disaster. Only a hard man could exist in the world he inhabited and he had been a fool to imagine he could change.

His feelings for Kathryn had made him soft, and he had relaxed his guard. He had not been aware of Maria. His instincts had let him down. In a mood of exhilaration and excitement, he had allowed a woman to murder his best friend.

It would not have happened at any other time! It would be his fault if Michael died. He should have been more aware. Instead of letting the girl live as a guest in his home, he should have kept her a prisoner and sent her back to her father immediately.

His love for Kathryn had made him weak. He had always known that he could not afford to love a woman, and now Michael lay close to death because he had betrayed his own rules.

His fists clenched at his sides. It would not happen again. He must be on his guard in future for, if a woman could come so close to destroying him and all he cared for, his true enemies would succeed where she had failed. Next time it might be Kathryn who paid the price.

* * *

Michael lay close to death for three days and nights. Kathryn stayed at Elizabeta's house to help nurse him. She saw Lorenzo only a few times, briefly, just to report on his friend's progress. Yet she sensed that an icy barrier had formed between them. Lorenzo was deliberately shutting her out.

What had she done to deserve this? Did Lorenzo blame her because Maria had attacked his best friend? She had asked that the Spanish girl might be allowed to stay with them at the beginning—but how could she have known what Maria was capable of doing? Surely he could not blame her for Maria's crime? And yet it seemed he must, for he had withdrawn from her. She had never known him to be so cold, so remote. Even at the beginning he had liked to tease her—now she felt that he had shut her out of his life.

After the third day, Michael's fever began to abate. He woke once when Kathryn was tending him, smiling at her as she bathed his forehead and gave him cool water to drink.

'You are very kind.'

'You saved Lorenzo's life. I would not have you die for it, Michael.'

'He is my friend—my brother.'

'Yes, I know.' She smiled at him. 'Sleep now. You have good friends to care for you.'

Michael closed his eyes. Kathryn turned to see Lorenzo watching her from the doorway. She thought his expression very odd, for it was a mixture of remorse and…she was not sure what else.

'How is he?'

'A little better, I think.' She moved towards him. 'I have stayed here for his sake and because we cannot expect to leave everything to Elizabeta, generous as she is. Once Michael is well enough, we can arrange for him to come home to us.'

'You think he will recover?'

'I pray that he will, Lorenzo.'

'I have no faith in prayers.' His expression hardened.

'Yet sometimes they are answered.'

'Perhaps.' His gaze narrowed. 'I am sending a ship to Sicily. What message would you have me send to your friends?'

'Tell them that we are married and that I am happy.'

'Very well.' He hesitated, then, 'What would you have me do with Maria?'

'If Michael had died, she must have been punished by the laws of Rome,' Kathryn said. 'Perhaps she should be. I do not know. I would wish to send her home, and yet perhaps she should be punished.'

'Her father is expected here tomorrow. I could let them go—take the ransom and be rid of her. Her father shall know what she is and that shall be her punishment. Is that what you wish?'

'You must do as you think best.'

'You do not beg for leniency?'

'She might have killed you,' Kathryn said. 'And she has sorely harmed Michael. She deserves some punishment…'

'For myself, I would have her cast into prison to rot.'

'Lorenzo! I would not have you speak so harshly.'

'Life has made me harsh, Kathryn.' An odd, wintry smile flickered in his eyes. 'Yet it seems that Michael will live, because of you, I suspect. Perhaps I shall let Maria's father deal with her, as he thinks best.'

'If she has lost the man she loves, I dare say she will suffer enough.'

Lorenzo inclined his head. 'I am summoned to an important conference. It may be some days before I return.'

'Take care, my love.' Kathryn went to him, putting her arms about him. He did not take her into his embrace, and she felt him stiffen, as if resisting. 'Lorenzo—have I angered you?'

'You have done nothing wrong,' he said. 'But I was at fault in marrying you, Kathryn. You deserve so much more than I can give you.'

'I love you. You must know that?'

'Unfortunately, I cannot afford to love you,' he said and drew away from her. 'It was a mistake to think that I could be a true husband to you, Kathryn. Forgive me. I should have sent you home to your father when we thought Lord Mountfitchet lost.' He put her from him. 'Everything I own is at your disposal, but do not expect me to love you.'

The hurt welled inside Kathryn. She could not answer him for he had wounded her beyond bearing. Tears were close. He must not see her weep for her pride's sake. She moved away from him, bending over Michael, bathing his forehead. When she looked round, she saw that Lorenzo had gone.

How could he reject her now? His loving had been so sweet and tender—how could it have meant nothing to him?

On the night of Elizabeta's masque she had been so sure that he loved her, but now…what had changed him?

Michael had saved his life at a terrible cost to himself, but with God's help he would recover. Why had Lorenzo set his face against her?

Kathryn could not know of the agony it had cost him to take the decision. She only knew that her heart felt as if it were breaking.

Michael's recovery was slow but sure over the next week. By the end of the week he was well enough to be moved to Kathryn's home.

'Are you sure you wish to have me?' he asked as she moved about the room, making him comfortable. 'I could go to an inn now that I am so much better. You do not need to nurse me for I am almost myself again and would not wish to be a trouble to you.'

'You will do no such thing,' Kathryn said. 'Veronique will have returned from her sister's by now and she will help me to care for you. Besides, Lorenzo is still away and you may bear me company.'

'He will be making preparations to put to sea soon,' Michael said and frowned. 'I should be with him…' He groaned as he tried to get up from the bed. 'No, it is no use. I am too weak. I should be of no help. I fear he will have to do without me for some weeks.'

'You must not strain yourself,' Kathryn scolded. 'Lorenzo would rather have you stay here in Rome until you are well again.'

'I fear I have no choice.'

'You will be better soon,' Kathryn said and smiled at him. She felt comfortable with him, for they had become good friends of late.

* * *

Lorenzo returned a few days after Michael was moved to the villa. He spent some time sitting with his friend, who had been brought out into the garden to enjoy the sunshine, and afterwards thanked Kathryn for caring for him so well.

'I had plans for Christ's birthday,' he told her. 'But I fear I must leave you again, Kathryn. I have a gift for you—and you will not be lonely. You have your friends, Veronique and Michael to bear you company.'

It was almost as if those nights of passion had never been, as if he were a stranger, a distant relative who was bound to care for her comfort, but found it a burden. She wanted to cry out that she would always be lonely without him, that she loved him and her heart was breaking, but she said nothing. Her grief was still too raw, and it was pride that kept her from weeping and begging him to let things be as they had been before that terrible night. Yet she held back her tears.

She loved him so much, but he did not love her. The knowledge was almost unbearable and yet she bore it bravely, refusing to shed the tears that burned behind her eyes. She would not beg him to love her.

Over the next few weeks, Lorenzo's visits were brief, and Kathryn thought that each time he seemed to withdraw from her more. It was as if they were strangers, as if he had never held her in his arms and kissed her. The ache in her heart grew harder to bear and sometimes she did not know how she could live with it. Perhaps it might be better if she had died when Maria tried to kill her, better than this life without Lorenzo's love.

One morning, after a brief visit from her husband,

Kathryn was alone in the garden and unable to hold back her tears. Why had Lorenzo turned from her? What had she done to make him look at her so coldly?

'Why are you crying, Madonna?'

Michael's voice made her turn in surprise. She had thought herself alone and was embarrassed to be caught giving way to her grief.

'Oh…' she said, wiping her face with the back of her hand. 'I did not hear you coming, Michael.'

'I am sorry to intrude,' he said. 'But will you not tell me what is wrong—or can I guess? I do not know how Lorenzo can treat you so coldly. He is a fool and so I shall tell him next time I see him.'

'No, you must not,' she cried. 'He has done nothing that should make you cease to be his friend. It is simply…' The hurt welled up inside her. 'He does not love me.'

She felt the touch of his hand on her shoulder. 'I am sure that Lorenzo does love you,' Michael said, his voice deep with emotion. 'It is just that he is afraid of his feelings—afraid to let go of the hate inside him.'

'But he was so loving to me until…' Her voice died away. 'He seems so angry, so cold.'

'Do not despair, Kathryn,' Michael said and his voice was soft, concerned. 'You know that I would do anything to make you happy.' As she turned to look at him, the warmth in his eyes sent a tingle down her spine.

'Michael…'

He placed a finger to her lips. 'Do not say it, Kathryn. I know that you love Lorenzo. But I wanted you to be aware of my feelings for you. If in the future you should need a friend, I shall be there for you.'

Kathryn's eyes filled with tears. He was kind and good and generous, and she had grown fond of him—but her heart was given to Lorenzo.

'Damn you!' Lorenzo said as Michael finished speaking. Three weeks had passed since his last visit to the villa, and Kathryn's eyes had grown sadder with the days. 'Who gave you the right to meddle in my affairs?'

'Kathryn is your wife and she deserves better from you,' Michael said. 'As for what right I have—we have been friends for years. If anyone has the right to tell you that you are throwing away something precious and good, then it must be I, deny it as you will.'

'You are in love with her yourself,' Lorenzo accused, feeling a prick of jealousy as he saw the truth in Michael's eyes.

'If she did not love you—if you had not married her— I should have asked her to be my wife,' Michael admitted.

'She would be better as your wife, Michael. I was wrong to marry her—selfish. I cannot give her what she needs. I cannot, dare not, love her.'

'Will you waste your life in bitterness?' Michael asked, his eyes narrowed and angry. 'I know that you suffered at that monster's hand, but nothing can change that. It is over. You are rich and powerful. You have a chance of happiness with Kathryn—throw it away and you will live alone with your regret.'

'You do not know what you ask,' Lorenzo said. 'If I love her…if I let go of what is inside me, I am nothing.'

'Then you are nothing,' Michael told him. 'And I am sorry for you.'

Lorenzo watched as he walked away, going into the house. Anger raged inside him, but with the anger was remorse, for he knew that Michael was right, and he knew something more. The path he had chosen was the coward's path. He was afraid to love Kathryn, afraid of what his life would be without her if he allowed himself to love her.

The stroke of an assassin's knife could take her as it had almost taken Michael. And yet, what was his life now— was it worth the living?

Lorenzo faced the truth at last. The hatred had gone, driven out by Kathryn's love. He had fought against her, but she was there inside him. It was love for her that had made him send Rachid's son back to him—a love that he could no longer deny, try as he might.

But had he destroyed her love for him?

Kathryn was in her chamber going through her gowns with Lisa. She looked round as the maid suddenly bobbed a curtsy and left the room, her heart beating wildly as she saw him. It was odd, but he had lost that cold angry look which had haunted her for weeks.

'Lorenzo?' She looked at him, her throat tight, unable to trust her senses. 'Is something wrong?'

'Have I made you hate me, Kathryn?'

'I could never hate you. Do you not know how much I love you?' She looked at him, her heart in her eyes, no pleading or reproaches, but simple love.

'You should hate me for the way I have treated you these past weeks,' he said. 'But I beg you to forgive me. It was because of Michael. I did not sense that Maria was there that night. Always, I have known when I was in danger of being attacked. It was a sixth sense, an awareness that has saved my life many times. I felt that in letting myself love you I was losing that part of me—and I was afraid. It might have been you whom Maria attacked. I have enemies, Kathryn. There may be others who would seek to harm me through you—and I was afraid that if I loved you, if I let myself soften, I might become weak and be unable to protect you.'

'Lorenzo…' Tears sprang to her eyes as she moved towards him. 'I thought you blamed me—had turned against me…'

'I do love you,' he said. 'But it is not easy for me to admit it or to show it. You accused me of being harsh, and it is true. I have had to be hard, to be ruthless. It is the only way I could live. But perhaps I could change, perhaps there is another way to live. I must keep my promise to fight with the Holy League, but I think…I have no heart to continue my feud with Rachid. It is not that I have forgiven him, but…it no longer seems important.'

'My love.' Kathryn moved closer, putting her arms about him. She laid her head against his chest as after a moment's hesitation, his arms closed about her. They stood in silence for several minutes, just holding each other, his lips against her hair. 'We could go home to England. My father would welcome us there. You could begin a new life.'

'Yes, perhaps,' he said and smiled oddly as she looked up at him. 'Once the Holy League has fought its battle with the Turks, these seas will be a much safer place. I might perhaps continue to trade in fine wines, Kathryn—but I do not think that I shall need to be constantly at war as I have been these last years.'

'I am so glad that you have told me what was in your heart,' she said, lifting her face for his kiss, which was sweet and tender, concealing the fires beneath. 'I have been so unhappy—I thought that I had lost you.'

His eyes were dark with self-condemnation. 'Forgive me, Kathryn. I was a brute to you…'

She placed a finger to his lips. 'No more. I understand. I have always understood what drove you, my love. Come, let us go down and walk in the gardens. We must make the most of our time together, for Michael tells me that you plan to leave soon.'

'I fear I must,' Lorenzo said. 'The fleet is gathering and my galleys are a big part of what is to happen—but we have a few days, my love.'

She held her hand out to him and he took it. 'Then I am content,' she said, looking up at him with eyes that told their own story. 'Your love is all I want, Lorenzo.'

Kathryn turned in her husband's arms, feeling the warmth and strength of his body. He had hurt her so desperately, but she was ready to forgive and to love, for she understood that he had been in turmoil. She would never quite understand what drove him, for only someone who had suffered as he had could know what he felt, but she loved and that was enough. She was his wife, his woman, and at last, she believed his love. From the first she had sensed that they belonged together, and it was this deep instinct that had carried her throughout the uncertain days. She belonged to Lorenzo and, whatever came between them, that bond would always hold her.

His arms went round her, drawing her close, his hands

stroking the slender arch of her back, caressing her, arousing her to passion. She gave herself up to the urgency of their loving. So much time had been wasted and they had so little left. His kisses brought her to a sweet ecstasy that consumed them both in the fires of love, and then at last, satiated and content, they slept in each other's arms.

And when Lorenzo woke with the dawn, he lay looking down at her lovely face, drinking in her beauty, absorbing every detail into his mind so that he would carry it with him in the weeks and perhaps months ahead when they would be apart.

Kathryn kissed Lorenzo, a long, sweet, lingering kiss that almost tore her heart from her body, and then stood back, letting him go. She knew that it might be many months before she saw him again, but it was the price she had to pay.

Lorenzo had paid his own price in loving her. He had fought his battle and come through it for her sake, and she could do no less for his. She would let him go with a smile.

'Promise me that you will take care of yourself, Kathryn.'

'I shall do nothing foolish,' she said. 'Veronique is here to bear me company, and my friends will visit me often. When I go shopping, it will be with them and a servant to watch over us.'

'I do not think Rachid will attempt to abduct you in Rome,' Lorenzo told her. 'I asked Michael if he would stay and guard you for me, but he says that he wants to fight by my side and I must accept his will. I am leaving men you can trust to watch over you.'

'You must not worry for my sake.'

'Nor you for mine,' he said and smiled in the old, teasing way. 'I shall return to plague you again, my love.'

'See that you do,' she said and tossed her head proudly. 'And now you must go. You have your duty to the League.'

'Yes,' he said. 'May God watch over you, Kathryn.'

'And over you, my love.'

She watched as he walked away, her heart aching. Her nails were turned into her palms and it took all her strength of will to let him go. He had come to her in love at last and it would break her heart if she should lose him now.

Chapter Ten

Their ships were sailing in precise formation. After weeks of talking and delay, Don John of Austria had given his orders and a mood of elation had spread throughout the fleet.

'At last we shall have some action,' Michael said to Lorenzo, when he came on board for a meeting. I had begun to think we should spend the autumn in wasted argument again.'

'This venture has been blessed by the Pope and we have a very capable commander in Don John. I believe that this time something good will happen.'

'I pray you are right,' Michael answered, looking thoughtful.

'There will be no more talk of turning back. If our information is correct, the Turks are settled for the winter at Lepanto.'

'Unless they retreat to Constantinople.'

It was a question their spies had been unable to answer for certain as yet, but if luck was with them they would catch their quarry at Lepanto.

'I must return to my own galley,' Michael said when their meeting had finished. He looked at his commander, noticing the shadows beneath his eyes. It seemed to him that Lorenzo had suffered some sleepless nights and he wondered what had caused them, for he knew that Lorenzo did not fear battle. However, he was wise enough not to mention it. 'God be with you, my friend.

'And with you,' Lorenzo replied. 'God protect us all if it comes to a battle.'

It was the first time he had ever replied in that way. There *was* a difference in Lorenzo. Michael had noticed it more often of late, though as yet he was uncertain as to what it meant.

Lorenzo woke from the dream with the images still fresh in his mind. At first he had been in a house—in a room. It was a room he knew well and filled with things he admired, in particular a banner of gold and a suit of black armour.

He had not dreamed of the house before. Always his dream was of a beach and a youth struggling against the men who finally succeeded in capturing him. Yet perhaps that particular dream was real. Perhaps it was a memory of the day he had been taken. If that were so, then all the other things he half-remembered might also be true.

Shaking his head to clear away the lingering thoughts, he left his cabin to join the men. It was a calm clear night and the news had come earlier that day. Their information had proved true. The enemy was at Lepanto, and it was said that they were in some difficulty. There were stories of plague aboard their ships and large numbers of dead, which had left them short of slaves at the oars. If this too was true, it would give the League the advantage they needed against the superior numbers of the Turks.

Lorenzo was eager for the battle to begin. Like all those who lived and sailed under the banner of Venice, he was angry at the way the enemy had attacked and pillaged Cyprus, but more than this was his desire to have an end to this conflict. Only then would he be free to return to Kathryn.

Kathryn awoke, got up and went over to look out of the window of her bedchamber. It was a beautiful sunny day, the sky a perfect cloudless blue. She had promised to spend it with her friends, and she knew it would be a pleasant day. The only cloud on her horizon was the lack of news from Lorenzo.

He had warned her not expect any messages from him. 'We shall be moving constantly,' he had told her, 'and there will be no way of sending you letters, my love—but you will know that you are always in my heart.'

Kathryn wondered if he was thinking of her now. She had dreamed of him, but the dream had been the old one, where she was swept away from him by an unstoppable tide of water, and she did not want to remember it.

If only she knew what he was doing, and if he was safe! If anything should happen to him now…but she would not let herself dwell on such things. Lorenzo had promised to come back to her and she would hold fast to that thought.

Lorenzo was in command of his own fleet. It was his condition for joining the League and it gave him the freedom to manoeuvre as he would. He had decided to stay close to Don John's personal ships, for he believed the overall commander to be not only a man of sense, but also a brilliant strategist.

On most of the galleys the men were chained to their oars, lashed by the bosun's whip to make them work. Lorenzo's men were free to choose. They had been trained to obey his orders to the letter, and though they could be punished for disobedience, they were more likely to be rewarded for bravery. Any prizes they took would be sold and divided amongst them.

A mass had been held throughout the fleet and everyone accepted that the battle was near. The Turkish fleet had been sighted and the nearest guess they had was that there were some three hundred vessels, the majority of them fighting galleys.

'They are spread out across the gulf,' Lorenzo said to Michael just before he returned to his own galley that morning. 'It will be a hard-won fight, my friend.'

'But we shall prevail!'

'If we have faith in our own ability.'

'Listen to that!' Michael said as the sound of strange music floated across the sea from the enemy ships.

By contrast, the combined fleet of the League was silent. The atmosphere was intense, dedicated, as if every man was prepared to die for the cause.

'Go to your men,' Lorenzo said his expression set. 'This day shall be remembered for all time.'

They were closing on the enemy now. The decks of the Turkish galleys were packed with men in rich clothes and wearing jewels; they were Janissaries and served the Sultan. Amongst them crouched the archers, their deadly weapons poised and ready to inflict the maximum harm.

The League was heavily outnumbered and no one knew better than Lorenzo what fierce fighters the Turks were. Amongst them, he did not doubt, were the ships of his enemy Rachid.

On board the Turkish ships the Janissaries were shouting and screaming, crashing cymbals and firing as the two fleets converged, hoping to confuse and scatter the League's ships. But the League held firm, waiting for the signal from their commander, which came in the end along with a change in the wind.

Suddenly the odds had altered. Now they were in favour of the League. It seemed that God was with them.

Kathryn could not rest. She had heard no news of Lorenzo for weeks and the waiting was at times unbearable. She had always known that it might be months before he returned to her, but she had hoped that there might be some news before this.

'It is the uncertainty I find so distressing,' Kathryn said to Elizabeta as they sat together at their sewing. 'Every day I expect that we may hear something, but there has been no word.'

Elizabeta nodded, stretching to ease her back. She was in the early stages of childbearing, though as yet it was hardly noticeable.

'My husband has contributed to the League's funds, as all men of conscience must,' she said. 'But I must tell you, Kathryn, that I am relieved he takes no part in this war. I know it must be very worrying for you.'

'I try not to be anxious,' Kathryn told her. 'Lorenzo promised that he would return to me and I must believe that.'

'Yes, of course,' Elizabeta said and smiled. She showed Kathryn the exquisite embroidery she was doing for her baby's shawl. 'I am sure he will return to you in time. After all, this is not the first time your husband has fought his enemies.'

'No, that is true.' Kathryn laid her sewing aside as she heard voices in the hall and then Veronique came into the salon with their visitor. 'Paolo,' she said and stood up to greet him. 'It is good to see you.'

'I knew you would be anxious for news,' he said. 'I came as soon as I heard—it seems that the League has won a great victory over the Turks.'

'A victory!' Kathryn could not keep the delight from her voice, her eyes lighting up from inside. 'I am so very pleased. But what else have you heard?'

'There have been casualties on both sides,' Paolo said carefully. He had heard that they were heavy, but did not wish to frighten her. 'They say that Don John's strategy was brilliant, but there was hard fighting. It was not won easily, surging this way and that, but the Turkish commander was killed and that helped to carry the day. Also, it is said that, on board the Turkish ships, the galley slaves broke free of their chains and joined in the fighting against their cruel masters.'

'You have no other news…for me?' She looked at him eagerly.

'I cannot tell you that Lorenzo is safe, Kathryn, for I do not know. But some of our ships may return soon and then we may learn more.'

'Yes, I understand,' Kathryn said. She was on fire with impatience to discover more, but knew she must control her feelings. 'It was good of you to come and tell me.'

'I knew you would be anxious,' he said. 'As soon as there is more news I shall tell you.'

Kathryn thanked him. She invited him to stay and take some wine with them, but he said that he had other calls to make.

'Well,' Elizabeta said after he had gone. 'Paolo brought good news, Kathryn. If the Turks are defeated, it means that the war is over, and that means Lorenzo should soon be on his way home to you.'

'Yes.' Kathryn smiled, her heart racing with excitement. 'I do hope so, Elizabeta. I cannot wait to have him home again.'

The battle against the Turks was won for the moment. Lorenzo did not doubt that they would grow strong again in time, but it had been a fierce fight and for the moment the enemy could do nothing but slink away to lick its wounds, which meant that these seas would be that much safer.

Lorenzo had lost three of his galleys in the battle of Lepanto. Crews from other ships had rescued some of the men, though inevitably some had been lost. At least his crew had chosen to fight of their own free will, which was not the case for all. However, they had captured several rich prizes, and that meant the men would be well rewarded for their work.

'What will you do next?' Michael asked as he came on board Lorenzo's personal galley. 'Are you returning to Rome at once?'

'Those galleys that have sustained damage should head for Sicily and make what repairs they can before returning home,' Lorenzo said. 'It is my intention to escort them there and to visit with Lord Mountfitchet for a few days before I return to Rome.'

Michael inclined his head. 'And what would you have me do?'

'Take the rest of the fleet back to Rome. Stay there until I return if you will, Michael. I shall be a week or so behind you. When I come, we shall discuss the future.'

'Is it in your mind to change things?'

'I am not yet certain of my plans. I will know more when I have spoken to Lord Mountfitchet. I may return to England, at least for a while.'

'Return to England?' Michael looked puzzled. 'Was that country once your home?'

'Did I say that?' Lorenzo frowned. 'I meant that I might take Kathryn to her home for a visit.'

He spoke with Michael for a little longer, and then they parted company. He was thoughtful as he gave the order to the stricken galleys. It would be safer if they travelled as a group, for they were vulnerable. However, his own galley was not damaged and he would be their escort to Sicily. And then…

What did he expect to learn from Lord Mountfitchet? Lorenzo was uncertain, but his dream had haunted him for a while now. In it he saw two young people on a beach. The youth told the girl to run and fetch help while he fought the men who sought to capture them…and there was also a picture of a house and a man the youth had called father. There were other things coming to him now, things that seemed so real that he could not think them dreams, and yet he was afraid to call them memories.

Was it possible that Charles Mountfitchet was his father? Or had Lorenzo simply taken things that Kathryn had told him and made something from them? Were these flashes that came into his mind at times true memories or merely imagination? It seemed unlikely that he could be Richard Mountfitchet, and yet of late something had been telling him that he must speak of his thoughts.

Kathryn would be waiting for him in Rome, but it would mean a delay of no more than a week or so, and he had a feeling that it was important for both of them that he should speak to Charles.

Kathryn was in the garden, picking flowers to take into the house, when she heard the ring of booted steps behind her and turned eagerly. Her heart took a flying leap as she saw her visitor.

'Michael!' she cried joyfully. 'I am so glad to see you back. Are you well? Is Lorenzo with you?'

'I am well,' he told her. 'I thank you for you inquiry, Kathryn—and I am happy to tell you that Lorenzo was well when I last saw him. He escorted some of our wounded galleys to Sicily, for they needed urgent repairs and were vulnerable. I believe that he intended to speak to Lord Mountfitchet before returning to Rome.'

'I had a letter from Lady Mary only yesterday,' Kathryn said. 'They have found land and a house in Sicily that suits them and they think they may stay there. It was Lord Mountfitchet's intention to speak with Lorenzo and ask for his advice, so it may suit him if Lorenzo calls there to see him.'

'Lorenzo has asked me to remain in Rome until his return.' Michael frowned. 'I think it is in his mind to take a trip to England, though he said his plans were not yet formed.'

'Yes, he did speak of making changes,' Kathryn said. 'I think he believes that it will no longer be necessary to have so many galleys to protect his ships in future, but we must wait and see what he decides.'

'Yes, of course. If you will excuse me now, I have other calls to make.'

'Will you dine with me this evening?' Kathryn asked. 'I have invited Elizabeta, her husband, Paolo, Isabella and her father and a few others. We should be pleased to have you join us. Perhaps you could tell us more of the battle, for we hear so many conflicting stories. It would be good to hear from someone who was there.'

'I should be delighted to do so,' Michael said, hesitated, and then added, 'It is in my mind that I might ask Isabella Rinaldi to marry me.' His cheeks became slightly pink. 'My father is most insistent that I take a wife. I have resisted it, for it would mean that I should have to change the way I lead my life. Perhaps, if Lorenzo intends to make changes, it is time I did so also.' He looked at her oddly. 'Do you think there is a chance that Isabella would look kindly on an offer from me?'

'I do not know,' Kathryn said. 'But I think she likes you.'

He nodded and smiled. 'Then I shall think seriously about making the offer. I shall see you this evening, Kathryn.'

'We shall look forward to having you with us.'

Kathryn stood for a while after he had gone, a rosebud in her hand. She would be pleased if Lorenzo was serious about taking her home, for she would be glad to see her father. But she was not sure that she would wish to make her home there for she was happy here in Rome.

She had written to her father many months ago to tell him of her marriage and assure him that she was well, but there had been no reply. At first she had thought that he must be too busy to write to her or that he was perhaps angry she had married without consulting him, but now she had begun to wonder if he had received her letter. It was strange that there had been no reply of any kind.

'It is good to see you again,' Charles said, offering his hand to Lorenzo. 'My sister wrote to Kathryn some weeks back, telling her that we were thinking of staying here in Sicily. We have found land we like, and a house—but I wanted your advice before I made the purchase.'

'It is one choice,' Lorenzo agreed. 'I believe it might be a good idea to buy land here, and establish vineyards of your own, but I thought you might consider living in Rome or Venice. I have plans to expand my wine-growing business, and perhaps to concentrate the shipping to England, Germany and France, where I have contacts. It was in my mind to ask whether you might consider being my partner? My business is expanding and I have plans to ship wines to more countries than before—but I shall need someone I can trust to help me in this venture.'

'Your partner?' Charles was surprised, but enormously pleased with the idea. 'I think I might, sir. Yes, I think I might. Had my son lived, I should have been content to sit back and let him take over my interests, but…' He sighed and shrugged his shoulders. 'I have reluctantly accepted that I may never see him again. And I am not sure that I would ever wish to return to England. I find the climate here suits me better. My only wish is that I might find some trace of my son.'

'He may be nearer than you think,' Lorenzo said, a sudden croak in his voice. 'Would you mind answering a few questions concerning Richard?'

Charles looked at him eagerly. 'Have you discovered something?'

'I am not sure. It may be nothing—but did you give your son a sword on his seventh birthday and tell him that it was time he learned to be a man?'

Charles looked shocked. 'I cannot remember if he was seven or eight—but it is true that I gave my son a sword on his birthday and I may have told him some such thing.'

'Tell me about the house you lived in then—has it a tower and a moat? Is there a room filled with armour from past times, and did Richard like to spend hours there?'

'Yes, all that you say is true,' Charles said and looked at him intently. 'Richard liked one suit of armour particularly. My father wore it at the battle of—'

'When Henry VIII met Francis I on the Field of Cloth of Gold, and your father rode with Henry that day.' Lorenzo's eyes narrowed. 'And did your son have an unusual pet—one that you did not approve of?'

'A pet…' Charles wrinkled his brow in thought for a moment and then laughed. 'Good Lord, yes! I had almost forgot. He brought home a wretched fox cub and…' His voice died away as he saw the look in Lorenzo's eyes. 'What happened then?'

'He took it up to his room and fed it with food he had stolen from the kitchens, and you found out and beat him for it...'

'I made him take it back to the woods where he found it.'

'But he did not,' Lorenzo said and smiled. 'He kept it in a part of the stables and saved food from his own plate to feed it until it was old enough to be released.'

'I never knew that.' Charles looked at him oddly. 'Only Richard could know all this...'

'I have wondered if it was a dream or imagination,' Lorenzo said. 'But when you spoke of the special suit of armour I knew that it was true.' His voice was hoarse with emotion. 'Forgive me, I do not know how to say this to you. When we first met I felt an affinity that I have seldom known with another man, but I would not believe in what my heart was telling me. I thrust it from me, but the dreams started to haunt me. I cannot tell you that I am your son, for I have no proof—but I believe that it may be so.'

'God help me!' Charles staggered back, falling into a chair. For a moment he sat with his head in his hands, and when he looked up at last the tears were running down his cheeks. 'I felt it too, but I did not believe it could be true.'

'Then you believe...you would own me as your son?' Lorenzo felt humbled, closer to tears than he had ever been in his life. 'I can give you no proof...'

'I think you have given me enough,' Charles said and stood up, moving forward to embrace his son, his body shaking with the sobs of emotion he at least could not hold back. 'Since we met it has been in my mind that if I had a son I should want him to be much like you. Indeed, though I had not made a conscious decision, I had come to think of you as my son.'

'Then I shall do my best to make you proud of me, Father,' Lorenzo said. 'It does not mean that I shall honour Antonio Santorini the less, for without his love and care of me I should have died many years ago. But in my heart I do believe that you are my true father, and I hope that if we return for a visit to England with Kathryn I may recover many more memories.'

'Then it is settled,' Charles said. 'We shall look at the land I thought to buy here and make our decision, and then we shall return to Rome and from thence to England.'

'We shall make our decision about the land, but I may go on ahead while you settle things here, Father. Kathryn will be anxious. Besides, my stricken galleys will be a few days making repairs, and they will escort you. The seas are much safer for the time being, but I doubt that we have rid them of all the Corsairs who have plagued us. I would have you make the journey in safety.'

Charles smiled at him. His heart was overflowing with love for this son new found, and he would have agreed to anything that Lorenzo asked of him.

'Kathryn…' Veronique came into the salon, looking flustered. 'You have a visitor…'

'A visitor?' Kathryn's heart raced. What could her companion mean? Was it Lorenzo? A man had followed close on the heels of Veronique and as she saw him she got to her feet with a glad cry. 'Father! Oh, I am so glad to see you. How came you here? I had no word…'

There was anger in his face as he looked at her. '*You* have had no word from me? I have waited months for a letter from you, Kathryn. I travelled to Venice, to the home of Signor Santorini, and learned there that you have married. What is this? Why have you behaved so ill towards me? I do not think I have deserved this from you, daughter.'

'Forgive me, Father,' Kathryn said. 'I would not have hurt you for the world. It is a long story and I must ask you to sit down while I tell it.' She looked at her companion. 'This gentleman is my father—Sir John Rowlands. Would you please order some refreshments for us, Veronique?'

'It is a pleasure to meet you, *madame,*' Sir John said. 'Forgive me if I was short with you earlier, but I was angry and anxious for Kathryn.'

'There is no need to be angry,' Kathryn told him as her companion smiled and left the room. 'I am sorry that you did not get my letter, for it would have explained all. Lorenzo married me because there was some question of my good name having been besmirched.' She shook her head as he fired up. 'No, no, listen to my story, I pray you, before you judge. Lorenzo has done nothing that should make you angry.'

'Tell me it all, then,' Sir John said. His anger had been caused by months of frustration and anxiety, but now that he was here and could see she was well, his feelings were a mixture of relief and pique.

As Kathryn's story unfolded his emotions ran the gamut between fury and distress. That his child should have been kidnapped! He was grateful to Lorenzo Santorini for rescuing her, but blamed him for having brought it on her in the first place. But when he heard that his old friend had been thought lost and Kathryn had been alone, he began to understand that she had been lucky. Had Santorini been another kind of man, her fate might have been very different.

'I see,' he said as she finished her story. 'And where is your husband, Kathryn? I should wish to meet him before I give you my blessing.'

'He has been fighting, Father. You must have heard tell of the terrible battle that took place more than two weeks ago?'

'Yes, I heard of it in Venice. I was delayed because of it, but surely he should be home by now?'

'One of his captains came to see me,' Kathryn said. 'Lorenzo went to see Lord Mountfitchet in Sicily. Michael said he would not be long. I am expecting him any day now.'

'Then I must wait in patience I suppose,' her father said. He smiled at her. 'Well, come, kiss me, daughter. I was angry, but now that you have told me all, I am prepared to forgive you.'

'Two galleys to the leeward, sir,' Lorenzo's second-in-command came to inform him as he was looking at some papers in his cabin. 'I'm not sure—but I think they are Corsairs.'

'Damn it!' Lorenzo buckled on his sword as he prepared to go outside and investigate for himself. The galleys were closing on them fast, and as he looked he saw that they were flying Rachid's flag.

Cursing himself for being caught off guard, Lorenzo gave the order for battle. It was two to one and it was his own fault, for he had been impatient to return to Kathryn. Had he waited another few days they might all have sailed together.

He had imagined that the Corsair's galleys would have gone back to Algiers to rest up for the winter and lick their wounds, but it looked as if they were hungry for a fight. Well, they would get one. He was outnumbered, but his men were loyal and, if need be, they would fight to the death.

Kathryn and her father were sitting in the salon drinking wine and eating biscuits when they heard the sound of voices in the hall. Kathryn jumped to her feet as Michael walked in, followed closely by Lord Mountfitchet.

'Kathryn.' Lord Mountfitchet's expression made her heart catch with fright. 'Forgive me, but I fear I have terrible news.'

'Lorenzo?' Her face was white and she might have fallen if her father had not been by her side. 'Something has happened to him…'

He put out his hand to steady her. 'Damn it, Charles! What is it?'

'John—I did not know you were here,' Charles said. He looked grey in the face, clearly much distressed. 'The news is the worst imaginable. Lorenzo insisted on setting out alone, for he was impatient to see Kathryn. He imagined the seas would be safe enough after the recent battle but…' He put a shaking hand to his face. 'I can scarce believe it. To have found him and then to lose him…'

'What are you talking about?' Sir John barked. Veronique had helped Kathryn to sit down and was giving her a drink of restorative wine. 'What has happened to Kathryn's husband?'

'We found the wreckage of his galley,' Charles said. 'It had been severely damaged and abandoned, though there was a man clinging to wreckage in the water. Somehow the poor devil had survived for two days. He was half out of his mind and is still in a fever, but he told us that the Corsair had taken prisoners—and that Lorenzo was either dead or a prisoner of his enemy.'

'No!' Kathryn cried, terror sweeping through her. 'No, not Rachid. He will surely kill him.' Tears trickled down her cheeks. 'There is such hatred between them....'

'Do not despair, Kathryn.' Michael spoke for the first time. 'I have already sent out ships to make contact with Rachid. We shall offer a ransom for him. I shall go myself to Algiers. I promise that we shall leave no stone unturned in the effort to find him.'

'Lorenzo...' Kathryn bowed her head as the pain of her grief almost overwhelmed her. 'This is my fault. I made him love me and...' It was what he had feared. Because of his love for her, he had thrown his natural caution to the winds. He had been impatient to see her. 'Oh, my love, forgive me!'

'What nonsense is this, Kathryn?' Her father looked bewildered. He rubbed at a spot in his chest as if it bothered him. 'How can it be your fault?'

'Excuse me,' she said, tears blinding her eyes. 'I would be alone.'

The men stared after her as she fled, but Veronique followed.

'What was all that about?' Sir John asked. He rubbed at his chest again. Sometimes he hardly felt the pain, but at others it became severe. He needed to take one of the powders that his physician had given him, but for the moment it must wait.

'Lorenzo told me his story recently,' Charles said. 'Please allow me to tell you what he related to me—and then perhaps you may begin to understand what this means.'

'I must go,' Michael said. 'There is no time to waste if we are to find Lorenzo alive. Please tell Kathryn that I will do everything I can.'

'Any ransom,' Charles said. 'I will give every penny I possess for his safe return.'

'I shall do what I can,' Michael promised and left them.

Kathryn stood at the window, staring out at the night sky. She was in too much distress to think clearly, but her heart felt as if it were being torn in two. She could almost wish that Lorenzo had died in battle; at least that would have been swift. To think of him at the mercy of his enemy was unbearable. She knew what it had cost him to put the past behind him, the agony of mind he had endured—and now he was once more a prisoner of the evil Corsair who had nearly killed him once before.

'Lorenzo…' she whispered. 'My love, my love—what have I done to you?'

It was her fault, for Rachid would not have caught him off guard before he fell in love with her. She had given him her love, but it was a poisoned chalice—it had led to his death.

Tears trickled down her cheeks. She let them fall. Her grief was so sharp that it was almost unbearable. If Lorenzo was gone from her for ever…

What must he be suffering? To find himself a prisoner of his enemy once more would be humiliating and soul-destroying. He knew what it was like to serve at the oar for three years, and, unless Michael was successful in his attempts to ransom him, he might die this time.

No, no, he must not die, for she could not bear to live without him. She was his woman, his wife, and her heart belonged to him alone. He must live—she did not know what she would do without him.

Lorenzo explored the tender spot at the back of his head carefully. He had been unconscious for some hours after he was captured, for he had been taken from behind and received a heavy blow to the back of the head, but he knew immediately that he was in the cabin of the Corsair galley. Why had he not been cast down into the pit with the other captives?

Did the pirate who had captured him know who he was? It was almost certain that he did—so was he being held for a ransom? Or had Rachid reserved a special fate for him? Yes, of course, that must be so. It was the only reason he had not been chained up with the other prisoners.

They had been enemies for a long time now and Rachid had not earned his name for nothing. He was called the Feared One because of his barbarity. It was unusual for his men to take prisoners unless they needed more galley slaves or captured someone they could ransom for a large sum of money. As a rule they killed ruthlessly, plundering the captured ships and often sinking them afterwards unless they considered them worth selling.

Lorenzo's head was throbbing as he lay considering his likely fate. He could either be sold as a slave, put to the oars, or held for ransom. But Rachid had good cause to hate him and it was probable that he was being kept alive so that he could suffer some form of torture before his death.

He had been a youth when he had been taken the first time, powerless to fight the ruthless men who had captured him. Finding himself chained to an oar with no memory of his life prior to his captivity, he had survived by instinct—an instinct that had served him well these past years. It would be different this time, for he knew exactly who he was and what had happened to him.

He knew that he must remain alert, while allowing his captors to think him still suffering from the blow to his head. Only if they believed he was ill and incapable of escaping would they give him the chance to make his break.

But he would do so when the chance came. He would rather die in the attempt than be a slave—or allow his enemy to humiliate him. The strongest man could break under torture, and he would rather die quickly and cleanly.

For a moment he thought of Kathryn. If he waited, perhaps Rachid would ransom him and he might be returned to Rome. He might see her again. A part of him wanted to take that chance, to put his faith in God and those he knew would even now be trying to arrange his freedom—but there was another part of him that refused to be sold.

Somehow he would fight free. If he died in the attempt,

then Kathryn would be a widow. She was beautiful and she would be rich, for he had left much of his wealth to her in a will he had made before the war—and she would find someone else to love in time.

'Kathryn, Kathryn, my love…'

His heart cried out to her as he whispered her name, but even for the sake of his love for her, he could not simply wait for rescue or death. He must try to save himself if he died for it.

'You. Infidel dog!' A rough voice spoke from the doorway. 'Do you want food and water?'

Lorenzo moaned, but made no answer. He sensed the man coming nearer and forced himself to lie still. To attack one man would do no good. He needed to wait for the right time.

The Corsair muttered something and slopped some water into Lorenzo's face. He had been waiting for it, because he had seen it done often enough. He muttered and jerked, but did not open his eyes. The man grunted and moved away, closing the cabin door after him.

Lorenzo ran his fingers over his face, sucking the few drops of moisture he managed to acquire by this method. He was thirsty and hungry too, but he needed to keep up the pretence for as long as he could manage.

Kathryn woke with tears on her face. She had dreamed of Lorenzo, dreamed that he was ill and in pain, and that he had called her name.

'Oh, Lorenzo,' she whispered as she got out of bed and went over to the window, gazing out at the night. 'Lorenzo, do not die and leave me. Come back to me, my love. I need you so…'

He was not dead. She would not let herself believe it, for if she did there would be an end to all hope. No, she knew that he was alive. He was out there somewhere and thinking of her—and somehow he would come to her. Surely he would find a way to come back to her? He must because she loved him.

It was no use, she would never sleep. She dressed and went out to the courtyard, welcoming the cool night air. Her heart ached for the man she loved, but there was no comfort to be had.

'Lorenzo...' she whispered. 'Please do not leave me, my love.'

Lorenzo knew that they had reached a port. The ship was no longer moving and he could hear shouting from the deck, the ragged cheer that comes from the throats of weary oarsmen who knew that they would at last be allowed some rest.

He was tempted to get up and look out of the porthole, but wary lest someone come and find him clearly recovered from the blow that had rendered him unconscious. He must wait for the right moment before attempting his escape.

It was a few minutes before someone came into the cabin and stood looking down at him. Then he felt someone kick him in the side.

'Get up, infidel dog,' the voice said. 'Rachid requests your presence.' Coarse laughter and then the sound of other men entering the cabin followed this command. 'We shall have to carry the dog,' the man said. 'Rachid will have our heads if he dies.'

Lorenzo let his body flop loosely as he was lifted bodily and carried out on to the deck. It was good to feel the fresh air on his face. He was very thirsty and it took all his strength of purpose to lie still as he was dumped unceremoniously on to the deck.

He sensed that the men had moved away from him and cautiously opened one eye. To his amazement, they had all walked to the prow of the galley and were staring at something happening on shore. This was his chance!

Lorenzo moved cautiously, crawling on all fours to the stern. He glanced over his shoulder but the Corsairs were all intent on watching whatever was happening on shore.

He thought that they were getting ready for someone to come on board—possibly Rachid. The thought of coming face to face with his enemy lent Lorenzo wings. He stood up swiftly, putting a leg over the side and finding a foothold, his other leg following just as the alarm was roused. Someone had seen him and shouted a warning. It was now or never.

He paused for a brief second before diving into the sea, but even as he hesitated he heard something just behind him and then a shot rang out. The ball embedded itself in his shoulder and he pitched face down into the sea.

Chapter Eleven

Kathryn was walking in the garden when Michael arrived later that day. She saw him talking with her father and Lord Mountfitchet and went quickly into the house to ask if there was any news.

'Have you found him?'

'No, Kathryn,' Michael said. His eyes begged for pardon for he knew that his words must bring her grief. 'Forgive me, I have no news at all. I made contact with one of Rachid's men, but he claimed to have no knowledge of an attack on Lorenzo's galley or of any captive.'

'But it was six weeks ago,' Kathryn said. 'Surely there must be some word by now? If he was taken back to Algiers—'

'My men and I visited the slave markets,' Michael told her. 'There was no news of him—they all denied having seen him.'

'Someone must have seen him…if he is alive…' Kathryn caught back a sob of grief. She was trying so hard to hold on to her hope to believe that he lived, but it was very hard.

'Do not give up hope yet,' Michael said. 'I have sent an envoy to Rachid, and if there is to be an answer it will come here to his father—but I shall go now to Granada to speak with Lorenzo's friend Ali Khayr. It is possible that he may have heard something—or that he may have contacts who could discover the truth of this.'

'But we have only one man's word that he was captured by Rachid's galleys,' Kathryn said. 'Supposing it was another pirate or…' She shook her head. 'No, I shall not believe he is dead. I am sure that he lives.'

'You always gave me hope when I had none,' Charles Mountfitchet said, a gleam in his eyes. 'And now I shall tell you that I believe he is alive, Kathryn. Lorenzo is not a green youth. He is a strong, resourceful man who has known suffering and survived, and I believe he will find a way to survive this time—no matter who his captors were.'

'I do hope you are right, sir,' she said, smothering a sob. Inside her head she was praying, begging for his life. 'I pray that he is alive and that we shall have him back with us soon.'

Sir John watched her anxiously, feeling her pain as if it were his own. He had experienced more pain in his chest of late and he knew that his time here was short. He must return home, for there were things he needed to do, yet he could not leave while Kathryn was so distressed.

Lorenzo opened his eyes. The woman bending over him had soft hands and a kind voice. She had been tending him for a long time now, though he did not know how long he had lain here in his fever.

'Are you awake at last?' the woman asked in her native

tongue and smiled at him. 'Allah be praised. We all thought that you would die. You were as good as dead when my husband fished you out of the sea.'

'Where am I?' Lorenzo understood her, for it was a language he had learned of necessity long ago. He wrinkled his brow and tried to remember what had happened to him, but for the moment his mind was confused. He felt too weak to think, but he swallowed obediently when the woman put a cup to his lips.

'My name is Salome,' the woman told him. 'My husband is a fisherman—we are but poor folk, sir. When my husband found you, you had been wounded and he thought you dead. He knew that someone was looking for you and he thought to claim a ransom for your body, but when he discovered that you were alive, he brought you to our home. Khalid would have given you to the Feared One had you been dead, but he would not give any living man to that monster.'

'I am very grateful,' Lorenzo whispered, his voice hoarse. 'You shall be rewarded. I have friends who will pay for my safe return.'

'I told my husband it would be so,' Salome said and smiled encouragingly. 'I have tended you for many days and nights, sir. Even when your wound began to heal your mind did not. You have been wandering in the past I think, for you spoke of being a child...of your father...'

'My father.' Lorenzo's face creased with grief as the memories flooded into his mind and it all slotted into place. 'He will be so distressed, and Kathryn...' Kathryn would think him dead. He tried to sit up, but the pain struck him and he fell back against the cushions.

'You are not yet ready to get up,' Salome said. 'Rest and wait, impatient one. When you are better we shall send a message to your friends and then you shall go to them. We are not greedy people, sir, but we are poor. A small sum for our trouble is all that we ask.'

Lorenzo smiled at her as his eyelids fluttered. 'I shall make you rich,' he murmured and then he slept.

'I must return home soon,' Sir John said as he found his daughter walking in the garden. His heart ached as he saw her so pale, her eyes dark with unhappiness. She was even more distressed now than she had been when Dickon was taken from her. 'I want you to come with me, daughter.'

'I cannot leave Rome,' Kathryn cried in sudden alarm. 'I must stay here in case…he is found.'

'Two months have passed now since Lorenzo was lost,' her father told her, his expression grave. 'I know you loved him, Kathryn, and if what Charles says is true—if he is Richard—then this is the second time you have lost the one you love most in the world. You will grieve for him, it is natural that you should—but I cannot stay here much longer. I must return home almost immediately. And I would have you safe at home with me.'

'No, I must stay here. I must wait for my husband.'

'I think that you should do as your father suggests.'

Kathryn turned as she heard Charles's voice. He had come into the garden and overheard them talking. 'I must be here if Lorenzo returns.' Her eyes filled with tears. 'Please do not make me leave him—please, I beg you. I must be here when he comes back…'

'I shall remain in Rome,' Charles told her. 'When I have

news I shall write to you. Lorenzo will know that you did not wish to leave. I shall tell him, Kathryn—but you would be safer at home with your father. Mary chose to stay in Sicily. She has kept poor William with her and has recently met a gentleman she likes and may marry. Had she been here, it might have been different—but I do not wish to leave you alone and I may have to travel elsewhere.'

'Then give me another week,' Kathryn begged. Her throat was tight with grief and she could hardly bear the pain. 'If there is no news of him by then, I must do as my father says…'

She turned away from them, controlling her tears with difficulty. Perhaps they were right and it might be better if she left Rome. It was for her sake that Lorenzo had travelled alone, because he had been impatient to be with her. He had feared that loving her might cause him to become soft—and it was that which had led to his capture or even his death.

Lorenzo had married her because she was distressed at losing her good name. She believed that he had loved her, but perhaps she was an evil omen to him. Had she not prompted Dickon to go down to the beach when they were children, pirates would not have taken him. Had she not made Lorenzo fall in love with her, he might even now be safe. The thought was like a dagger striking deep into her heart and made her stagger as she realised what love of her had done to Lorenzo not once, but twice.

'Forgive me, my love,' she whispered. 'But perhaps it is best.'

She raised her head, fighting her grief and the longing deep inside her. 'Very well, Father,' she said. 'If there is no news within a week, I shall go back home with you.'

* * *

Lorenzo was resting when Salome came hurrying into the room. The pain in his shoulder was much easier now, but he was still too weak to do much more than walk about the house. He could not go out into the gardens for fear that someone might see him. He had already stayed too long and his presence in this house might mean danger for the good people who had nursed him back to health.

'Is something wrong?' he asked as he saw Salome's anguished look.

'They are looking for you,' she said, a frightened expression in her eyes. 'Men came to the village earlier asking for a man of your description. My husband fears that someone will betray us. They are offering money for news of your whereabouts, *signor.*'

'Then I must leave your house,' Lorenzo said, 'for I would not bring harm to you. I fear I have nothing to give you for your kindness, lady, but you shall be rewarded as soon as I return to my home.' He thought of a small gold ring on his finger and slipped it off. 'Take this as a token of my good will. I owe you much more and, God willing, I shall live to repay you.'

'My husband had no thought of repayment when he took you from the sea, but he grows old and soon will be able to work no more.'

'You shall be rewarded,' Lorenzo promised, 'and now I must leave before they come looking for me here.'

'You must wear my husband's clothes,' Salome said. 'I have brought you something to darken your skin, else you will be noticed at once for your skin has the pallor of ill health. If I do not offend you, lord, you should keep your head down lest your eyes betray you.'

Lorenzo thanked her again for her advice, slipping on the long, shabby robe she offered over the remnants of his own clothing. The sea had taken most of his garments, leaving only his breeches.

He left Salome's house through a small gate at the back of the garden, avoiding the main street of the fishing village. It was late in the afternoon, the sun dipping over the sea in a blaze of gold, and he knew that dusk would soon cloak him in darkness.

He had not been idle these past weeks and he believed that his best chance of escape was to reach Algiers, where he might mingle with the crowds frequenting the waterfront. It was a busy port and there might be merchant ships from Portugal or Holland. With luck he could find work. If he could reach Spain, he had friends who would help him.

Lorenzo had been walking for some half an hour or more when he was alerted by the sound of hoofbeats coming fast up the lonely road. He realised at once that it could only be the men who had visited Salome's village earlier, and looked about for somewhere to hide.

The rocky hillside offered no protection. Perhaps he could simply bluff it out by pleading ignorance. He must remember to keep his head bent, and to act in a humble manner befitting his lowly status.

As the riders came nearer, Lorenzo moved to the side of the road. Perhaps they would simply ride by and ignore him.

His hopes were short lived as the leading horseman reined in and shouted to him. 'You there—dog! Have you seen anyone passing this way? A man not of our people?'

'No one has passed this way, sir,' Lorenzo kept his head bent humbly, thankful for the shabby robe that covered his hair. With luck they would ride on by thinking him merely a poor fisherman.

'How long have you been on this road?'

'All day, sir.'

The man looked back at his companions, who had brought their mounts to a halt, and an argument began between them. Some were for returning to the village, others for going on.

'The old woman lied,' one of the horsemen said. 'We should return and persuade her to tell us the truth. Perhaps if we split her lying tongue the fisherman will speak. The beating you gave him did not break him—but it may be different if you turn your attention to her.'

Lorenzo listened in horror. He could not condemn Salome and her husband to the kind of torture these beasts might inflict. His sense of honour would not permit him to escape while others suffered in his place. Throwing back his hood, he looked up at the leader.

'I am Lorenzo Santorini,' he said. 'I am the one you seek.'

For a moment the man stared at him in stunned disbelief, then a gleam of greed came to his rascally face.

'We have searched for you many weeks,' he said and grinned. 'Rachid has promised much gold to he who finds you.'

'Then you are a rich man,' Lorenzo said, his face cold

with pride. 'Do not waste time with the old ones. I have friends searching for me. They are only a few leagues distant from us.'

An expression of consternation came into the man's eyes. He turned to his companions, some of whom had already dismounted and were eyeing Lorenzo warily. They clearly expected him to put up a fight, but he stood unresisting, letting them take him. Their greed for Rachid's gold would save Salome and her husband from further suffering.

Lorenzo offered his wrists for binding. He expected to be led behind the horses as in a Roman triumph, and was surprised when a mount was provided. Their leader took the reins of his horse, but he was neither abused nor insulted.

'Rachid wants you alive,' his captor told him. 'You do well not to struggle, for I have no wish to harm you.'

Lorenzo inclined his head but said no more. His pride would keep him strong. Most men broke under torture. All he could hope for was a quick death.

'Goodbye, Kathryn,' he murmured softly. 'Forgive me, my love. I would have come to you, but the price was too high.'

Kathryn watched as the cliffs of her homeland came into view. Soon they would be home and her heart was breaking. She had been forced to admit that Lorenzo was dead, for if not he would have found a way to contact his friends these past weeks.

Charles was remaining in Rome. He had refused to give up hope and Michael had promised to continue the search, but she knew that neither of them truly believed that he would be found. There had been no trace of him since his capture.

'Lorenzo, my love…' Kathryn blinked back her tears as her father came to join her on the deck, looking towards the shore and the foaming water as it rushed against a coastline that could be treacherous and had sent many a sailor to a watery grave.

'We shall soon be home, my dear,' he said, noting her pale face and sad eyes, purpled by shadows that robbed her of the carefree beauty which had been hers. 'Perhaps then you may feel better.'

'I do not believe that I shall ever feel better. I loved him, Father. I loved him so much that…' She left the words unfinished. In truth, she wished that she might die, but she did not want to hurt her father.

'I understand your grief, Kathryn. When your mother died I thought that my world was at an end, but I learned to live without her. I took solace in my children.'

'I have no children.'

'But you are young enough to marry again. Lorenzo left you a fortune, so the lawyers tell us, though as yet we have no details. You will have no trouble in finding another husband, Kathryn.'

She did not want another husband, and talk of the fortune Lorenzo had left her was anathema to her. No money could ever heal the hurt inside her!

'Please do not speak of it,' she begged. 'Money means nothing. I shall never marry again.'

'I pray you will not speak so foolishly,' her father said, a note of anger or distress in his voice. 'Your grief is natural, daughter, but it will pass in time. Believe me, you will be happy again.'

Kathryn turned away. Her father did not understand. She had given her whole self to Lorenzo. Without him she was only half a woman. She could never love again and she did not wish to marry without love.

Sir John saw the grief in her face and wished that he had never allowed her to travel with Charles Mountfitchet. He cursed the ill luck that had caused her to marry a man he thought unsuitable. Charles was a fool to believe in Santorini's tale. No doubt it was a ploy to inherit the estate and the title. Santorini had money, but to be an English lord was something many men might aspire to, he imagined. And the man had lost many ships during the war. He had probably thought that it was a way to restore his losses.

Having never met Kathryn's husband—something that rankled in his mind—he had no way of knowing whether Santorini was wealthy enough to bear those losses. He had taken a dislike to the man he considered had stolen his daughter. In his opinion, it was for the best that Kathryn should be left a widow. He did not like to see her grieving, but she would get over it in time. And he did not have much time left to him. Before he died, and he knew that it was coming slowly, he must see his daughter safe—even if it meant forcing her to obey him.

Kathryn could not read her father's thoughts, but she sensed that he did not sympathise with her love for Lorenzo. At the moment she felt too distressed to argue with her father. As time passed he would surely accept her decision, for she could never remarry.

Her heart had died with Lorenzo, for she felt that he must be dead. Only death would have kept him from returning to Rome.

Lorenzo could not believe that he was still alive. Two weeks had passed since he was captured and as yet he had not been ill treated, nor had he been summoned to Rachid's presence. He had expected it would happen immediately and that he would first be humiliated and then tortured, but thus far his jailers had given him food, water and a grudging respect.

He was confined to a room that had bars at the windows and the door was kept locked at all times, other than when his jailer brought him food. Yet it was not the filthy dungeon he had expected to be cast into and he wore no chains about his wrists or ankles. Indeed, he had been given all he needed for his comfort, including water to wash, clean clothes and a soft divan on which to sleep. He had everything he needed other than his freedom.

What was in Rachid's mind? Lorenzo wondered. Was his enemy being fiendishly clever, lulling him into a state of acceptance before inflicting some terrible torture?

He paced the room restlessly. Thoughts of escape were constantly in his mind and yet he hesitated. Rachid was planning something. Perhaps he was like a cat toying with a mouse, daring Lorenzo to try and escape.

He tensed as the door opened. His guards were always regular with his meals, but this was the middle of the afternoon. Something was about to happen.

Lorenzo was fully alert. This might be his only chance to escape. He resolved to try if there was any slip on the part of his guards. Salome and her husband were no longer involved. It was merely his own life at stake now and he would prefer a quick death.

A man entered the room, surprising Lorenzo as his body tensed. It was not the guard who had been bringing him food and water, but a much older man, richly dressed with a bright gold turban.

'My master requests the pleasure of your company, lord.'

Lorenzo smiled grimly. So the summons had come at last.

'Requests?' he asked, a wry twist to his mouth. 'And supposing I choose to decline your master's invitation—what then?' A gleam of defiance was in his eyes, for if he must die he would prefer that it came swiftly.

'That would be a cause of much regret to my master, sir.' The old man smiled oddly. 'I believe you will find this meeting to your advantage. You have nothing to fear.'

'Do you expect me to believe that?'

'You have my word. I am Mustafa Kasim and I am guaranteeing your life—and your safety.'

Looking into his eyes, Lorenzo was puzzled. This was not what he had expected from Rachid. However, life had taught him to be a fair judge of character and somehow he believed this man, believed in his honesty.

'Very well, I shall accept your word, sir.'

'Thank you,' Mustafa Kasim said. 'Please follow me if you will. My master is waiting.'

Lorenzo followed in his wake, walking through what seemed the endless rooms and passages of Rachid's palace. The walls were built of thick grey stone, the floors tiled with a dull grey marble. Even on the warmest summer day this place would strike cold into the bones, but Lorenzo held himself erect, refusing to shiver.

He could not know what would happen when he finally came face to face with his enemy, but clearly he was not to be tortured or executed just yet. Perhaps Rachid had decided to hold him for ransom.

Until this moment Lorenzo had expected his enemy to be ruthless in exacting payment for all the ships sunk, the slaves rescued and given their freedom. He had believed that Rachid must hate him, for he had waged a merciless war on his enemy and could expect no less.

Mustafa had stopped outside an impressive door, which was fashioned of heavy carved wood studded with iron. He rapped on it once with a metal wand he carried and the heavy panels swung back, manipulated by two huge black slaves dressed in rich clothes. The room they were about to enter was very different from the rest of the fortress. The walls were hung with an array of dazzling silks in vibrant colours and the floor was covered with thick silk rugs. Several divans stood about the room, but there were also tables made of alabaster and silver, statues of marble and of gold, a veritable fortune of small items that were of immense value everywhere, almost as if a magpie had gathered them together. Clearly Rachid was very rich.

'My lord,' Mustafa said and bowed respectfully. 'He you have commanded is here.'

Lorenzo glanced towards what appeared to be a kind of throne. Rachid lived, as a king might, in his own little empire. The throne was made of solid silver and decorated with precious jewels. He knew a desire to laugh at such ridiculous opulence, but controlled it as the man, dressed in the robes of a caliph, rose and came towards him. Looking into his face, he was surprised. This man was not the enemy he had fought for so many years but his son: the young man he had exchanged for the Spanish girl.

'So we meet again.' The younger man smiled oddly, pleased by Lorenzo's confusion. 'You look surprised, Signor Santorini. You did not expect to see me?'

'I expected your father.'

'My father?' Hassan laughed. 'I am sorry to disappoint you, *signor.* My father cannot greet you. He died two weeks ago, on the day of your arrival here.'

'Rachid is dead?'

'Have I not said so? You must forgive me for keeping you waiting so long, *signor.* My father's death was unexpected and caused me a few problems.' He waved his hand to indicate the wealth in the room. 'There were others who wished to share in these things, which are rightfully mine. They have been dealt with, but it took a little time.'

Lorenzo repressed a shudder. For a moment he saw something in the younger man's eyes that made him go cold. At that moment there was no doubting he was Rachid's son.

'However, you wish to know why you are here?'

'I believed I was brought here at Rachid's command?'

'He intended to have you killed...very slowly I believe. You forced him to exchange a woman he wanted for me— a poor exchange, in his opinion, but one he was obliged to make.' Hassan's eyes glinted with anger, and he seemed to be waiting for Lorenzo's reply, but when none came he went on. 'However, I am not my father. I like beautiful things, as you see. Women, jewels, silks—all these things please me. I do not like blood. My father forced me to command one of his galleys, but now he is dead.' Something in Hassan's eyes told Lorenzo that he was pleased rather than distressed at the fact of his father's death. 'You could have killed me when you took our ships. Will you tell me why you spared me?'

'I thought that you did not deserve to die. You are not your father, his sins are not yours.'

'No, I carry my own sins, not his.' Again Hassan's eyes glittered. 'You were merciful when your men would have killed me. Now I shall be merciful. You gave me my life, I give you yours. You may leave my house when you choose. One of my galleys will take you wherever you wish to go in safety, that is my promise to you.'

'If you mean that, I would go to Rome.'

'Ah, yes. You have taken a wife.' Hassan nodded. 'I too am about to take my first wife. We have much in common, Signor Santorini. You will do me the honour of dining with me this evening. Tomorrow you may leave.' He indicated one of the divans. 'Please sit, *signor.* Tell me about your wife.'

Lorenzo sat, thinking furiously. He did not yet quite believe in his good fortune. This might be some deceit that was intended to lull him into a false sense of security so for the moment he must be very careful. Hassan was Rachid's son and might be capable of the same cruelty as his father. It seemed that he was sincere, but Lorenzo would remain alert until he was safely back in Rome. Rome meant Kathryn. He smiled and looked at the younger man.

'It is because of my wife that I sent you back to your father...'

* * *

'Do we really have to have such a large gathering?' Kathryn asked. She had no desire to sit down to a banquet with thirty or more guests, nor did she wish to dance and make merry.

'We are celebrating your brother's betrothal,' Sir John said, giving her a severe look. 'You would not wish to appear lacking in your good wishes towards Philip and Mary Jane?'

'No, Father, of course not. Mary Jane is a sweet girl and I have told Philip how happy I am for him, but—'

'I shall hear no excuses, Kathryn. I have forgiven you for your earlier neglect of duty towards me, but I insist you oblige me in this matter.'

Kathryn turned away, feeling his harshness like the sting of a whip. She had never known her father to be so stern and it hurt her deeply. He did not seem to understand that she was suffering terribly. She loved Lorenzo so much that sometimes her grief was almost impossible to bear.

Leaving her father, she fetched her cloak and went out walking. It was bitterly cold, the wind whipping about her slight body, tugging at her clothes as if it wished to tear them away. Kathryn shivered, her face pinched and white. It was so much colder here on this Cornish coast than in Rome; there the winds had been warm, the air perfumed by sweet flowers, and she longed to be back there. She shuddered as she felt the icy wind touch her face, glancing up as the storm clouds gathered overhead.

Such grey skies! How could she bear to go on living in this cold grey world without Lorenzo? It would be so much easier to die, for if there was an afterlife, as the priests promised, she might be with her lover.

Her footsteps took her beyond her father's estate, to the cliffs above the cove where her beloved Dickon had been stolen from her so many years ago.

Was it possible that Lorenzo and Dickon were the same person? Charles Mountfitchet certainly believed it was so and Kathryn recalled the way her heart had recognised him the first time she gazed into his eyes—eyes so blue that no others compared. Yet she had rejected the thought, believing him a highborn Venetian, the true son of Antonio Santorini. She had not been willing to accept that such a man could be her lost love, and yet now…

It seemed that she had lost her love for the second time. But why should she go on alone? Why should she bear this pain another moment? She had only to take two steps forward and she would go crashing down into that swirling venomous sea, where she would be instantly crushed against the jutting rocks.

'Kathryn? Kathryn! No, you must not!'

She turned as she heard the voice, her face suddenly alight with hope. For a moment she thought the man hurrying towards her was Lorenzo, but then she saw that it was Michael and she went to meet him, her heart racing. Perhaps he had news!

'Kathryn!' Michael said, his face anguished by concern. He had thought she meant to jump. 'I thought for a moment that you meant to…'

'Have you news?' she asked, her hand reaching out to him in supplication. 'Have you heard from him?'

'I am sorry.' He looked at her sadly, devastated that he

must tell her what would hurt her. 'I have been told that he was shot while trying to escape and fell into the sea. I believe our search is at an end.'

'No…' Kathryn moaned and swayed as the despair swept over her, engulfing her senses. 'Lorenzo, no!' She had known it must be so, but to hear the details was unbearable. 'My love…'

Michael caught her to him lest she fall. He held her as she sobbed out her grief against his chest, his lips murmuring words of comfort against the perfume of her hair.

'My sweet love,' he said softly. 'Forgive me. I know it is Lorenzo you love, but I am here. I would love and protect you, heal your hurts.'

'I cannot…' She looked up at him, her eyes dark with grief. 'I shall never love another. Never marry again.'

'Hush, Kathryn. I do not ask it. I ask only to be your friend and perhaps one day you will look on me kindly. When your grief has healed.'

Kathryn could not answer him. Her heart felt as if it had been cleaved in two. Everyone spoke of her grief healing one day, but they did not understand. No one knew how she felt. Michael was being kind, and she loved him as a friend, but he could never take Lorenzo's place in her heart. It was impossible.

'Come,' she said, lifting her head, pride battling with the urge to give way to this pain inside her. She must try to put off this heavy grief. She must make an effort for the sake of her friends and family. 'We must go back to the house, sir. My father will wish to speak with you.'

Charles was at dinner when he heard a flurry outside the door. The sound of voices raised in excitement and disbelief alerted him and he was on his feet, expectant as Lorenzo walked into the room.

'Praise be to God!' he cried, his voice husky with emotion. Tears stung his eyes and spilled unchecked as he went to embrace his son. 'I feared I might never see you again, my son. They told us you had been shot while trying to escape in the port of Algiers.'

'And so I was,' Lorenzo told him, his eyes bright with devilish laughter. 'But it seems that God must have been looking after me, for I was plucked from the sea more dead than alive by a poor fisherman and nursed back to health by that man's good wife.'

'We shall reward them,' Charles said. 'They shall never know poverty again.'

'It is as good as done,' Lorenzo said. He looked long and deep into his father's face. 'You have suffered for my sake, Father, but I shall try to cause you no more worry. Rachid is dead and I have no quarrel with his son. Hassan and I have made our peace. We shall make war on each other's ships no more.'

'Come, share the meal I was about to eat and tell me the whole story.'

'Yes, of course.' Lorenzo glanced about the room and frowned. 'You are alone. Where is Kathryn?'

'Her father came to Rome, looking for her. He had not received her letter telling him that you were married and was angry, I think. When the news came that you had been lost he was convinced that you were dead and insisted that she return home to England with him. Kathryn did not wish to go, Lorenzo, but she felt she must obey her father.'

Lorenzo's eyes glinted with anger and frustration. 'She should not have gone with him,' he said harshly. 'Her place was with you at this time.'

'Do not be angry with her, my son,' Charles pleaded. 'I know that she grieved for you terribly. It broke her heart when she learned what had happened to you.'

'And yet she did not wait to see if I would return.'

Lorenzo had been on fire to see Kathryn and his frustration made him harsh.

'I told you, her father made her go.'

'I might have expected more loyalty from my wife. She might have defied him if she had wished.'

'I swear to you that she did not leave willingly.'

Lorenzo nodded. 'At least you stayed, Father.'

'I had nowhere else to go. My one hope was that you would come back to me. I prayed for it, planned for it— and it seems that my prayers have been answered. You are alive and I shall thank God for it the rest of my days.'

'Yes, I truly believe that we have been blessed.' Lorenzo smiled. The bitterness from the past had disappeared with his doubts about his identity. He knew himself this man's son, remembered much of his lost youth. 'Do you recall when we used to go hawking in the woods at Mount-fitchet? Sometimes I would follow the hawks for miles and you waited for me to return. I always did in the end, though you had thought me lost.'

'Yes, you always came back,' Charles replied and smiled at him. 'But you spoke confidently, as though you had remembered all?'

'I think it may have been the blow to my head when I was captured, or perhaps that the abduction brought back memories, forcing me to face the past. Perhaps I had forgotten because I did not want to remember.' His father nodded, understanding. 'Memories had been coming to me in drifts for a while, but always vague, seeming like dreams. I did not know I was Richard Mountfitchet before I was captured. I suspected it might be so, but now I know for certain.'

'I was certain in Sicily,' Charles said and looked at him steadily. 'I think when you were a boy I did not always show my faith and love for you, Lorenzo, but in future I intend that it shall be different. God has granted me a second chance and I shall make the most of it.'

'We have both been lucky. I see now that I might have fared far worse than I did. Something kept me alive and perhaps that was God's love.'

Charles nodded, but said no more—Lorenzo must find his own way back to the faith he had lost. 'So what will you do now, my son?'

'It was in my mind to return to England with Kathryn. I thought we should visit her father before settling in Venice. That is still my intention. My life is here now, sir. England does not have much to offer me—though it might be different if you were there. What are your own plans?'

'As we discussed them in Sicily. I believe I shall stay here in Rome until you return, Lorenzo. I have travelled enough of late and I like it here.'

'I shall leave my business affairs to you until I return, Father,' Lorenzo said. 'But before I leave I must speak to Michael about the future. If I am to make changes, I would have him with me.'

Charles hesitated, looking awkward. 'Michael is not

here. He went to England. I believe it was his intention to see Kathryn. We heard that you were shot trying to escape and I think he means to tell her that there is no hope of finding you alive.'

What he left unsaid was his conviction that Michael was in love with Kathryn and would have her for himself if he could. It could not help matters, for Lorenzo was already angry enough. He just hoped that he would not arrive too late.

'Then I must not delay,' Lorenzo said, a brooding expression in his eyes. He needed no telling that Michael cared for Kathryn—he had observed it himself. 'I shall spend this evening with you and then I must sail for England.'

Chapter Twelve

Kathryn looked at herself in her hand mirror. She was wearing a gown of green silk that her father had presented her with as a gift especially for that evening. She had asked that she be allowed to wear the black velvet she had chosen for her mourning, but Sir John had given her a stern look.

'You will not come to your brother's betrothal wearing black. It becomes you ill, Kathryn, and would be seen as an insult by Philip's betrothed and her family. You are a young and beautiful woman. You should make the most of your beauty, daughter.'

'Do not forget that I am in mourning for my husband, Father.'

'You grieve for a man by the name of Lorenzo Santorini, daughter. If Charles is right, that man does not exist. Therefore, I am not certain that your marriage was ever a true one. However, you *are* my daughter and as such will not disgrace me by appearing before our guests as a black crow.'

'That is unfair!' Kathryn cried, hurt almost beyond bearing by her father's unkindness. Why was he being so cruel to her? Had she not enough to bear without this hurt? 'Lorenzo married me in good faith. I was and am his true wife.'

'You wed without my blessing and I could dispute it if I wished,' he reminded her coldly. 'You will oblige me by forgetting that unhappy period of your life. It is my sincere hope that you may marry again soon.'

'I do not wish to marry.'

'It is my wish that you shall be properly settled, Kathryn. People will whisper behind their hands about this odd marriage, but if you marry again they will be silenced. It is in my mind that a marriage shall be arranged by the end of your official period of mourning, and the contract may be made before that if we choose.'

Kathryn did not answer him. She could not for fear that she might say something that would anger or hurt him and cause a wider breach between them. She was greatly upset by what she considered his harshness and his words had brought her to the edge of tears. How could he force her to think of marrying again when her heart was broken? It was a cruel suggestion and she could hardly believe that the father she had loved so much could do this to her.

But she must not let anyone see her tears this evening. It was to be a special celebration for her brother, of whom she was fond. Raising her head, Kathryn prepared to go downstairs to greet her father's guests. She must be brave and smile this evening, for Philip was to be betrothed to a girl he admired and liked.

'Do you love Mary Jane?' Kathryn had asked her brother earlier that day.

'Love her?' Philip had wrinkled his brow, giving her a strange look. 'I am not sure what you mean by love, Kathryn. I have known Mary Jane all my life. We are friends and I think her a sweet, pretty girl who will make me a good wife and bear my children. She is of good family and will bring me a small estate as her portion. I do not think I can ask more of my marriage.'

Kathryn had not known how to answer that declaration. She could never be content with such an arrangement, though she knew that it was commonplace amongst men and women of her class. It was not for her, though if she had never known Lorenzo perhaps...but she had! Her heart contracted with the familiar ache. It might have been better if she had never met him. She would rather die now than live with another man as her husband. She belonged to Lorenzo and could never be another's.

The betrothal ceremony was over. Philip and Mary Jane were dancing while everyone else looked on, smiling in approval, feet tapping to the merry music the minstrels played.

'It will be your turn next, Kathryn,' said a lady standing to her left. 'Sir John will find you a husband, my dear, and you may put all this nonsense behind you.'

'I am still in mourning for my husband, Mistress Feathers.'

'Oh, you will soon discover that one man is very much as another. I have been married three times and there was nothing to choose between them. Money, power and children will bring their own content. Love is merely a myth.'

Kathryn felt her throat closing and the tears were close. This insufferable woman knew nothing of love! She could feel the grief welling inside and knew she could not stay in this room another moment.

She turned and left the hall, which echoed with laughter and music. Snatching a cloak that lay carelessly on a chest in the anteroom, she went out into the chill of the night air and began to walk, tears trickling down her cheeks as the grief spilled over.

'Lorenzo, my love,' she whispered to the night. 'Come back to me…oh, please, come back to me. I cannot bear this life without you.'

'Kathryn! Please wait!'

She turned as she heard Michael's voice calling to her. She had hoped to be alone, but the one person she could bear to be near at the moment was Michael. He had been with them in Venice and in Rome. He understood her better than any other, and he cared for her—which it seemed her father did not.

'You should not be out here on this bitter night,' Michael scolded her. 'It looks as if it will snow before morning. If you continue like this, you will become ill.'

'If I am ill, my father cannot force me to marry a man I neither know nor love.'

'He would surely not be so unkind!'

'He has spoken of it. Everyone tells me I must forget Lorenzo and put the past behind me, but I cannot. I love him. I shall always love him.'

'But to force you into marriage…' Michael hesitated. He had not intended to speak so soon, for he knew that Kathryn was suffering. But he had fallen deeply in love with her during the time she had nursed him back to health, and he could not bear to see her so unhappy. 'Your father has been courteous to me. Do you think he would accept an offer for your hand from me?'

'I cannot marry you. It would not be fair to you, Michael. I like you very much. You are a good friend— but my heart is with Lorenzo. I fear it always will be.'

'I meant only to save you more unhappiness. I would take you back to Rome, to your friends. You were happy there, Kathryn.' He moved towards her, looking into her face, her eyes, his hand reaching out to touch her cheek. 'It would not be a true marriage at first. I would be patient, Kathryn. I would wait until you felt able to be my wife in truth.'

'Oh, Michael,' she said brokenly. 'You make me ashamed. You are so good, so kind—but if I accepted your offer I might ruin your life. Supposing I could never love you, could never give you what you wanted?'

Tears were trickling down her cheeks. She could taste their salt on her lips. Michael put his arms gently about her, not imprisoning her but holding her in a comforting embrace, his lips moving against the fragrance of her hair.

'I love you, Kathryn. I would wait for ever and count it a blessing to be of service to you.'

She gazed up at him, tears hovering like crystals on her lashes. 'But you spoke of asking Isabella Rinaldi to be your wife?'

'My father wishes me to marry and I must oblige him, for he grows old and it is important to him. Isabella is pretty and I like her—but I love you. I have loved you since I first saw you, but I knew you saw only Lorenzo. I did not imagine that there was hope for me then…' He left the rest unsaid, for to remind her would only cause her more distress.

'Oh, Michael.' Kathryn wiped away her tears. 'I pray you, give me a little time to think. Perhaps…I do not know.'

She could not bring herself to say she would marry him, and yet she would rather it was Michael if she must marry again. Yet was it fair to take what he was offering her, knowing that she would never be able to give him more than second best?

'Say no more for the moment,' Michael said and smiled, taking her by the hand. 'Come back with me now, dearest one. I cannot let you walk alone in this bitter chill. Lorenzo would not demand that your life be sacrificed to grief, Kathryn.'

'I wish I was in Rome.' Kathryn sighed. 'It was so much warmer.' She smiled, feeling better than she had in weeks, allowing him to lead her towards the light and heat of the great hall.

The music had stopped quite suddenly. People had started talking, whispering excitedly one to another. She sensed that something had happened to change the mood of the evening. Kathryn's nerves tingled, feeling a prickling sensation at the back of her neck as Michael led her into the room. Everyone seemed to be looking in the same direction, at something—someone! Her heart stood still as heads suddenly turned towards her and Michael, and then the guests were parting, like the sea for the Israelites departing from Egypt, suddenly silent. She gasped as she saw that a man dressed all in black was walking towards her.

She felt as if she were in a dream, her head spinning as

she saw him clearly. Her senses were reeling. Could it be—or was she in some kind of feverish nightmare? Her face had drained of colour and suddenly the ground came zooming up to her. As she fainted, two men moved to catch her.

It was Lorenzo whose arms surrounded her, sweeping her up as she would have fallen, lifting her effortlessly. His face was grim, eyes dark with anger as he looked at Michael and saw the jealousy that the other man was unable to hide.

'She is mine. Do not forget that.'

'We thought you dead. Kathryn has grieved enough.' Michael was defensive, angry in his disappointment, for he knew that he had lost all chance of her. 'I merely sought to comfort her.'

'We shall speak later.'

Lorenzo turned away, carrying Kathryn's limp form in his arms. He had such an air of command, such burning anger in every line of his face that when he demanded Kathryn's chamber, servants hurried to conduct him there.

Sir John watched the little scene from across the room. He had hoped for a match between Michael dei Ignacio and his daughter, but one look at Lorenzo's face had told him that it would be both futile and dangerous to attempt to deny him. He had come to claim his wife and nothing would stop him.

Sir John moved to confront him as he strode from the hall. 'My daughter, sir?'

'Is safe enough with me.'

'You wed her under a false name.'

'Not so. Antonio Santorini adopted me. I am legally his

heir and bear his name. My father has agreed that I shall keep it at least until I inherit his title—which I pray will be many years in the future.'

Kathryn moaned and fluttered her eyelashes.

'Take her to her chamber,' Sir John said, a hint of bitterness in his voice. 'She has made herself ill with her grief.'

Lorenzo inclined his head. He followed the servants up the stairs to Kathryn's chamber. Servants fluttered ahead, clearly impressed by this stern-faced, aristocratic man who had declared himself her lawful husband to an astounded company. Covers were pulled back so that he might deposit his precious burden on clean linen. But when they lingered, their eyes large with curiosity, he dismissed them with an imperious wave of his hand.

Kathryn was stirring. Her lashes were wet. She had been crying earlier—and yet she had been holding Michael's hand when he first saw her enter the hall. He felt a surge of murderous jealousy against his friend. Had Michael stolen her love from him? For a moment as he saw them together in the hall he had contemplated murder.

Kathryn's eyelids moved. She opened her eyes, gazing up at him for a moment in bewilderment as though she did not believe what she saw, closing them once more as a tear squeezed from beneath her lashes.

'I am sorry that the sight of me made you faint, Kathryn.'

She opened her eyes again. 'Is it truly you, Lorenzo? They told me there was no hope—that you were dead.'

'And if I had been?' His voice was made harsh by anger. 'Would you have married Michael?'

'No!' She edged herself up against the pillows. The faintness had gone now, but she had a nasty taste in her mouth and her head ached. 'Why are you looking at me like that? You know I love you. You must know it!'

'Do you? You had been somewhere with Michael—in the midst of your brother's betrothal feast you slipped away with him. Why would you do that if you were not lovers? It is some months since you thought me lost, but I had hoped you would not have forgotten me so soon.'

'You cannot think that I would betray you so easily?' Kathryn was shocked, hurt. He had looked at her this way once before, as if he hated her. He blamed her for what had happened to him. 'My father said that I must marry again. I did not wish to—but Michael said he would be patient...' She faltered as she saw the fury in his eyes. He was so very angry! 'He did ask me to marry him a marriage in name only for the moment. I told him I needed time to consider.'

'You could not believe he meant that?' Lorenzo's voice lashed at her like a leather thong. 'He would take you any way he could, but he wants you the way a man wants his woman. The way I want you, Kathryn.' His hot eyes scorched her, making her tremble all over.

'I did not wish to marry again.'

'Yet you would have let them persuade you had I not returned. I thought your love stronger, Kathryn.'

'It is,' she said. He must believe her! She gave him a pleading, desperate look. 'You know I love you. I have always loved you.'

'Even when we were children?' he asked. 'You forgot your poor Dickon when you fell in love with Lorenzo—

and you would have forgotten him as easily again once Michael was your husband.'

The reproach in his voice stung her, but he was unfair. 'That is not true! You know it isn't, Lorenzo. I am yours. I have always been yours…'

'Yes, you are mine, that much is true.' He rose from his seat on the side of her bed, causing her to look alarmed.

'Pray do not leave me!'

'You need to rest. We shall talk another time, for now I shall call your women to attend you. In the morning we leave for Mountfitchet.' His eyes were cold, remote. 'We are married, Kathryn, though your father would have had it otherwise. You will come with me. I do not give up what is mine, nor do I easily forgive.'

Kathryn stared after him as he left the room. He was insisting that she go with him and yet he was angry with her. He blamed her for his capture, because his love for her had made him careless, and he had decided to withdraw from her again.

She had longed, prayed for his return, hoping that he was alive despite all the odds, yet now that he had come to her, he had closed the door, shutting her out once more. It could only mean that he no longer loved her.

The journey to Mountfitchet Hall took only half a day's journey by horseback. It was bitterly cold, little flurries of snowflakes drifting into their faces, but not yet settling on the hard ground. Kathryn rode by her husband's side, glancing at the stern cast of his features from time to time. Two of her women and ten of Lorenzo's own men accompanied them.

When they reached Mountfitchet, she noticed that Lorenzo seemed to know exactly where he was going and wondered if he had been to the estate before coming to her father's house. They were greeted eagerly by Lord Mountfitchet's servants, who treated him respectfully as their master and seemed delighted to see him.

'Did you call here before you came to us?' she asked him when the greetings were over and they were alone in the private parlour that was situated to the right of the Great Hall.

'No, I came straight to you. Why do you ask?'

'You seem so at home here.'

'It was my home for fifteen years, Kathryn.' His eyes were intent on her face, though not as cold as the previous evening.

She opened her eyes wide in surprise. 'Have you recovered your memory? Charles told us that you had some vague memories, but you seem so sure…'

'I remember everything, Kathryn. Just as it happened.'

'You recall that day on the beach—the men who took you?' He nodded. 'Do you hate me for what happened to you?'

'Why should I hate you?' He looked puzzled.

'Because it was my fault. I dared you to go down to the beach to see what they were doing.'

'I was old enough to make up my own mind, and I knew the dangers better than you.'

'You told me to run away and fetch help while you fought them, but by the time the men looked for you it was too late. I have always blamed myself for not staying to help you fight them.'

'You were a child. What could you have done against such men? Would you rather I had let them take you too? Can you imagine what might have been your fate—where you might be now had you lived?'

Kathryn turned her head away so that he should not see her eyes, should not see the hurt he inflicted. 'Do not mock me, Lorenzo. I cannot bear it.'

'You mistake me. I do not mean to hurt you—but I should not have wished such a fate for you, that is all.'

'If you will excuse me, I should like to go to my chamber and rest.'

'Of course.' He inclined his head, respectful, cool—almost a stranger. 'I have things I must do while we are here. My father left the business of the estate for me to order as I thought fit.'

Kathryn glanced at him. 'Do you think of living here?'

'Would that please you?'

'I was happy in Rome.' She raised her head proudly. 'At least, I was happy for some of the time.'

'What does that mean, Kathryn?'

'Whatever you would like it to mean,' she said, a flash of pride in her eyes. She was suddenly angry. She had mourned him sincerely and he had no right to treat her this way! 'Since you think so ill of me I shall not try to explain.'

She turned and walked away from him, leaving the room. Her heart was racing wildly and she wondered if he would follow her, compel her to answer him, but he did not.

Why should he? He did not want her love. He found it a burden. In Rome he had told her that he had never wanted to love her. Somehow he had conquered his emotions. He had claimed her because she belonged to him, but he did not truly want her.

Alone in the room Kathryn had just vacated, Lorenzo was haunted by the scent of the perfume she had left behind her. Throughout his captivity the memory of her scent, her softness, her sweetness, had made him determined to live, and now that he was with her he could not break down this barrier between them—a barrier he knew was of his making.

Had his jealousy driven a wedge between them? He had noticed her silence on the journey, her pale face, the accusation in her beautiful eyes, and knew it was his fault. In his first anger at seeing her so close to Michael, he had been too harsh. He cursed his ill temper. He had learned to be harsh of necessity. Once, he had been a very different man. Could he be as he had once been again? Could he learn to laugh and be happy?

He must and would try to make Kathryn happy! He could not know if it was too late to recover the brief happiness they had known in Rome, but he would try to win her.

And if that was not possible? Lorenzo asked himself if he would be prepared to give her up.

No! His mind rejected the idea instantly. She was his! He would not give her up. Somehow he would make her love him again.

Kathryn was walking in the gardens when she heard her husband's voice calling to her. She stopped, waiting for him to come to her. She had seen him only at mealtimes or a brief moment in the evenings, for he had seemed to be working ever since they had arrived at Mountfitchet.

'Kathryn,' he said as he joined her, 'is it not too cold for you to be walking?'

'It is a little chilly,' she agreed. Her restless mood had driven her outside, but she would not tell him that.

'Shall we return to the house?' he said, offering her his arm. 'I have some news. A letter has come from Queen Elizabeth of England. It seems that she has heard of us and some of what has befallen us. She wishes to know more about the battle of Lepanto.'

The letter had expressed curiosity about Lorenzo too, for the Queen had heard that Corsairs had captured him from her shores, and she always took an interest in such matters. Indeed, it was said that the Queen liked to have bold and handsome young men about her.

Kathryn felt a chill about her heart. Was he going to leave her once more? 'Are you to visit the court, then?'

'We shall go together, Kathryn. It is time that I gave a little time to my wife's pleasure. We shall buy you some pretty things in London. Perhaps you would like a ring or a rope of pearls? I have given you few gifts. There was never time for such things.'

Kathryn gazed into his eyes, trying to understand this new mood. Did he not know that his love was the most precious gift he could give her? She wanted for little else.

'You were always generous, Lorenzo. I never wanted for material things when I was in Rome.'

'But I gave you nothing more. Is that what you are saying, Kathryn?'

'Sometimes you gave me more.'

'Kathryn…' He was interrupted by the arrival of a servant who came hurrying towards them, clearly the bearer of an urgent message.

'Yes, what is it?' Lorenzo was impatient, for he had believed he was at last breaking through the barrier she had been keeping in place these past days.

'A message for the lady Kathryn, sir,' the servant said. 'Sir John, her father, has been taken gravely ill and would fain speak with her once more before he dies.'

'Before he dies?' Kathryn looked at her husband in alarm. 'What has happened? I did not think him ill before we left.'

'We shall return at once,' Lorenzo said as he saw her concern. 'Do not worry, my love. I am sure this seems worse than it is.'

He had called her his love, and in such a voice! Kathryn's heart beat wildly—but for the moment she could not think of herself. Her father was ill and she must go to him.

Tears were in her eyes as she let Lorenzo hurry her into the house. She had not been happy in her father's house these past weeks for he had seemed unlike the loving father she had known and loved, but she could not bear that he should die with bad feeling between them.

Sir John was lying with his eyes closed when Kathryn entered the room. As she approached the bed, he opened them and looked at her.

'Kathryn, my dearest child—forgive me.'

'Father…' The tears were very close though she struggled to hold them back. 'There is nothing to forgive. I love you.'

'I have been harsh with you,' he said, his voice little more than a whisper as she went to his side, reaching for his hand to hold it gently in her own. 'It was only because I wanted to make sure you were safe when I was gone. I was fearful for you if I should die before you were wed.'

'You must not die, Father. I love you. I do not want you to die.'

'I have known for some months that I could not live many years, my dearest child. It is the reason I made you come home with me. I could not leave you alone and defenceless in Rome and I believed if I could see you safely wed to a good man I could die in peace. You might have lived in your brother's house, but that would be no life for you. Now that you have your husband to protect you, I may die easily—if you will forgive my unkindness to you, daughter?'

Kathryn bent to kiss his lips. 'I love you,' she said. 'You have always been a good and loving father to me. It hurt me when I did not understand your harshness, but now…' She bit back the sob that rose to her lips. 'If my forgiveness will ease you, you have it, my dearest father.'

'Thank you, Kathryn,' he said and smiled. 'Sit here by my side for a little. It is good to know you are near.'

Kathryn's eyes stung with the tears she would not allow to fall. She had felt estranged from her father because of his apparent intention to force her to marry against her will, but now that she understood his reasons, all she could feel was grief that he was dying, and regret that she had not seen the signs of illness in him.

She sat with him for most of the night, leaving his bedside only when her brother came to take her place, insisting that she must rest for a few hours.

'Lorenzo says you must get some sleep,' Philip told her when he came to take her place. 'I shall call you if need be.'

'I had no idea he was so ill.'

'Do not blame yourself, Kathryn. He hid it well, even from me in the beginning. I begged him to let me come to Venice and find you, but he insisted on making the journey himself. I think it took the last of his strength. He has been failing ever since you returned.'

She had been too caught up in her grief for Lorenzo to notice! Regret mingled with her grief as she went to her bedchamber. She had hoped that Lorenzo might come to her there, for she needed his arms about her, but he did not. For a while she lay sleepless, tossing and turning in the feather bed, and then at last she slept.

Lorenzo came to her the next morning as she was dressing. Her heart caught with fright as she saw his grave expression.

'Is he worse?'

'He is certainly no better. I have spoken with the doctors and they do not hold much hope of his recovery. I am sorry, Kathryn. I know this must cause you pain.'

'Yes, it does,' she admitted. 'We had not been on the best of terms of late, and that makes it harder somehow.'

'You had quarrelled with him because of me?'

'Yes…' She smothered a sob. 'I did not understand why he wanted me to marry again so soon. He thought it would make me safe when he was gone.'

'I am sorry to have been the cause of anger between you.'

'There is no need,' she replied. 'I was grieving for you and because of that I did not notice that he was ill.'

'Did it hurt you so much when you thought I was dead?' His eyes were on her face, seeking out the truth.

'Yes, of course,' she said, looking steadily into his eyes. 'It broke my heart. I thought it would have been better if I had died. One day I walked to the top of the cliffs where…I think I might have thrown myself into the sea then if Michael had not come.'

'He saved your life, then?'

'He stopped me from committing a sinful act, for it is a sin to take one's own life—but still I had nothing to live for until you returned to me.'

'Kathryn…' His voice was hoarse with emotion, remorse strong in him. 'And then I was harsh to you. Forgive me if you can. When I saw you enter the hall holding Michael's hand I thought the worst, and—'

He was prevented from continuing by the arrival of a servant.

'You are wanted, Mistress Kathryn,' the girl said. 'Sir John is dying and asks for you.'

'Oh, no!' Kathryn cried and Lorenzo caught her hand, holding it tightly. 'Come with me, please?' She gave him a look of such appeal that it almost tore the heart from him.

'Of course,' he said. 'I shall always be there when you need me, Kathryn. We shall not be parted again in this life if I can help it.'

She smiled at him, but her eyes were filled with tears. They hurried to Sir John's bedchamber. It was obvious that he was failing, for he looked deathly pale as he lay with his eyes closed, and Philip was kneeling by the bed, head bent in prayer. Sir John opened his eyes as Kathryn approached.

'My dearest child,' he said. 'Come, kiss me one last time.'

She went to his side, bending over him and pressing her lips to the papery softness of his cheek, her tears spilling over.

'Ah, do not cry, my dearest,' Sir John said. 'I am ready to die now that you are safe.' He looked beyond her to Lorenzo. 'You, sir. I pray that you love my daughter as much as she loves you.'

'I love her more than I have ever loved anyone.'

'Then I am content.'

Sir John closed his eyes. He had been holding Kathryn's hand, but his fingers lost their grip and fell away.

She gave a little sob as she realised he had stopped breathing, but then Lorenzo was there beside her. He drew her gently to her feet and into his arms, holding her as she wept against his shoulder.

'He is at peace now,' he said to comfort her.

'He is with our mother,' Philip said. 'I think it was what he wanted.' He bent over his father, closed his eyes and placed coins over them, and then drew the sheet over him. 'We should leave him to the women now.'

Her husband and brother led Kathryn from the room. She was glad of Lorenzo's arm about her waist, supporting her, but for the moment she wanted to be alone. The tears were draining her and she had no strength to fight them.

'Would you excuse me for a little?' she asked. 'I need to be alone for a while.'

'Yes, if it is your wish.'

Lorenzo watched her walk away from him, her back straight, head high. His heart ached for her and would have offered comfort if she had asked, but it seemed that she preferred to be alone.

She had told him that she loved him still, but he felt very alone at that moment. Perhaps in her heart she had not quite forgiven him.

Kathryn wept until there were no more tears left in her. She felt drained, exhausted, and fell into a deep sleep. When she woke again it was night. A fire had been lit in her chamber and someone had placed a coverlet over her, but the bed was empty beside her.

Suddenly, she wanted Lorenzo here with her. She had needed to be alone to let go of her grief, but now she longed for the comfort of his strong arms about her. He had not come to her, but she would go to him.

Throwing back the covers, she got out of bed. She went across to the fire to light a taper and touched it to a candle in her chamber-stick. She was approaching the door when it opened and Lorenzo entered. He stared at her in silence for a moment.

'I thought you were sleeping.'

'I was.' She drew a deep breath, then continued, 'But when I woke I wanted you. Will you not lie beside me, Lorenzo? It is a long time since we were together as man and wife.'

'I was not sure you wanted that.'

'How could you doubt it? Have I not always welcomed you to my bed?'

'I would not blame you if you hated me,' he said, his deep blue eyes intent on her face, his expression grave but questioning. 'It was because of me that you were kidnapped. I was unkind to you in Rome when I feared to let myself love you and then I was the cause of an estrangement with your father...'

'Hush, my love.' Kathryn moved towards him, her perfume seeming to surround him, capturing his senses. She put her fingers to his lips, smiling up at him so tenderly that he caught his breath. 'I have sometimes been angry with you, and sometimes I have broken my heart for the loss of you, but from the moment I first looked into your eyes in Venice I have loved you. My heart knew you as Dickon then, though my mind would not have it so. But Lorenzo Santorini or Richard Mountfitchet, I shall love you all my life.'

'Kathryn...' His eyes gleamed as he moved to take her in his arms, holding her pressed against him. 'I do not deserve such love from you. I am not worthy of you.'

'Perhaps not,' she teased, a wicked expression on her lovely face. 'But you may strive to be so for the rest of our lives.'

'The rest of our lives?' There was laughter in his face as he gazed down at her, his hold tightening, hot eyes devouring her with a passion that made her breathless. 'For this life and the next,' he murmured huskily. 'I love you, Kathryn. I love everything that is you—your smile, your laughter, and your scent...your lips that haunt me when I sleep.'

'You are no longer afraid that loving me will make you weak?' she asked anxiously. 'You said that it was the rea-

son you withdrew from me in Rome and I have wondered—'

'That was a fool's notion,' he replied hushing her with
the softest of kisses. 'Your love made me stronger,
Kathryn. I was determined to live for you. Besides, it was
because of that love that I am here with you now.'

'What do you mean?' she asked, feeling puzzled.

'The man I was before I loved you would not have spared
Rachid's son. It was Hassan who spared my life after his
father's death. He is a Corsair and I think there is something
of his father in him, but when we talked I discovered that
he is a very different man. We have made a truce. Neither
of us will attack the other's ships. It means that I may carry
on my trade without the need for so many war galleys.'

'Do you trust him? Will he keep his word?'

'I believe so. For years Venice had a similar treaty with
the Turks. Before I left Rome I heard rumours that the
Doge may make some sort of pact again. A tribute of gold
so that we may trade in peace. Some would think it a be-
trayal of the League and all that it stood for, but Venice
grew strong on trade and without it we would be nothing.'

'And shall we live in Venice?'

'You were happy in Rome,' Lorenzo said. 'Venice is the
base of my wealth, Kathryn, and I must continue to trade
from there. Yet I do not see why we should not have a home
in Rome. My father will live in Rome for he likes it there,
and I shall spend much of my time there.'

'And when you go to Venice I shall go with you,'
Kathryn said, 'for I would not be parted from you again.'

'Nor I from you,' he said and drew her closer. 'I do not
think life would hold me if I lost you, my love.'

She looked up at him then, a naughty sparkle in her eyes. 'Then lie with me, Lorenzo. I want to feel you close to me, holding me, loving me.'

'You are sure?' The heat was in his eyes, testament to his burning desire, but still he hesitated. 'You wanted to be alone…'

'Only for a little,' she said. 'I have wept for my father, but I shall put my grief aside now. There have been too many tears. I want to be with you, Lorenzo, to be happy and loved.'

'You are loved, my dearest one, and I shall do all I can to make you happy.'

'If I have your love, I shall be happy.' She smiled and took him by the hand, leading him to the bed.

Their loving was sweet and tender, a sealing of the promises they had made each other. Later, they made love again, a hot, hungry coupling that made her cry his name over and over as he thrust himself deeper into the warm moistness of her welcoming femininity. And when it was over at last, there were tears on her cheeks.

Lorenzo wiped them away with his fingertips. 'Did I hurt you, my precious? I wanted you so much…'

'Never,' she said, kissing away his doubts. 'You have never hurt me when you love me. My tears were because you gave me so much pleasure.' She smiled up at him. 'Perhaps we have made our son this night, Lorenzo.'

'When children come they will be welcome,' he murmured against the silky perfume of her hair. 'But it is you I adore, my Kathryn.'

She sighed with content as his lips nuzzled against her throat. She was safe and happy in his arms, and something told her that a child would be born of such sweet loving.

Chapter Thirteen

'I think you are bigger than I was with my son,' Elizabeta said, laughing as Kathryn pouted and placed a hand to the small of her back. 'Poor you. These last few weeks seem for ever, do they not?'

'Not as long as the time we spent at Queen Elizabeth's court,' Kathryn said and frowned. 'She seemed delighted with Lorenzo and demanded his attention day and night. I believe she would have kept him with her for ever if she could. I thought that we should never get away.'

'Well, now you are here, and I am pleased that you will stay in Rome for the birth.'

'Yes.' Kathryn sighed. 'I long to give Lorenzo a son, but I cannot wait to be back to my normal size again. I feel so huge!'

'It is always the same,' her friend agreed, 'but Lorenzo thinks you are beautiful, so do not worry. He never looks at another woman.'

Kathryn smiled. She did not need to be told that her husband was faithful to her. He had shown his love for her in so many ways these past months that she no longer doubted him.

She believed he had still been a little jealous of Michael when they first returned to Rome, but now Michael was married to Isabella and living in Venice. He had Lorenzo were still friends, though Michael had his own fleet of ships now. Lorenzo no longer needed so many galleys, for his ships sailed without fear of attack from his old enemy. It seemed that the seas of the Mediterranean had become much safer since Lepanto.

Lorenzo was out on business, which continued to take much of his time, though he had promised he would not leave Rome until after their child was born.

'I shall be near when you need me,' he told her. 'And we shall stay in Rome so that you have your friends about you.'

Kathryn was glad of Elizabeta's company that morning. She stood up, walking about the walled garden, stooping to smell a beautiful red rose. It was as she straightened up again that the pain suddenly struck her.

She gave a cry of mingled surprise and alarm, looking at her friend in consternation. 'I think…oh…' She gasped as she felt another strong contraction. 'The baby…' Her eyes reflected fear as she looked at Elizabeta. 'I thought there were another few days left…'

'I am not surprised if you are coming early,' Elizabeta said. 'You have been carrying low for the past week or more. Some babies do come a little early, Kathryn. There is no need for alarm.'

'Oh…' Kathryn breathed hard as the pain ripped through her, much stronger now and more urgent. 'I think I should go to my room.'

As she went into the house, she met her father-in-law. Charles looked at her white face and realised what was happening. He summoned a servant as Kathryn bent over with the pain.

'You must go to bed, my dear. I shall send for the physician—and a message will be delivered to Lorenzo. You need him to be here with you at this time.'

'Thank you.'

Kathryn bit her lip, refusing to give into the fear and pain, which was coming often now. She was glad of the assistance of her maids. They helped her to undress and to lie on her bed, packing pillows at her back to try to make her comfortable, and bringing towels when her waters broke.

Elizabeta came to sit with her, holding her hand as the pains racked her body, making her writhe in agony and cry out.

'You are doing well,' she said. 'Your pains are much stronger than mine were at this early stage. I think your labour will be shorter.'

Kathryn could not answer. She had never felt such terrible pain and could not stop herself screaming as it became intense once more, and she experienced a strong desire to push.

'It is coming,' Elizabeta cried. 'Oh, my dear friend, I can see the head. Push harder now and it will soon be over.'

Kathryn did as she was bid. The pain then made her scream long and loud, and it was this sound that Lorenzo heard as he entered the house.

His father met him, restraining him, as he would have gone to Kathryn. 'Wait a little, my son. She has her women and Elizabeta.'

'She needs me. I must go to her.'

At that moment they heard a wailing sound and looked at each other in relief. 'It is over. Kathryn…'

Lorenzo broke from his father's hold and started towards his wife's room. As he reached it another terrible scream broke from her.

'Kathryn?' He looked towards the bed and was met by a warning look from Elizabeta. 'We thought the babe was born?'

'Your son was impatient to make his way into the world, sir—but it seems there is another child. And this one may take its time.'

'Another child? Twins…' Lorenzo turned pale, for such births were more difficult for the mother. He went to the bedside, reaching for Kathryn's hand as she writhed in agony. 'My poor love, forgive me.'

Kathryn shook her head to deny his fault, but the pain was too intense for her to speak to him. She clung on to his hand, her fingers digging into his palms as the pain struck again.

'Our son. Call him Dickon,' she whispered hoarsely. 'If anything should happen to me…'

'Nothing will happen!' He looked about him impatiently. 'Where is the physician? Has no one sent for him?'

'He was sent for at once,' Elizabeta told him, 'but your son came quickly.' She showed him the babe wrapped in soft swaddling. 'Is he not beautiful?'

'Yes, but I would to God he had been the only one,' Lorenzo said, his face white with concern. He watched as Kathryn moaned and writhed, frustrated that he could do nothing to help her. 'Damn the man! Where is he?'

'Here, Signor Santorini, at your service.'

The physician entered, a small, dapper man dressed in dark clothes and carrying a wooden box, which contained the instruments of his trade.

'She is in such pain,' Lorenzo said. 'Do something to help her!'

'If you would please leave the room. Only one lady should remain while I examine your wife, *signor.*'

Lorenzo seemed as if he would refuse, but Elizabeta gave him a speaking look. 'I shall stay with her. You can trust Signor Viera. He was very good when I was in labour. Kathryn will do well now that he is here.'

Lorenzo bent to kiss Kathryn's forehead, which was damp with sweat. 'I shall return soon,' he promised.

Outside the bedchamber he found his father waiting anxiously for news. 'Is all well?' he asked.

'Kathryn has given birth to a healthy boy, but there is another child and this one does not come so easily.'

'God have mercy!' Charles crossed himself. 'At least the physician is with her now.'

'For what good it may do us,' Lorenzo snarled. He had little faith in doctors and was consumed with fear that he might lose the woman he loved more than life itself.

It was several minutes later that the doctor came out to them.

'The second child has turned the wrong way. I must turn it and perhaps use my instruments to bring it out. If I do, the child may be damaged. It is a risk, but unless I help your wife she may die in the struggle to give birth.'

'Save Kathryn,' Lorenzo said. 'I pray the child will not suffer too much harm—but you must save my wife.'

'It shall be as you say.'

Lorenzo stared as the door closed behind him once more. He belatedly tried to follow, but Charles stopped him.

'The birthing chamber is no place for you, my son.'

'Kathryn needs me.'

'I know how you feel, but you must leave this to Elizabeta and the doctor. When your mother died giving birth to a stillborn child, I wanted to be with her, but she did not want me near her. Go to Kathryn as soon as it is over, Lorenzo.'

Lorenzo was torn by his desire to comfort his wife and the wisdom of his father's words. He paced the hall outside Kathryn's chamber like a caged beast, each minute seeming like an hour. And then, at last, when he thought he could bear it no longer, the door opened and the doctor came out to him.

'Your daughter is very weak, *signor.* She may not live the night. Your wife is well, but will need to rest. She has suffered some damage and it may be that she will not be able to have more children.'

'But she is well? She will live?'

'She needs rest, but she will live,' the doctor told him. 'You may go into her now, *signor.*'

Kathryn lay with her eyes closed as he approached the bed, but she opened them and smiled as he bent over her to kiss her softly on the lips.

'We have a son and a daughter. Is that not clever of me, Lorenzo?'

'You are wonderful, my darling,' he said and looked at her with love. 'Thank you for my son, Kathryn. He is a most precious gift.'

'And your daughter? Are you not pleased with her?'

'Of course…' He hesitated, but thought it best to be honest. 'Doctor Viera told me that she is delicate. We may lose her, Kathryn. But you will live and so will our son.'

'She shall live too,' Kathryn said. 'And we shall call her Beth.'

'I pray that you are right, my darling.' Lorenzo kissed her again. 'You should sleep now, Kathryn. I love you and our babies and I shall come to you again soon.'

He watched as she lay back against the pillows, dark shadows beneath her eyes, worn out by the fight to give birth, and whispered a silent prayer. He gave thanks for her life and that of his son.

'If you are merciful, God,' he murmured aloud, 'watch over our Beth this night, I pray you.'

Elizabeta beckoned to him and he crossed the room to gaze at the face of the tiny girl she held for him to see.

'Is she not beautiful?'

'Very. She is like her mother.'

'And as such, she is a fighter. I think the doctor is wrong,' Elizabeta said. 'She was sucking my thumb strongly just now. I shall summon the wet nurse to attend her and then we shall see.'

Lorenzo felt a wave of tenderness as he bent to kiss the tiny scrap of humanity that was his daughter. 'Live, my little one,' he said. 'Live for yourself, for your mother and for me.'

It seemed to him then that the child smiled at him, and he felt her little fingers curl about his heart, binding him as surely as he was bound to the woman who had given this tiny scrap life.

* * *

It was a beautiful day and the first time that Kathryn had come down in more than two weeks. Lorenzo had insisted on carrying her to her chair in the garden, placing cushions at her back and a rug over her knees. She looked about her, catching the scent of a full-blown dark red rose, and lifting her face to the sun as a feeling of content surrounded her.

'I am quite well now,' she told him with a smile.

'You are still a little tired,' he replied. 'You must rest for three weeks as the doctor told you.'

'He makes such a fuss,' Kathryn said and pulled a face at him. 'Did he not tell you that Beth would not live through the night? And does she not thrive?'

'Thanks to our good friend Elizabeta and the wet nurse.'

'I should have liked to nurse her myself,' Kathryn said wistfully, 'but Dickon is so greedy there would not be enough milk left for her.'

'She thrives as she is,' Lorenzo said. 'And you make much fuss of her when you hold her. She will learn to know that she is loved, Kathryn.'

'She likes you to hold her,' Kathryn replied with a tender smile. 'She stops crying instantly when you pick her up. I think she knows you are her devoted slave, Lorenzo.'

'She is so like you,' Lorenzo said and laughed ruefully, knowing that the babe had him curled about her little finger. 'I cannot resist spoiling her, because she is so beautiful.'

Kathryn sighed with content as she looked up at him. He was so different now to the man she had married, always laughing and teasing her, making up stories to entertain her, just as he had when they were children. She knew that Dickon had come back to her at last. He was Dickon and he was Lorenzo, the two now blended into one whole, a man she could love, respect and lean on in the years to come.

'We are so lucky,' she said, 'to have each other and our children.'

'God has blessed us,' Lorenzo said. 'Once I thought he did not listen to our prayers, but now I know that I was wrong.'

Kathryn reached out for his hand. Her fingers moved to the hard welt of scarred flesh, tracing it gently. Lorenzo no longer wore his wristbands. He had no secrets to hide. The past was gone, if not entirely forgotten.

'I love you,' Kathryn said.

'As I love you,' he replied. He looked up and smiled as his father came out to join them in the courtyard. 'I have everything that any man could want.'

FREE

2 BOOKS AND A SURPRISE GIFT!

We would like to take this opportunity to thank you for reading this Mills & Boon® book by offering you the chance to take TWO more specially selected titles from the Historical Romance™ series absolutely FREE! We're also making this offer to introduce you to the benefits of the Reader Service™—

- ★ **FREE home delivery**
- ★ **FREE gifts and competitions**
- ★ **FREE monthly Newsletter**
- ★ **Books available before they're in the shops**
- ★ **Exclusive Reader Service offers**

Accepting these FREE books and gift places you under no obligation to buy; you may cancel at any time, even after receiving your free shipment. Simply complete your details below and return the entire page to the address below. You don't even need a stamp!

YES! Please send me 2 free Historical Romance books and a surprise gift. I understand that unless you hear from me, I will receive 4 superb new titles every month for just £3.65 each, postage and packing free. I am under no obligation to purchase any books and may cancel my subscription at any time. The free books and gift will be mine to keep in any case.

H6ZEE

Ms/Mrs/Miss/Mr...................................Initials ....

BLOCK CAPITALS PLEASE

Surname ....

Address ....

....

....Postcode ....

Send this whole page to:

The Reader Service, FREEPOST CN81, Croydon, CR9 3WZ